FRAGILE HEARTS BY THE LOCH

LOCH LANNICK BOOK 8

HANNAH ELLIS

Published by Hannah Ellis
www.authorhannahellis.com
Postfach 900309, 81503 München
Germany

Cover design by Katherine Newton

FRAGILE HEARTS BY THE LOCH

CHAPTER ONE

Jess's gaze had been fixed on her favourite colleague from the moment he'd walked into the staffroom. After a two-week break from work, getting back to seeing him on a daily basis felt like being given water after a trek through a desert. Her eyes lapped him up. Eventually, he turned and looked right at her, raising a hand to wave across the room. Butterflies took flight in her stomach. His smile always did that to her. In reply, she made a jerky hand movement that started as a wave but ended with her touching her forehead. Apparently she'd lost control of her limbs. She dropped her chin to her chest, hoping he wouldn't catch the burn of her cheeks.

After more than six months working at Portree High School, she should really feel more comfortable in the staffroom, but every day felt like her first. Her co-workers were pleasant enough, but at twenty-three years old she was the youngest member of staff. It was her first teaching job and she'd moved from Aberdeen for the position. To start with it had felt like an adventure, but she soon felt lost and overwhelmed. It hardly felt like any time since she'd been a secondary school pupil, and now she was a teacher.

Imposter syndrome had kicked in as soon as she started the

job and wasn't showing any signs of subsiding. Even though she knew she was perfectly qualified to teach, the voice in her head constantly told her otherwise. It was hard to say whether the voice was louder when she was in the staffroom, surrounded by colleagues who were far more qualified and experienced than she was, or when she was standing in front of the pupils, wondering if they could sense her fear.

Her cheeks still felt flushed when someone sat heavily beside her, making the couch cushion sink. Now she was going to have to make polite conversation.

"Do you want to be friends?" the young woman asked. Her lips were coated in red lipstick and her eyelashes were so dark and long that Jess wondered if they were fake, though they didn't look unnatural. She was smartly dressed and her blonde hair was styled in a neat bob.

Jess squinted at her in confusion. "I'm sorry, what?"

"I'm new," she said, her bright lips stretching to a wide smile. "First day today. I don't know anyone, but I was thinking that it's a school and back in my schooldays it was easy to make friends. You just set your sights on someone and waltzed up and asked them. I chose you because you look young and fun. I'm Ava, by the way." She thrust her hand out.

"Jess," she replied, shaking the woman's hand and trying to judge her age; she guessed Ava was a few years older than herself, maybe late twenties. "Are you taking over from Theresa? In the office?"

"Yes. It's just a temporary position. She wants to come back after maternity leave. I've done a lot of office work and tend to jump from one temp job to another. I worked in a school once before but it was a few years ago, and that was a primary school. So what do you say, will you take me under your wing and help me get settled?"

"I'm pretty new myself," Jess said. "I feel as though I'm still figuring things out too."

Ava leaned in and lowered her voice. "You can at least give me the lowdown on the other staff."

Automatically, Jess's eyes strayed across the room, searching *him* out.

"I wanted to ask about those two," Ava said, following her gaze.

Jess chastised herself for being so obvious. "What about them?"

"They're cute. Tell me everything you know. Who's the one on the right?"

"Chris Duffy. Sports teacher. He's okay but he's quite arrogant."

"I should have known he'd be the sports teacher. I guess you can get away with being a bit arrogant when you look like that."

Jess shrugged; he definitely wasn't her type.

"What about the other one? He's probably arrogant too with an arse like that?"

"Oh my God!" Jess snorted a laugh and felt her cheeks heating up again.

"Come on! Don't pretend you haven't noticed how well his jeans fit."

Jess had absolutely noticed how good he looked in the jeans and shirt combo that was his standard work attire.

"I bet all the young girls love having him as a teacher," Ava went on. "It would definitely have given me a positive attitude towards school if I got to look at him every day. Not sure I'd have learnt much, though. It'd be hard to concentrate on anything other than his bum!"

"Stop it!" Jess said, putting a hand over her mouth.

"Tell me about him then. Give me all the juice."

"Rory Kennedy. English teacher."

"And?" Ava glared at her. "What's he like? Does he love himself?"

"No." Jess smiled. "He's not arrogant at all. He's lovely."

"I'm not sure what this says about me, but I think I'd rather he was arrogant. I like a bad boy."

"He's definitely not a bad boy."

"Is he single?"

Jess chewed her bottom lip, mulling over the question. "Sort of," she finally said.

"What on earth does that mean?"

"It's complicated. I'm not really sure what the situation is—"

"He's coming over," Ava said excitedly. "Oh my goodness, that smile has made my insides all quivery. Act naturally!"

"That's an oxymoron," Jess said, remembering a conversation she'd had with Rory a while back when she'd been helping him come up with oxymorons for one of his lessons.

"Oh no. Are you a brainy type? I suppose that was inevitable. It's a room full of teachers after all. Do you teach English too?"

"No. Chemistry."

"Wow. Super brainy. No wonder you think I'm a moron!"

"I didn't say that." Jess laughed at the teasing in Ava's eyes. "I said it's an *oxy*moron. If you're acting, it can't be natural. Therefore acting naturally is an oxymoron."

"Yeah, I get it." Her eyes drifted to Rory.

"Hey!" He beamed at Jess as he perched on the arm of the couch. "Nice tan! I guess the sun was shining in Italy."

"Yeah, it was great."

"You've been in Italy?" Ava asked. "How lucky are you?"

"I went with my sister," Jess said.

"It was weird not seeing you for two weeks." Rory gave her shoulder a squeeze. The physical contact made her feel shaky.

"This is Ava," she said in a bid to shift the attention away from herself. "She's taking over from Theresa in the office."

"Nice to meet you." Rory leaned across Jess to shake Ava's hand and introduce himself. The whiff of his aftershave was heavenly, and Jess had to restrain herself to stop from leaning closer into him.

"Jess has been filling me in on the staff," Ava said with a mischievous glint in her eye. "Telling me who the morons are!"

Rory slipped from the arm of the couch into the small space beside Jess. "I thought we agreed that he's just old and set in his ways," he whispered. "Calling him a moron might be a bit harsh."

"I wasn't saying anything bad about anyone." She shifted in her seat but there wasn't much room, and Rory's leg remained pressed against hers.

"She hasn't mentioned me yet then?" he said. "You've not had her complaining about me dragging her to the pub on Friday nights?"

Ava grinned. "There hasn't been any mention of the pub, although I have to say I've never needed dragging to any bar."

"There are a bunch of us who go for drinks on Fridays," Rory said. "Celebrate making it through the week. You should come with us. You'll definitely need a drink after your first week here."

"You're worrying me," Ava said. "Jess had me thinking it was a decent place to work, but now I'm not so sure."

"I'm kidding. It's great really." He gave Jess's leg a nudge. "Remember our first week? You got so drunk on that first Friday night out."

"The hangover still haunts me." She smiled at the memory. "We started working here at the same time," she told Ava.

"We bonded over being newbies together," Rory added.

"Sounds cosy." There was a hint of mischief to Ava's voice. "Oh, no. The boss is here. Am I supposed to be at her side with a clipboard or a notepad or something?"

"She's really nice," Jess said, looking at the head teacher, Imogen Corley, who'd just walked in.

"She'll mingle for a few minutes," Rory said. "Then you'll get your formal introduction and we'll all give you a little clap to welcome you."

"That sounds embarrassing!"

"It is," Jess said, remembering how self-conscious she'd been when she was the new member of staff. At least Rory had been in the same boat. Imogen looked their way and beckoned to Rory.

"What have I done?" he said out of the corner of his mouth as he stood up. "I always feel as though I'm about to get into trouble whenever she wants to speak to me."

"Yeah, right." Jess rolled her eyes. "You're the teacher's pet!"

"See you later," Rory said and left them alone again.

Ava turned to face Jess. "Okay, spill the beans. Are you and he together?"

"No," Jess said, shocked by the question.

"Are you sleeping with him?"

Her cheeks felt as though they were on fire. "No. Why would you ask that?"

"Because of the chemistry between you. You seem to have a very friendly relationship."

"Well, we are friends."

"Don't try and tell me that's all. Come on. Tell me the real story …"

"There's nothing to tell." Jess looked across the room to where Rory was chatting to Imogen Corley. He was a lovely guy and a good friend.

Sadly, that really *was* the whole story.

CHAPTER TWO

It shouldn't have been a surprise that the Easter holidays threw Arran's routine off. Spending so much time with Rory was bound to cause more confusion for him. Elspeth had to remind herself to be patient with him several times on Monday afternoon when the questions about when he'd see Daddy were incessant and grated on her nerves. Rory had taken Arran to Edinburgh to visit his parents for a few days over Easter, as well as having him to stay at his place in Portree for some of the holiday.

When Rory had moved out, they'd agreed that they needed to keep life as stable as possible for Arran. That meant they'd been determined to keep things amicable. Rory had made things easy for Elspeth when they'd split up. It was typical of him to put other people before himself. And that meant Elspeth spent most of her waking hours engulfed in guilt for splitting up with him and breaking up their family.

"Is Daddy coming to read me a story?" Arran asked, looking at her over the dinner table.

"No. I told you he's not coming today. He's got to work again, and you're back at nursery, so you'll see him at the weekends and on Wednesday nights like before."

He dropped his knife and fork so they clattered onto the plate. "I want Daddy to read me a bedtime story."

"He read the story almost every night for the last two weeks. It's my turn."

"I don't want you to read to me. I want Daddy."

Elspeth's jaw clenched. "You'll see him on Wednesday. He'll come and read your bedtime story then."

"That's not fair!"

"Sorry," she murmured, feeling like the worst mother in the world. She'd known when she ended things with Rory that it would hurt Arran. She'd struggled on with the relationship for as long as possible for Arran's sake, until she finally felt as though she'd break.

"I want Daddy," Arran said again, glaring at her.

"I know you do. But he's not here today. Eat your dinner and then we'll go up and get you in the bath."

"I don't want a bath. I want Daddy." He slipped off his chair and went to the living room. Elspeth ate a few mouthfuls of her dinner, more to give them both a moment to calm down than from hunger. When she followed him, he was curled on the couch, cuddling a big toy dinosaur that Rory had bought for him a couple of years before.

"Do you want to play a game with me?" Elspeth asked, hating that he looked so sad. She'd almost rather he had a tantrum than go into one of his quiet moods. It was tempting to suggest putting the TV on to cheer him up, but Rory had decided TV should be restricted to weekends, and Elspeth had tried to keep that rule in place even after Rory had moved out.

"I want to play dinosaurs," he said.

"Is the stegosaurus going to be the king of the dinosaurs?" she asked as Arran uncurled himself from the cuddly toy.

"Yes." He dragged the stegosaurus across the room to the box filled with dinosaurs of all shapes and sizes. It kept him entertained until Elspeth coaxed him upstairs to get ready for bed. He'd had a story and was all tucked up when he asked for

Rory again. His eyelids drooped as his sad little face asked repeatedly for Daddy.

"You'll see him soon," Elspeth said, stroking his hair and staying beside him on the bed. As he drifted off to sleep, she reminded herself that it was the school holidays that had unsettled him and everything would be better when they got back to the regular routine.

Thankfully, Arran woke in a better mood the next morning. There was no mention of Rory as they got dressed and ready for the day. They were just putting their coats on when a knock came at the door. Her dad stepped inside.

"Do you want me to take him to nursery?" Keith asked.

"No, thanks. I'll take him. I thought we'd walk up for a change."

"Are you sure? I'm going to work now anyway. I'm happy to take him."

"I know," Elspeth said, not sure why she was irritated with him. "But I feel like the walk."

"Won't you be in a rush to open the cafe?"

"I'm not opening today." She handed Arran his hat and looked impatiently at Keith, who was now blocking their way.

"What do you mean you're not opening? It's Tuesday. You always open on Tuesdays."

"I realise that. But it means I only get one day off a week. Excuse me for deciding I'd like to have two days off. That's actually quite normal, you know?"

His eyes narrowed. "What are you going to do with yourself?"

"I don't know. What do most people do with their weekends? Chill out, do nothing."

He stepped outside when Elspeth ushered Arran out. "So it's a general thing? Not just today?"

"Yes. I think so. I updated the opening hours on the social media pages. I just need to change the sign in the window of the cafe."

"Right, okay then. It seems like you've got it all decided."

Elspeth's shoulders drooped. "Should I have asked you first?"

"No. It's fine." He walked up the drive with them until he reached his car. "Are you sure you don't want me to drive him?"

She shook her head. "No. We'll see you later."

"Bye, Grandad!" Arran said, waving at him. He chatted away to Elspeth as they walked, telling her about his friends at nursery and pointing out things they passed on their walk – a squirrel scurrying from tree to tree and various birds. They were near the pub and about to cross the road when they caught sight of Lexie coming out of her house. Arran called out to her and waved enthusiastically. When she headed their way, they continued on to meet her halfway.

"How are you?" she asked, scooping Arran up for a cuddle when he ran at her.

"Good!" he replied happily. "Where's Nick?"

"He's already gone to work," she told him, then looked to Elspeth. "How are you?" She did the annoying head tilt that everyone seemed to do now when they asked how she was.

"Fine," she said as brightly as possible. "Glad that the school holidays are over."

"Aye, we've hardly seen you, but I guess the cafe's been busy. I feel as though I've been working non-stop too. I've been cursing Leana on a daily basis."

"Me too. It was quite rude of her to jet off to America." Leana and Alasdair had finally decided to take a holiday and visit the members of Ghost Moon in Los Angeles. From the messages, they were having a great time. It was mostly Leana who Elspeth had turned to when she and Rory had broken up. When Leana had left, she had realised just how much she relied on her for someone to talk to.

"Only a few more days," Lexie said. "Then she'll be back. I'm so jealous of her trip."

"I want to go to America too," Arran declared.

"Me too!" Lexie grinned at him. "Or anywhere hot and sunny with a beach. I'm not fussy."

"Do you and Nick want to come over for dinner one night?" Elspeth asked.

"Yes. I'm working at the pub every evening this week though."

"Maybe next week then. Arran will be with Rory at the weekend."

"Message Nick. He'll be happy to have you cook for him."

"Yeah, okay." Having someone else around in the evening would take Arran's mind off the fact that Rory wasn't there. "I'll get in touch with him."

"I've got to get to the activity centre." Lexie set Arran down and gave Elspeth a quick hug. "Give me a shout if you want to go out at the weekend."

Elspeth half-heartedly said she would, then took Arran's hand as they set off again towards the nursery. When they arrived he shot off to join his friends and barely gave Elspeth a backwards glance. On the way home, she slipped around the back of the pub and dropped down to the loch. The uneven path was deserted and Elspeth enjoyed the solitude. New leaves were sprouting on the trees and several clusters of bluebells had shot up beside the path. Birds sang in the trees, but stopped abruptly at the sound of barking when Elspeth was almost home.

"Hello!" she said to Jasper, who bounded towards her. Crouching, she patted him down, then rubbed her cheek against his and laughed when he licked her face. "Nice to see you too!"

After darting away, he returned and dropped a tennis ball at her feet. She threw it in the direction of the cottage before walking up to the cafe. He barked loudly when he brought it back.

"Give me two minutes," she called to him through the open door. "I'm not working, I just need to change the opening times."

Carefully, she removed the sheet of paper from the window

beside the door. She'd print out a new one later, but for now she simply crossed out the opening times for Tuesday and wrote closed instead. It felt quite satisfying.

"How about a walk?" she said to Jasper when she locked the cafe again. He jumped around her legs excitedly. "Not far though. Just a quick one." They continued on the path, stopping to look through the trees as they reached Leana and Alasdair's house. Next week she'd be able to go for a morning walk and call in for a coffee with Leana. The thought of coffee made her turn back. Jasper bounded happily between the trees and the path, never venturing too far away from her as she ambled along.

At home, she found her mum and Isla sitting at one of the tables outside the cafe.

"You stole my dog," Isla called.

"Sorry." Elspeth stroked Jasper's head, then sat beside her mum. "We went for a quick walk."

"Aren't you opening today?" Christine asked her.

"No." She rolled her eyes. "And Dad's already made me feel like the laziest person in the world so please don't give me a lecture. It's not so ridiculous for me to take two days a week off, is it? And it's not as though I'm closing the place at the week-end. We don't generally get much business on Tuesdays anyway."

"I don't have a problem with it," Christine said. "Why are you being so defensive?"

"Because Dad was asking me what I was going to do all day, as though I'm completely lazy."

"I'm sure he didn't mean it like that. He tends to blurt out whatever springs to mind without thinking it through."

"So you're going to close on Mondays and Tuesdays from now on?" Isla asked.

"That was my plan, but maybe I should have checked with you and Dad," she said to her mum. "I honestly don't think it will make much difference to profits."

"You don't have to check with us. It's fine. I think it's a good idea. I'm always telling you that you work too much. Both of you do."

"I like working a lot," Isla said.

"I used to," Elspeth said. Recently, she'd lost her enthusiasm for the cafe.

Christine stood. "Speaking of work, I better get going. Do you want me to leave the car for you if you're not working today?"

"No." Elspeth shook her head. "I don't plan on going anywhere. The cottage could do with a good clean so I'll probably get on with that."

"That doesn't sound like much of a day off," Christine said as she walked away. "Do something fun instead."

"You can hang out with me if you want," Isla said.

Elspeth smiled lightly. "Everyone's been walking on eggshells around me since Rory and I broke up, but I never feel more like a charity case than when you're nice to me!"

"I think that's offensive," Isla said. "It sounds as though me being nice is something out of the ordinary."

"Well …" Elspeth flashed a cheeky grin and decided not to comment further. "What are you doing today? Did you ask me to hang out as a ploy to get me cleaning sea glass for you?"

"It's a very therapeutic job!" Isla insisted. "I'm actually going out on the boat first. I need to build up my sea glass supplies. But if you tag along with me to collect sea glass you also need to help me clean it."

"Go on, then."

"Don't do me any favours! This is supposed to be me looking out for you. At least pretend to be grateful."

Elspeth leaned closer to Isla, smiling sweetly. "Oh, thank you so much. You are so kind and thoughtful."

"All right." Isla shrugged her away and stood up. "Don't go over the top. I'll meet you at the boat in ten minutes."

At least spending the day with Isla would keep her from sitting around feeling sorry for herself. And if she could get Nick to come over for dinner, that would help keep Arran distracted from missing Rory.

As she typed out a message to Nick, she tried not to dwell on the fact that her plans only ever seemed to be about making it through the day.

CHAPTER THREE

Leana pulled her sunglasses low on her nose to peek out at the sunlight dancing on the surface of the water. Spending her days on a sunlounger by the pool was blissful but she was about ready to get back to reality. They'd been away for three weeks now. One week had been spent on a short road trip over to the Grand Canyon, with a stop at Vegas on the way. The rest of the time had been spent in the large house in Beverly Hills with the members of the UK's most successful band, Ghost Moon.

"What day is it?" Leana asked as a shadow fell over her.

Alasdair checked his watch. "Almost three."

"Not what *time*. What day? I've completely lost track. Is it tomorrow we fly home?"

"It's Tuesday today," he replied. "We fly on Thursday."

"So tomorrow's our last full day," she mused.

"Yes." The wicker sunlounger creaked as Alasdair perched beside her. "Unless I can convince you to stay longer."

She smiled lightly at the joke he'd made a few times now. It took a moment for her to register the serious set of his features. As she sat up, she adjusted her bikini top and reached for the glass of fresh lemonade beside her. "What are you talking about?"

"There's no reason for us to rush back, is there? We could change the flights and stay longer."

"I thought the band were off on their tour of California next week?"

"They are, but Josh said we could tag along with them."

Leana stared at him in disbelief. "I need to get back to work."

"Mary and Angus will manage without you for a bit longer. And there's no real reason for me to rush back." His fingers trailed over her stomach before reaching around her back and pulling her closer to him. He was only wearing a pair of swimming shorts, and his bare chest pressing against her made her insides flutter. "It's been really great spending so much time with you," he muttered before brushing his lips lightly across hers.

"You make it sound as though we hardly see each other usually."

"It's different being on holiday. It's more relaxed." He kissed her lightly. "And I really like that we wear less clothes."

"I quite like that too," she said, pushing her hands into his hair as she kissed him.

A groan from nearby reminded Leana that Austin, the band's bass player, was asleep on one of the other sunloungers. Previously Leana hadn't been his biggest fan, but she'd warmed to him on their visit.

"You two are nauseating," he grumbled as he stumbled bleary-eyed from his sun lounger.

In what seemed to be his daily routine, he'd had several beers at lunchtime, then fallen asleep. Leana winced as he lurched towards the pool, sure he was about to fall in. Instead he found his balance and put one foot into the water, dragging it along to kick water up at them. Ducking behind Alasdair, Leana only got a few drops over her and laughed at the mischief on Austin's face. While they'd been there, a day hadn't gone by that someone hadn't been thrown in the pool.

It was clear what was coming as Alasdair extracted himself

from Leana. Laughing, Austin took off at a run, but Alasdair caught him quickly and dragged him easily over to the pool. They both ended up crashing into the water, splashing Leana in the process.

"You're so childish," she said, standing and watching them dunking each other. Her breath caught in her throat when her legs slipped out from under her. For an instant, she thought it was the wet surface that had caused her to slip – until she registered Josh's arms scooping her up. "No!" she said, wriggling to get away but knowing the attempt was futile. "Why are you so obsessed with throwing people into the pool?" As he took strides to the edge of the pool, she gave up on trying to escape and instead tightened her grip on him and held her breath as he jumped with her in his arms.

When they surfaced, he spat a mouthful of water at her. She turned away from him to avoid a direct hit.

"Because it's funny," he said. "And I didn't start it that time. I only joined in."

Austin spluttered as he swam away from Alasdair and pulled himself out to sit on the edge of the pool. "Leana and Alasdair needed to cool down!"

"You're just jealous," Leana remarked. Swimming to Alasdair, she looped an arm around his shoulders and kissed him until both Austin and Josh splashed them.

"What's happened to you?" Josh asked, lying back to float on the surface of the water. "You used to be all shy and squeaky clean."

"I might have spent too much time around you," she said, amused.

Alasdair had one hand on the edge of the pool and one arm around her. "I'm not complaining," he said and gave her a quick peck.

"I *am* jealous actually," Austin announced, reaching for his sunglasses. "Whatever happened to my girlfriend? Didn't I have a girlfriend?"

"She got bored of you," Candy, the band's drummer said, walking outside with a can of Diet Coke in her hand. "But that was weeks ago. Have you only just noticed she's gone?"

"I should find someone new," he said. "Let's go out tonight and find me a new girlfriend."

"You use the word girlfriend far too loosely," Candy said.

"Girlfriend's the wrong word, I'm just being polite. That's what hanging around with Leana for too long does to you."

"Do you want to go out tonight?" Candy asked, looking to Leana.

She nodded in reply. They'd had a mix of low-key nights out and evenings hanging out at home. Leana had been sure she'd get sick of hanging out with the band quickly, but it had been surprisingly relaxed. In America, they'd achieved moderate success while still keeping some semblance of anonymity. Not being harassed by the public and paparazzi every time they went out seemed to have a stabilising effect on the three of them, and Leana had found them much easier to be around than she previously had.

"Can we go to one of the places by the beach again?" she asked.

"No!" Austin groaned. "Don't make me go for a civilised dinner at Venice Beach. I'm a rock star, you know. I don't want to hang out by the boardwalk."

"I want to go to the beach," Leana said firmly. "I love people-watching on the boardwalk."

"Fine!" Austin said. "I'll go, but I warn you now I'm going to spend the whole evening complaining about how bored I am and how I'd rather be in a dark and dirty club."

"I'll pretend to believe you," Leana said, pushing off from Alasdair. "I better do some laps if we're going out for dinner."

"You're an awful person to be around," Austin said, slipping back into the pool. "Twenty laps and that's it."

Leana grinned at him. "I didn't say anything about *you* swimming."

"Yeah, right. Like I can relax when you're swimming your laps and being all sporty. Come on, I'll race you."

"She'll beat you again," Alasdair said, setting off on his own laps.

∼

Josh suggested a steakhouse for dinner. His PA had reserved a table outside with an ocean view. Sitting in the warmth of the spring rays, eating good food and watching people going past, Leana felt utterly relaxed. She rested her head on Alasdair's shoulder as the sun hovered low on the horizon.

"I can't believe you're leaving again in two days," Candy said, popping a chip in her mouth even though she'd just announced she was full to bursting. "The time's gone far too quickly."

"God knows when we'll see you next," Josh said. "I'm guessing it'll be at a wedding."

"Whose wedding?" Alasdair asked, taking a swig of his beer.

Josh shook his head. "Yours, you clown! Who else is likely to be getting married?"

"We don't have any plans to get married."

"Surely you're gonna get around to it at some point," Josh said.

"I think you should." Austin moved his chair back from the table and stretched his legs out. "A decent party's just the excuse we need for another trip to Scotland." He winked at Leana and she smiled back at him. That was about as close as he'd get to admitting he approved of her. At one time all of the members of the band had seemed to be against their relationship.

"You probably shouldn't hold your breath," Alasdair said, draping an arm along the back of Leana's chair.

Candy leaned with her elbows on the table. "Why not?"

Under the scrutiny of everyone around the table, Alasdair

shifted in his seat. When he glanced at Leana, she raised a quizzical eyebrow. She'd like an answer to the question too.

"It's probably not our thing." He reached for his beer bottle and turned it in his hand.

"Marriage?" Josh asked, seeming as confused by the statement as Leana.

"Yeah." He looked to Leana. "We're happy as we are, aren't we?"

She stared at him for a minute before nodding. In front of their friends probably wasn't the best time to get into a discussion about it.

"Shall we go and find somewhere more fun?" Austin asked, looking around. The steakhouse was definitely a tame venue for a night out, but he had been surprisingly civilised during their visit. It turned out that he was quite a softie underneath all the bravado.

"Leana wanted to look around Santa Monica pier," Alasdair said. "Last time we were here we all ended up too drunk."

"Getting drunk's the sort of fun I was thinking of," Austin said. "Not walking around a pier full of fairground rides and children."

Alasdair stood up. "Shall we see you back at home then?"

Josh picked at the label on his beer bottle. "Leaving me with the bill, are you?"

"That was my plan." Alasdair pulled his wallet out of his pocket. "Do you want me to get it?"

"I was messing with you," Josh said. "How bad would I feel letting my pauper friends pay for dinner?"

Candy patted him on the shoulder. "You know they're only friends with you because you're rich?"

"The thought has crossed my mind!"

"That should be obvious," Leana said, taking her denim jacket from the back of the chair. "It's not as though we'd be friends with you for your personality."

Josh gave her a crooked smile. "I miss the days when you were shy and nervous around us."

"I don't think I was ever nervous. I just didn't like you."

Josh and Austin affected mock wounded looks with both of them clutching their chests dramatically.

"Have a good night," Leana said, chuckling.

"You too," Josh called as they walked away.

Stepping onto the boardwalk, Leana and Alasdair dodged out of the way of a couple of middle-aged men rollerblading dressed only in speedos.

"It's not *that* warm," Leana remarked under her breath as she watched them weave in and out of people. Between the beach and all the people, she wasn't sure where to look, and her eyes roamed constantly from one mesmerising sight to another.

Alasdair took her hand. "I don't want to be all smug, but I always knew that if you spent more time with the band you'd get on well with them."

"They seem different here," Leana said. "Not as arrogant. They're almost like normal people."

"That sounds mean!"

"I mean like regular people rather than obnoxious celebrities."

"I think it's a lot to do with expectations." He paused to stroke a Dalmatian that came sniffing around them. "In the UK everyone expects them to act a certain way. It's all part of the image. Over here not many people know who they are. Not being recognised everywhere they go means they can relax and have a normal life. It's why they've stayed longer than they originally planned."

Leana had got that impression from the conversations she'd had with them over the last couple of weeks. Living in America seemed to suit all three of them.

"Not working so much doesn't seem to have much of an impact on their income," she remarked. "Josh is very generous."

"It's the money from the royalties. I'm fairly sure he'd never have to work again if he didn't want to. The money will keep coming in."

"It's made it a very cheap holiday. We've hardly spent anything." Apart from the road trip they'd taken, they hadn't paid for much at all. Josh had even paid for their flights over. And they'd flown first class.

"We could always stay longer and use up our dollars," Alasdair said, stepping closer to her to avoid a bunch of teenagers speeding past on skateboards.

"I can't. Not just because of work. I'm worried about Elspeth too. She's having a crisis and I felt bad enough about leaving in the first place."

"I thought you said she was fine?"

"She says she's fine. Mum and Isla tell a different story. Everyone's worried about her."

"I'm sure she'd be okay without you for a bit longer. You could call her every day."

"I said that when we arrived but it's not easy with the time difference. It's not the same anyway. I want to be there."

"Okay," he said.

The sun was disappearing from the horizon when they reached the pier. Not that it mattered; everything was lit up with bright and colourful lights. Leana's eyes flittered around, taking in the stalls with various games and prizes of over-sized cuddly toys. Lights flashed and machines whirred and let out beeps and bings. The smell of fatty food hit them at the same time that Leana side-stepped to avoid a small child with a puff of candy floss that was bigger than his head.

A little further along, a rollercoaster rumbled above their heads, its occupants squealing as it gathered speed.

"Do you want to go on a ride?" Alasdair asked.

"Maybe."

"The big wheel or the rollercoaster?"

She craned her neck to look up. "I bet there's a great view

from the top of the Ferris wheel." Pulling on Alasdair's arm, she set off towards the ticket booth.

"I'm not sure why I agreed to this," Alasdair said as they stepped into the gondola with seats opposite each other and colourful umbrella-style covers overhead.

"It's cosy," Leana said, her legs resting against Alasdair's as she sat facing him. It took a moment for it to stop rocking, then it lurched again as the wheel began to move. "It's faster than I expected," she said, peering out along the lights on the coastline as they reached the highest point.

"It makes me feel a bit queasy." They descended again and Leana was surprised by how quickly they were back to where they started. "Let's get off," Alasdair said.

"No, I want to go round again. I forgot to take photos."

"I really don't like it," Alasdair muttered, but it was too late – they were on their way up again.

Leana had just pulled her phone from her pocket when the wheel stopped abruptly, making the gondola lurch before settling into a steady rocking motion.

Holding her phone up, Leana began snapping away. Given the lighting, the photos weren't great, but she continued to take more while they were stopped. "That was good timing," she said. "It's easier to take pictures when it's not moving."

"Why have we stopped?"

She peered over the edge. "Just letting people on and off. It's actually really cool watching people from up here. It's like a miniature village."

Alasdair whispered her name like a question, but she was too busy looking at the world below them to take any notice.

"Leana?" he said again, louder.

His sombre tone made her turn and look back at him. "Are you okay?" she asked, as he stared straight at her.

"Can you just sit still?" he asked, swallowing hard.

"Yeah, okay. Why do you look so nervous?" She stared at him for a moment. He was usually very chilled out, so it was unnerving whenever he got stressed. As he took a deep breath, Leana slapped a hand over her mouth. "Oh my goodness! Are you going to propose?"

He closed his eyes. "Am I *what*?"

"Is that why you were being coy about marriage earlier? Because you wanted it to be a surprise?" She put a hand to her heart, then moved to sit next to him.

The colour drained from his face as he groaned.

"Alasdair?" She took his hand and squeezed it. "What's going on?"

"Please stop moving," he said through gritted teeth.

"Okay." She stayed still. "I'm not sure what's happening here."

Taking his hand from hers, he covered his face. "I think I'm going to vomit. Seriously, why has it stopped for so long?"

She leaned around him to look. "There are more people getting on."

"Sit still," he growled.

"Sorry. Do you really feel ill?"

"I need to get off."

"It's going again now," she said, as it set off again.

The muscles in Alasdair's jaw remained tight as they continued down to the ground. Leana waved at the attendant, letting him know they wanted to get off. As soon as he opened the door, Alasdair stumbled out and meandered quickly through the crowd. Leana caught up to him at the edge of the pier, leaning against the rail.

"Hey," she said, putting a hand on his shoulder. "Are you okay?"

He shook his head and lowered himself to the ground, where he hung his head between his knees. Crouching beside him, Leana softly rubbed his back.

"You're really pale," she said when he finally looked up.

He managed a small smile. "Don't ever take me on a Ferris wheel again."

"I don't intend to. And if you'd have vomited up there I'd probably have disowned you."

"It was the swaying, and the creaking. And it's bloody high and looks like it's held together by rusty chains and rubber bands."

"I'm sure it's safe."

"You're always overly optimistic."

"Apparently so." She frowned. "I thought you were going to ask me to marry you at the top of the Ferris wheel."

"Why would you think that?"

"It would have been romantic."

"You're really expecting me to propose?"

She shrugged.

Slowly, Alasdair stood up. "I still feel woozy. Can we go back to the house and talk about this later?"

"Yeah, okay."

Putting the conversation off wouldn't make any difference, especially since she had a niggling feeling it might challenge her optimistic nature.

CHAPTER FOUR

During their stay in LA, Leana and Alasdair had got into a routine of sleeping longer in the mornings. On that last morning they were both awake early. Leana lay with her back to Alasdair as her mind whirred, wondering if they were on a completely different page with regards to their relationship.

"I really don't want to leave tomorrow," Alasdair said, breaking the silence. She'd known he'd been awake for a while, but clearly they'd both been caught up in their thoughts. Turning over, she looked at him expectantly. "Touring around California with the band would be incredible. They're going to San Diego next week and playing a few gigs in bars and pubs. Then they fly up to Sacramento, then drive onto San Francisco, playing lots of small gigs. After San Francisco, they'll head back down the coast with a few stops along the way. Josh said I could even play some gigs with them. Since we've come all this way, wouldn't it be cool to see as much as we can?"

"It would be very cool. But I *can't*." Immediately she was annoyed with him. "I have to be back at work next week. I realise you think my job is unimportant, but I like to think I'd be missed if I didn't go back."

Alasdair shifted to sit up against the pillows. "I didn't say your job is unimportant. Just that Mary and Angus would probably understand if you asked for more time off."

"But you know how I feel about stuff like this. I'm not delusional enough to think no one else can do my job or that the place would fall apart without me, but Mary and Angus are expecting me back and I don't like to let people down. I want to get back for Elspeth too."

Alasdair nodded.

"Now I feel as though I'm spoiling your fun," she said.

"No. It's fine. I understand." He ran a hand over her hair.

"Sorry. I'm also ready to get home. The holiday's been great, but I want to get back."

"How would you feel about me staying?" he asked hesitantly.

"And I'd fly back alone?"

"Yeah. I'd really like to tour with the band again and play a few gigs."

"I guess you could." She wasn't overly keen on the thought of making a long-haul flight on her own, but she also didn't feel she could demand he come with her.

"You don't want me to?" he said quickly. "If you'd rather I didn't, then I'll fly back with you. I know you hate the flight."

"I'd manage," she said. "How long would you stay for?"

"The band will be on the road for six weeks."

Leana tried her best to hide her disappointment. "And you want to go with them for the whole time?"

"Yeah. I'd like to."

"Okay." She wasn't sure it was okay with her, but she hated to come across as a clingy girlfriend, and it wasn't as though she couldn't manage without him for a while. "If you want to stay you should."

"Really?"

"Yeah." She could definitely have sounded more encouraging, but at that moment she felt a little sideswiped by the suggestion.

"Thank you." He shuffled down the bed and cuddled up to her.

"You don't have to thank me," she said frostily. "I'm your girlfriend, not your jailer."

"I know, but if you didn't want me to I wouldn't stay."

"It's fine. I guess it makes sense. You don't really need to get home for anything, and it'll be good for you to see more of California."

"It would be way better if you came too."

"Obviously," she said, breaking into a smile as he nuzzled her neck. When he moved to kiss her, she pushed him away and looked at him seriously. "Did you mean what you said at dinner, about not wanting to get married?"

He propped himself on an elbow and the crease of his brow told her he was wishing she hadn't brought the subject up. "I didn't really see it in our plans."

"Right." She stared at the ceiling. "And when you say you don't see it in our plans, you mean you don't want to get married?"

He winced and looked thoughtful as though he were choosing his words carefully.

Pushing the sheet off her, Leana sat up. "Is it marriage in general or being married to me that isn't appealing?"

"If I was going to marry anyone, it would be you." He sat up and dragged his fingers through his hair. "But it's not something I'm that keen on, to be honest. Do you want to get married?"

She nodded slowly. "I definitely thought it was part of our plan."

"You've never mentioned it."

"I mention it all the time!" Her voice came out louder than she'd intended. "I've been dropping hints for ages. You must have noticed. With Isla getting married, and Lexie, I feel as though all I've done is drop hints."

"I didn't realise you were serious."

She screwed her nose up, struggling to get her head around the conversation. "Why do you think I would joke about that?"

"I just thought it was banter."

"So you don't want to marry me?" Tears pricked her eyes and she moved from the bed, needing to put some distance between them.

"I'm not sure I see the point. I love you and I plan on us being together forever, but I don't need a piece of paper and a party to prove that."

At the window, Leana slid the curtains back and looked out over the garden that was dotted with palm trees. She was fairly sure no one ever ventured further than the terrace and the pool. When she turned back, Alasdair was sitting on the edge of the bed looking at her intently.

"I'm going to have a shower," she said, pushing tears from her cheeks as she strode across the room.

"Wait!" Alasdair followed, stopping in the doorway. "I'm sorry. I didn't mean to upset you."

"Why haven't you ever mentioned this before? We've been together for almost three years. We have a house together. Surely at some point you could have let me know that you don't want to get married."

"I assumed that since we have the house and we're so settled that we're fine as we are. Why change things when everything's good? We're happy, aren't we?"

"That's not the point. I would have liked to have known that being with you meant never having a wedding or being married. You should have mentioned it earlier to give me chance to decide …" She trailed off.

"Chance to decide if you want to be with me?" he asked slowly. "So if I don't want to marry you, you might decide you don't want to be with me?"

"I didn't say that." They stood in a deadlock for a moment. "But what happens if I say I definitely want us to get married?" she asked eventually.

"Do you definitely want us to get married?"

"I always thought we would. And now you're saying you don't want to. If we want different things, I'm wondering who's going to be the one to give in."

"Obviously it's something we should discuss."

"Why is that obvious to you *now*? I don't understand why you didn't think this was worth mentioning before."

"Because I didn't realise you were so set on getting married."

"But it's what couples do. You should have assumed."

He took a step back and sighed loudly. "I don't want to do something just because it's what people do. That's a really stupid reason to get married."

"That's not my point," she said, her tone so fierce she was almost shouting. "I meant you should have assumed that I wanted to get married because it's a normal thing that people want from a relationship. The reason I want to marry you is because I love you and I want to stand up in front of everyone close to us and promise that we'll love each other forever."

He pressed the pad of his thumb against the bridge of his nose. "Declaring it in front of everyone seems a bit pointless."

"Well it's good to know where you stand on the matter. Thanks for filling me in." She swung the bathroom door shut and locked it, ignoring Alasdair when he called out to her.

The warmth of the water spilling over her eventually washed away all her tears. She felt emotionally drained when she forced herself out from the warm spray.

Alasdair was waiting in the bedroom, dressed in a pair of swim shorts. "Can we talk about this calmly?" he asked.

"We can try." She avoided eye contact as she moved to the dresser and picked up the bottle of sunscreen. Even in the gentle spring rays, her fair skin could burn quickly. "I'm not actually sure what to say. You really don't want to get married?"

"No."

"And you wouldn't even get married just because it's what I want?"

"Would you expect me to?"

She slammed the sunscreen down again without even opening the bottle. "Yes, I think I would. And it seems as though you'd expect me *not* to get married because *you* don't want to."

"That's not the same thing."

"Of course it is," she snapped.

"No. It's not! You're asking me to do something that I disagree with on principle."

"In that case, to answer your question, no, we can't talk about this calmly. You don't want to get married and I do. I'm not sure what we do about that."

Alasdair glared at her. "How about we carry on as we are? That would be an easy solution."

"Easy for *you*."

"What else can we do? Are you going to leave me if I don't agree to marry you?"

She bit down on her lip, determined not to cry again. "I don't know."

"You don't know?" His features tensed. "Are you serious? That's the state of our relationship? You'll leave me if I don't agree to marry you?"

At that moment, marrying him was the last thing in the world she wanted. "I didn't say that. You're twisting things. But it sounds to me that you only want to be with me if it's on your terms."

"You're being ridiculous." After a moment he moved to the door. "There's no point in discussing this now. I'm going for a swim."

CHAPTER FIVE

L eana sank onto the edge of the bed, then flopped back and let out a long breath. After rehashing their argument in her head she contemplated calling Elspeth, but decided against it. She had enough to deal with and didn't need to hear Leana ranting about Alasdair.

Hiding away in the bedroom all day was tempting, but she supposed she ought to go downstairs and be sociable. She just wasn't sure how she'd manage to pretend everything was fine. In the end she stayed where she was until a light knock came at the door and it inched open.

Candy smiled at her. "I drew the short straw and was assigned to come and check on you."

"I guess I should be thankful it wasn't Austin." She watched as Candy closed the door softly behind her, then walked to the window and closed that as well.

"Josh feels bad for bringing up marriage last night."

"Oh, no." Leana sat up. "You heard us?"

"We were out on the patio. We could only hear the really loud bits, but I think we got the main points."

"Now I really have to hide all day."

Candy sat beside her. "For what it's worth, he surprised me too. I thought you two would get married without a doubt."

"I can't believe this is only just coming up," Leana said. "Somehow he doesn't think he should have brought it up sooner."

"The two of you have really never talked about marriage before?" Candy asked, looking shocked by the idea.

"Only in a very light-hearted way. Honestly, I just assumed he'd propose at some point." She felt her throat tighten with emotion. "I'm such an idiot. I even thought he was going to propose last night. We were on the Ferris wheel and for a moment I really had it in my head that he was going to."

"That's totally the sort of thing I would have expected too." She went to the window and looked out. "I think he's being an arse to be honest."

"Thanks!" Leana was grateful to have someone to chat it through with. She'd never have suspected that Candy would end up as an ally, but it was nice to have someone to make her feel that she wasn't being unreasonable.

"How about we go and hang out by the pool for the day and everyone will pretend they didn't hear your domestic?"

"I can't face it. Any chance you feel like a shopping trip or something?"

Candy jutted her bottom lip out. "Please don't put me in the middle. I don't want to take sides."

"I'm not asking you to. Just get me out of here for the day. Please. Say we need a girlie shopping trip."

"Neither of us do girlie shopping trips."

"I need to buy souvenirs," Leana said, getting desperate. It was a lie, but it sounded like a believable excuse on the eve of her leaving.

"Isn't it going to make things worse if you avoid Alasdair?"

"You heard us arguing. Do you think things can get worse?" She shook her head. "I don't think I can be around him at the moment. At least give me time to cool off."

"Fine. I'll get us out of here for a while. Let's go."

The room fell silent when they walked downstairs. Alasdair was sitting at the breakfast bar in the open-plan kitchen while Austin and Josh lounged on couches in the living area.

"We're going out for a bit. Leana needs to buy souvenirs. Anyone want to join?"

"Nope," Austin said immediately. Josh shook his head while Alasdair took a sudden interest in his coffee.

Candy picked up a set of car keys from the table. "See you later then."

Finally, Alasdair met Leana's gaze and gave her a half-hearted smile, which she couldn't bring herself to return. She wandered outside after Candy.

"Where do you want to go?" Candy asked as they got into the white convertible Audi on the drive. She pressed a button to retract the roof and another to open the gates at the end of the drive.

Leana pushed her head into the head rest. "I don't care."

"Great. You make me go out and now you're going to make me choose where we go. Have I ever told you how annoying you are?"

Leana smiled at the teasing in her voice. "Sorry to ruin your day."

"You're not really going to force me to go shopping are you?"

"No. Whatever you want. I just need some time away from Alasdair."

"I like to drive." Candy tapped buttons on her phone until music blared through the car speakers.

"Fine by me," Leana said.

They didn't speak again as they meandered down the hills and along the interstate to reach Highway 1. Leana focused on the glorious rocky shoreline beneath the bright blue sky and tried not to dwell on Alasdair. It turned out to be an impossible task.

Her mind wandered constantly, trying to get her head around all that he'd said.

She remembered watching Isla getting married the previous year and being so sure that it would be her turn next. How many times had she imagined the white dress and the bouquet and exchanging rings and promises with Alasdair in front of their friends and family? How on earth hadn't she realised he didn't share that dream?

Tears stung her eyes and she turned to look out of the window so Candy wouldn't see her pained expression. If her future with Alasdair didn't involve marriage, what did that mean for them? She loved him and was certain that if he'd been upfront about it sooner, she'd have accepted that they wouldn't get married and be perfectly happy as they were. If she hadn't spent the last few years imagining a wedding and a life of wedded bliss, it wouldn't feel like she was losing something now.

What got to her the most was how adamant and rigid he was about it. While she'd be willing to compromise on a small wedding or even eloping, he didn't seem as though he was willing to budge at all. And if he wasn't willing to make compromises for the sake of her happiness, what sort of relationship did they have anyway?

Candy switched the music off, breaking Leana from her thoughts. "Are you crying?" she asked.

"No." Hastily, Leana wiped at her cheeks and did her best to get herself under control.

"Yeah, right. It's your last day here. Don't spend it being a blubbering wreck."

"I'm not sure I can help it."

Candy reached over and patted her leg. It was amusing to watch Candy trying to comfort her. Clearly, it didn't come naturally, but Leana appreciated the effort and forced herself to smile. "I'm getting a bit hungry," she said, realising she needed to spare Candy from her bad mood.

"Great," she said, with a note of relief. "I know a place for lunch."

∼

They arrived back at the house late in the afternoon. Alasdair, Josh and Austin were sitting around the pool sipping from bottles of beer. At the sight of Leana walking out there, Austin and Josh muttered their excuses and disappeared into the house. Candy also made herself scarce.

"Hi," Alasdair said. "How was shopping?"

"We just drove up the coast and went for lunch."

He nodded and moved to sit beside her when she perched on the edge of a sunlounger.

"I'm sorry about earlier," he said, reaching for her hand.

"Are you?"

"Yes."

"I keep thinking about everything, and I'm not even sure what to say."

"Me neither." He grazed his thumb over her knuckles. "Josh and Austin had quite a lot to say about it. I've spent the day getting lectures and being called all the names under the sun."

"That's a surprising turn of events."

"Yeah." He looked her right in the eyes. "I should have spoken to you about marriage before. And I shouldn't have been so abrupt this morning. I felt a bit cornered."

"The idea of being married makes you feel cornered?"

"No. It's not like that. I want to be with you forever. I'm fully committed. That's not the issue."

"I'm not entirely sure what the issue is then," she said calmly.

"I just don't see the point in getting married. It's like trying to prove something …"

"It's a celebration," Leana said. "What's the problem with celebrating finding the person you want to be with forever?"

"I don't see the need to celebrate in front of loads of people with a lot of outdated traditions."

"I think we're going to go round in circles with this conversation," she said wearily.

"Does getting married really mean that much to you?"

"Yes. Otherwise this wouldn't be an issue, would it?"

With a sigh, he leaned forwards, his elbows propped on his knees as he dragged his hands through his hair. "I guess if it really means that much to you, we could get married. I don't want a big wedding though."

Leana sat quietly, trying to find something to say that wouldn't lead them straight back to shouting at each other.

"I'm trying to meet you halfway," he said.

"That's definitely not halfway. You begrudgingly took about half a step in my direction."

"Well I can't suddenly fall in love with the idea of getting married. What do you want me to say?"

"Nothing." The trickle of the filter system on the pool sounded suddenly loud. "Can we put this conversation on hold? It's my last day here and I don't want to spend it arguing. I want to swim and lie in the sun enjoying the end of our holiday. It's not as though we're going to figure this out today so we may as well leave it for now."

He tucked her hair behind her ear and kissed her softly. "I love you. So much."

"I love you too," she said sadly.

The remainder of the afternoon went by pleasantly enough. Josh, Austin and Candy reappeared and the atmosphere was only slightly awkward as they chilled out by the pool. No one was keen to go out that evening, so Josh called the chef in to prepare a meal for them.

When Alasdair went up to shower before dinner, Leana followed him upstairs.

"Have you changed your flight?" she asked. With all the drama of the morning, the subject of him extending his stay had been put to one side.

"No. I thought I should probably fly back with you tomorrow."

She was tempted to suggest it might be good for them to have some time apart but wasn't sure how that would go down. "Okay. If that's what you want."

"I don't want you to fly home alone with things the way they are between us."

"If you want to stay, you should stay."

He gave her an odd look. "I feel like this is a test and whatever I say is going to be wrong."

"You don't have to come home because we had an argument."

"I don't want things to be awkward between us. I want us to work all this out and that's not going to happen if I stay here."

"But if you come home, you're going to be annoyed with me that you're missing out on travelling with the band."

"Probably." His features softened and he flashed her a crooked smile.

"You should stay," she said, moving to wrap her arms around him. "We'll figure things out when you get home."

"Are you sure you don't mind me staying?"

The stubble at his jaw scratched at her cheek. "I don't mind."

Taking a step back, he looked at her in earnest. "And we'll figure all this out when I get home? I know things were pretty heated this morning, but as far as our relationship goes, this is only a tiny bump in the road, right? We'll find a way to get past this and we'll be fine?"

"Yeah. I think so."

"You don't sound sure and it worries me."

"We'll figure it out. I just need some time to get my thoughts in order. I guess we both do."

He wrapped her in a hug and they stood in a quiet embrace

for a few minutes. Leana took comfort in the familiar scent of him. There was no way she wanted to lose him. But she was clearly going to have to adjust her expectations. Hopefully the time apart would give them both a chance to figure out what they really wanted and what sacrifices they were willing to make.

CHAPTER SIX

The small group of staff from Portree High School were spread across three tables in one section of the Merchant Bar. Arriving last, Jess and Ava had taken a small round table and shifted it towards the rest of their group. Jess was happy to be slightly apart from the rest – aside from Rory, she considered them colleagues rather than friends.

"I have to say, I'm very surprised by this place," Ava said, leaning slightly in Jess's direction.

Jess scanned the modern airy room, trying to figure out what anyone would find surprising about it. "How so?" she asked.

"There are a lot of hot young guys. I expected it to be full of old men in flat caps, but it seems as though there could be a decent nightlife here."

"What are you two talking about?" Rory asked, joining them with a fresh pint. He'd been chatting with Leo, the history teacher, when they'd arrived.

"We're talking about men," Ava said. "Maybe you could help by pointing out the single ones."

Rory looked at Jess in amusement before turning to scan their colleagues.

Ava grimaced. "Not *those* men."

"I haven't lived on Skye very long," Rory said as he looked around the room. "Less than a year. I don't really know many people."

"What about the barman?" Ava asked.

"That's Craig." Rory sipped his pint. "I think he's single but I'm not sure. Nice guy."

"He's gorgeous," Ava said. "Maybe taking a job on Skye wasn't such a bad idea after all. What about the two guys at the end of the bar? I presume one of them is with the woman, but maybe one of them is available. They're both fit."

Rory looked surprised when his gaze landed on them. "When did they get here?" he said as though talking to himself.

"You know them?" Jess asked.

"Yeah. That's Logan and Isla."

"Oh." Jess had heard a lot about Logan and Isla, so it was interesting to put faces to the names.

"Who?" Ava asked.

"Sorry." Rory gave a quick shake of the head. "They're my … erm … my … friends."

"Really?" Ava raised an eyebrow. "You don't sound too sure."

"Yeah. They're friends," he said more confidently. "Anyway, they're married. The other guy is Logan's friend, Gary. I think he's single."

"I've seen him out in Portree before," Jess said.

Rory nodded. "I think I see Gary every time I'm out in Portree."

As though he could feel them looking, one of the guys turned, and then the other. The taller of them set off towards them.

"Hey!" he said. "How are you?"

"Good," Rory replied. "How about you?"

He smiled widely. "Glad it's Friday."

"These are my colleagues," Rory said quickly. "Jess and Ava. This is Logan. He's my … friend."

Logan burst out laughing. "You could say it like you mean it!"

"Sorry. I wasn't sure how to introduce you."

"Yeah, it's a bit complicated," Logan said. "You could say we're …" Pausing, his lips twitched as though playing around with different descriptions. "We're illegal brothers!" he finally said. "I quite like that."

"You're what?" Ava asked.

"I wanted to say brother-in-law," Logan explained. "But we're not really. We operate outside of the law!"

"How much have you had to drink?" Rory asked.

"I'd say just enough!"

"I reckon so. Shall we settle on being friends?"

"No." Logan shook his head. "We're family." He looked between Jess and Ava. "His son is my nephew. I don't know why there isn't a simple way of saying that."

"Logan!" the woman at the bar shouted. "Your food's here."

"Gotta go." He smiled at them before wandering away again. At the same time, one of their colleagues called to Rory and he moved away to chat, promising he'd be back in a few minutes.

"Rory has a kid?" Ava asked Jess quietly.

"Yeah. A four-year-old."

"Is he together with the mother?"

"No."

"I suppose that explains why you described his relationship status as complicated. The baggage is the problem, I presume? You don't want to date a guy who has a kid?"

"That's not the problem." Jess wasn't sure she knew Ava well enough to have this conversation, but she was also desperate to find someone to confide in.

"What then? You clearly fancy him."

Jess frowned. "Is it that obvious?"

"From where I'm sitting it's not subtle. Although I'm pretty perceptive so it doesn't mean anyone else has noticed. Spill the beans before he comes back."

"I accidentally friend-zoned myself," Jess said, trying to stop her gaze from wandering to Rory.

"No. That's not really a thing."

"It is," Jess insisted. "When he split up with his girlfriend he was devastated. So I offered a shoulder to cry on. We went out for dinner a few times and I listened to him tell me about his ex and his son and all about his ex's family. I swear I know more about them than my own family."

"I see," Ava said. "That *is* a problem."

"I don't know what to do about it," Jess complained, hoping that Ava was worldly-wise and ready with a quick fix.

"I'd say move on and set your sights elsewhere. It sounds as though you absolutely friend-zoned yourself."

"I really like him," she confessed. "Surely there's something I can do?"

"There is one thing." Ava's eyes twinkled mischievously. "Ask him out on a date. Then at some point during the date, stick your tongue down his throat. That'll probably clue him in to how you feel."

"Be serious," Jess groaned.

"I'm very serious. If he thinks you only see him as a friend, you need to change that. The sooner the better."

"It doesn't matter anyway." Jess turned to watch Rory laughing with Tom, the maths teacher. His smile made her heart flutter. "He's not over his ex, so I've got no chance. He sees me as a friend because he's still got feelings for her."

"I take it she was the one to break things off?"

"Yeah." Jess's brows drew together. The situation always puzzled her. She couldn't fathom why anyone would break up with him. He was sweet and kind and perfect. Not to mention gorgeous with a smile to die for.

"When did they split up?" Ava asked.

"A few months ago. He moved out at the beginning of the year."

"About time he moved on then. You should go for it."

"I'm not good at chasing guys. I've never been the one to make the first move."

Ava dipped her eyebrows. "Sometimes you have to take the initiative. And if I were you, I wouldn't wait too long. He's kind of charming. There's no way he'll be single for long."

"I have a bookcase that needs assembling."

"What's that got to do with anything?"

"I ordered a bookcase a while ago. Rory said when it arrived he'd help me put it together. So I was thinking of using that as an excuse to invite him over for dinner. But it's pathetic, isn't it? I could probably assemble it myself."

"No, that's a good idea. Get him to help, then cook him dinner and share a bottle of wine. Then snog him and see where things go from there."

"I'm worried it's bad timing, but maybe you're right that I need to be more proactive." She twirled the stem of her wine glass and smiled as Rory headed back to them.

"Do you want another drink?" he asked.

Jess finished her wine and nodded. "I'll get them. What do you want?" she asked Ava.

"Sprite, please."

"Don't you drink?" Rory asked sitting beside her.

"I'm driving," she said. "Which is annoying because I'd love a glass of wine."

"Taxi?" Rory suggested.

She shook her head. "I live on the mainland. Just over at Kyle of Lochalsh, but it'd cost me a fortune in a taxi."

Jess left them chatting and went to get more drinks. The barman was at the other end of the bar, serving a couple of guys. He gave her a nod which she took to mean he'd be over in a minute. Drumming her fingers on the bar, she looked along at Isla and Logan. It felt slightly creepy that she knew so much about them. Rory had talked a lot about his ex-girlfriend's close-knit family, and she'd always found them a little intriguing.

Mostly due to the way Rory spoke of them with so much affection even after he'd split up with Elspeth.

The guy with them caught her looking, and she snapped her gaze away quickly. She could feel his eyes on her, and when she glanced again, he was sidling up beside her. His eyes sparkled with mischief and his smile was endearing.

"I don't think I've seen you around before," he said.

"Do you say that to everyone you haven't seen before or should I feel special?"

He eyed her intently, his lips twitching in amusement. "You should feel special."

"Even though I've seen you around loads of times? We've been in the same pub together often, but up until now you've never noticed me. That definitely doesn't make me feel special." Hoping that would send him away with his tail between his legs, she switched her attention to the barman and ordered drinks. Finally, she looked back to find his eyes were still on her.

He leaned casually on the bar. "So you've noticed me?"

She couldn't help but laugh. "You're really cocky, you know?"

"People have mentioned it. I'm Gary, by the way. But maybe you already know that."

"I didn't know that," she lied. "I'm Jess."

"Would you like to go out for dinner with me sometime, Jess?"

Before she could answer, Isla called out to him. "Stop being a pest! Leave the poor woman alone."

"You're not *my* wife," he called back to her. "You've got a perfectly good husband to nag. Leave me alone."

"You know the rules," Isla told him.

"Go away!" He returned his attention to Jess. "Dinner sometime?"

Jess caught Isla shaking her head and mouthing an apology to her. "What rules?" she asked, curiosity getting the better of her.

"Ignore her. I don't know what rules she's talking about. She's crazy."

The barman set the drinks on the bar and Jess passed him the money. "I'd like to know about these rules," she said to Gary.

He sighed heavily. "My relationship history is a bit of an issue for Isla. To help me make better choices she decided to give me some unwanted advice … which included some rules for dating."

"Such as?"

Gary opened his mouth to speak but Isla interrupted him. "Such as not pestering women at the bar when they're clearly not interested."

"Shut up!" he growled, taking a couple of steps closer to Jess. "I'm really sorry about her. She's a nuisance."

"To be fair, that seems like a good rule. What else?"

"Stupid stuff like taking things slow, not sleeping with women on the first date."

"This sounds like good advice. Maybe you should trust your friend."

"You might be right. So how about dinner?"

"That would depend if you're going to take your friend's advice. I need to know what kind of night it would be. Are you going to be a gentleman and not try and get in my knickers at the end of the night?"

He nodded slowly. "Yeah. I'll be on my best behaviour. We'll go for dinner and get to know each other, no expectations."

She hesitated for a moment. "No thanks."

"What?"

"It doesn't sound very appealing. What with the definite lack of sex." Her face broke into a grin at the look on his face.

"Wait one second …" He held a hand up and turned his head, calling to Isla. "I presume the rules change if I fall in love?"

"I guess," she said with a puzzled look. "Why?"

"Because I just fell in love."

"You're such a numpty," Isla said to him as he returned his attention to Jess.

"Please go out for dinner with me," he said as she picked up the drinks from the bar.

"Not interested. Sorry."

"But I love you!" he said, sticking his bottom lip out. "Come back. Please."

She shook her head and walked across the room feeling fairly pleased with herself.

"What the heck just happened?" Ava said as she slid the drinks onto the table.

"Did he ask you out?" Rory asked, his lips stretched to a tight smile.

"Yeah. I told him I'm not interested."

"Why? He's cute," Ava said. "And what did you say to him? He can't take his eyes off you."

Jess refused to look, but enjoyed the warmth of the confidence boost. "He's not my type. He seemed a bit desperate. It's not a good look." She winced slightly and reached for her wine. She should really heed her own advice and try not to seem desperate around Rory. Confidence was much more attractive. She needed to be confident and somewhat aloof. Except that was a lot easier said than done.

"I was telling Ava she should look for a place around here," Rory said, changing the subject, "instead of driving an hour to work and back every day."

"You don't have a spare room, do you?" Ava asked. "I can't afford my own place. I'm staying with my parents at the moment and enjoying cheap rent."

"Sorry. My place is small."

Ava sighed. "Rory said one of the teachers is looking for a flatmate but I'm nervous about moving in with someone I work with if I don't know them well."

"You don't know *me* well," Jess pointed out.

Ava pulled a face. "Don't be silly. You're my best friend."

"Harriet's nice," Rory said. "You should ask her about her spare room."

"Yeah, she's all right," Jess agreed.

"I'll go and talk to her. See if I can suss out if I could live with her." She picked up her drink as she stood. "The one in the blue top?"

Jess and Rory nodded in unison, then watched Ava walk away.

"She seems nice," Rory remarked.

"Yeah. I like her." As they fell silent, Jess's heart pounded and her mouth felt dry. She was sure she'd struggle to speak, even if her mind hadn't gone completely blank. It was painful trying to find something to say to fill the silence.

"Have you got much planned for the weekend?" Rory asked.

The flat-pack bookcase that was taking over her living room sprang to mind. It would be a perfect opportunity to ask him to help her with it. He was probably too busy though. "Not a lot," she said. "How about you? Is Arran coming over?"

"Yes." His face lit up. "I'll pick him up in the morning and he'll stay with me tomorrow night so I get all of tomorrow and Sunday with him."

"That's good." She gulped at her wine. There was no point in asking him out anyway since he'd be busy all weekend. Unless he had time on Sunday after Arran left. She could ask him to help her with the bookcase on Sunday evening. That was a good plan. Or it would be if she could get the words out. "What will you do with Arran?" she asked, stalling.

"Nothing special. Probably go for a walk and go to the play-ground. Apart from that, just hang out at home."

Jess smiled nervously as Rory continued to blether on about Arran and what he liked to do and how he could be fussy about food. It was kind of cute how animated Rory was when he talked about his son, but Jess was a little distracted, trying to find a convenient moment to ask him about the bookcase.

Ava joined them again before Jess managed to make any plans with Rory.

"Harriet seems nice," she said. "And the rent's cheap. I'm going to meet up with her tomorrow and have a look at the flat and get to know her better, but I think that might work out well." She clinked her glass against theirs. "Here's to lots of drunken Fridays if I don't have to drive home at the end of the night."

CHAPTER SEVEN

E lspeth had too much wardrobe space. It was something she noticed every time she put any washing away or got any clothes out. The absence of Rory's things made her stomach twist uncomfortably. She'd found another of his T-shirts at the bottom of the washing basket too. She wasn't sure how there was anything still lurking after him being gone for four months. That must be about the last of it.

At the sound of the front door opening and Arran's delighted squeals that Daddy was here, she pulled on the cardigan she'd been looking for and picked up Rory's clean T-shirt from the bed. Pausing, she contemplated keeping it, but when she held it to her face she was disappointed that it only smelled of washing powder. Holding onto his things didn't make any sense anyway. It wasn't as though she needed a reminder of him; she saw him several times a week. She also had Arran as a permanent reminder.

Descending the stairs, it occurred to her that Rory should probably knock instead of letting himself in. At the same time, she imagined how strange it would feel for him to wait on the doorstep. It had been his home too until recently, and part of her liked that he was still so relaxed around the place.

"Daddy's here!" Arran said, his arms hooked around Rory's neck as he hugged him hard. Anyone would think he hadn't seen him for months, not just two days.

"I can see that." Elspeth smiled in a bid to disguise how uncomfortable she felt. She'd expected the awkward atmosphere would wane once they got used to the new arrangement, but if anything it seemed to get harder every time Rory arrived to pick Arran up or drop him off.

"How are you?" she asked him as brightly as possible.

"Good, thanks. You?"

"Great."

"The weather's lovely." He shifted Arran in his arms. "I expect you'll have plenty of customers in the cafe today."

"Yeah." She tipped her head at Arran's bag by the door. "There are his things. You don't need anything special, do you?" It was the same conversation every time, and she hated how wooden she sounded.

"No, I don't think so."

"I found another T-shirt of yours." She tucked it into the top of Arran's backpack.

"Can we go to your house now?" Arran asked, pressing his cheek against Rory's. Elspeth averted her gaze. It made her heart ache watching them together. The fact that Arran always seemed to prefer his time with Rory cut deeply too.

"Yes," Rory said, picking up the backpack. "Let's leave Mummy in peace."

"Have you got anything planned for the weekend?" she asked, opening the door for them.

"No." His slight hesitation made Elspeth wonder if he had an exciting programme of events planned to further cement him as the favourite parent. "We'll just see what we feel like, I suppose."

Elspeth leaned to kiss Arran and was overwhelmed by the familiar scent of Rory's aftershave. "Have fun," she said, amazed that her voice remained level. "Love you," she whispered.

Arran beamed at her. "We love you too, Mummy."

She forced a smile and ignored the tightness in her chest.

~

The box with the bookcase taunted Jess when she got up on Saturday. She'd already been downstairs for a cup of tea but had taken it back to bed to tackle the endless supply of marking in comfort. She'd given one of her classes a test that week and was pleasantly surprised by how well the majority of them had done. It gave her a small boost that she probably wasn't as incompetent at teaching as she thought she was.

If only she was competent when it came to DIY too. The pile of books in the corner of the living room really deserved to go on shelves. First she made herself a late breakfast, then got to work unpacking the box and laying out all the pieces. Methodically, she pored over the instructions, reading through them twice and then laying out the sections of the shelves and the corresponding screws. Surely she could manage it alone.

She was getting on pretty well when her back began to complain at being constantly hunched over. Stretching, she stood and walked to the window. After the dark and dreary winter, the arrival of spring was welcome. As a seagull glided on the wind over the row of small back gardens, she felt the urge to get outside and make the most of the good weather. The bookcase would wait until later. Spreading the job out wasn't a bad idea either – less chance of her losing her patience with it. So far it felt like a satisfying project, and she hoped it stayed that way.

The streets of Portree were noticeably busier than they had been over winter. Down at the harbour people milled about, and a queue snaked out of the chip shop. Jess wandered along, taking in the view across the water and the boats bobbing on gentle waves. Whichever way you looked was pretty: over the water or out towards the mountains or the row of brightly coloured houses along the harbourside.

After buying a takeaway coffee, she stood by the harbour wall, leaning on the railing to watch the comings and goings.

She saw Rory before he saw her – walking hand in hand with his little boy, who was carrying a red bucket. They were both smiling as they chatted away.

"Hi!" Jess called as they got near to her.

Rory's head shot up and his smile stretched wider. "Hello," he said warmly, then casually kissed her cheek. "What are you up to?"

"Just out for a walk. I needed some fresh air and thought I'd make the most of this weather." It was still fairly fresh but the brilliant blue sky was uplifting.

"We're doing the same." He glanced down at Arran, who moved his head to Rory's thigh and looked warily at Jess.

"You must be Arran?"

"Yes," he replied quietly.

"This is Jess," Rory said. "She works with me at the school."

Jess smiled down at him. "I like your bucket."

"I'm going to find sea glass for Auntie Isla. And shells for Mummy."

"That sounds great. I hope you find lots."

"You're very welcome to help us," Rory said.

She shifted her weight, not sure if it would be intrusive to encroach on their time together. "I don't know if I'm very good at finding things."

"It's easy," Arran said. "All you have to do is look. Then you find stuff."

"That does sound easy." She looked to Rory. "Are you sure that's okay?"

"Of course. Come on." They followed when Arran pulled on his hand to lead the way. A little further along, stone steps led down to the stony beach. Rory tilted his head in Jess's direction.

"I tend to find a comfy rock to sit on and watch him. He can spend hours pottering around looking for shells and sea glass."

"You've got to help too!" Arran said, looking at him accusingly.

Rory grimaced at being caught out. "I will. I bet I'll find the most."

"No," Arran said seriously. "I'm the best at finding things."

"Except for your shoes when we're trying to leave the house!"

Jess found it enchanting to watch Rory in Dad mode. It was lovely to see the ease of their relationship.

Wandering along the beach searching for sea glass was wonderfully engrossing. The gentle breeze tangled her hair and pinched her cheeks until she felt utterly exhilarated.

"You're really bad at this," Rory said after a while.

Dragging her eyes from the rocky beach underfoot, she grinned at him. "I'm trying! Here …" Bending, she picked up a shell and held it out to Arran.

"It's broken," he said, frowning at her. "You haven't found any sea glass. I found one and Daddy found two."

"I'm the winner," Rory said proudly.

Arran looked at Jess. "You're a loser."

"Arran!" Rory hissed. "That's not very nice."

"But she lost," he said innocently.

"You're right," Jess said lightly. "When it comes to finding sea glass, it seems as though I am a loser."

"Sorry," Rory said as Arran wandered away from them. "I never know what he's going to come out with next."

"It's nice that he's still at an age when he can call someone a loser and genuinely not mean any offence."

"I guess that's not going to last much longer. He starts school in August and it's already making me nervous. He's growing up too fast."

"I bet he'll love it. He seems very curious."

"He is," Rory said, his smile full of affection as he watched Arran amble along the beach.

"I'm sure he's very clever like his Daddy," Jess said, then cringed at how cheesy she sounded. She'd been having such a good time that she forgot to feel self-conscious around Rory, but that changed in an instant.

"A little genius," Rory said cheekily.

Automatically, Jess gave his arm a gentle nudge as they fell into step, following Arran. They hadn't gone far when she caught a flash of light on the ground. "Hey, Arran!" she called as she bent to pick up the dainty piece of sea glass. "I'm not such a loser after all."

He made his way back to her, and his eyes widened when he reached her. "It's red," he said in amazement. Funny how excited kids could be. It was only a scrap of battered glass, but his eyes lit up as though it was treasure. As she held her hand out, he peered at it but didn't reach to take it. "The red pieces are special," he told her with an air of wonder.

"Really?"

Rory nodded. "It's the rarest kind of sea glass."

"We've never found red sea glass before," Arran said.

"Never?"

"No." Rory cupped her hand, pulling it towards him and looking at it with same sense of wonder that Arran had. "Even Isla doesn't find red pieces very often."

"Is it yours now?" Arran asked her.

"I found it," she said, her heart beating erratically from Rory's touch. "Finders keepers, right?"

Arran nodded solemnly. "I want to give it to Auntie Isla."

"Oh." She did her best to keep a straight face. "What will Isla do with it?"

"She makes jewellery," Arran said.

"And what does she do with the jewellery?"

Arran looked questioningly up at Rory.

"She sells it," Rory replied.

"So this is worth something?" Jess asked, brushing grains of sand from the glass. Again, Arran looked to Rory, who gave a curt nod. "Okay. I'll give it to you for ten pounds."

Rory's laughter was quick and melodic.

"I haven't got ten pounds," Arran said flatly.

"Maybe your Daddy has?" She flashed Rory a mischievous grin.

"He hasn't," Rory replied.

She locked eyes with Arran. "Five pounds?"

"For a chemistry teacher, you give a good lesson in economics," Rory said, then beckoned to Arran to come closer to him. "If you'll excuse us, I think I'll give him a quick lesson too." Crouching, he whispered something in Arran's ear, then straightened up, looking at her smugly.

"You've got pretty hair," Arran said loudly.

Jess pressed her lips together but couldn't quite suppress her laughter and ended up snorting in a fairly unattractive way. "You think I can be won over with flattery?"

"I thought we'd give it a go. Time for plan B then." Rory crouched and whispered in Arran's ear again.

"Do you want to have dinner with us?" Arran asked.

That took her by surprise. She looked at Rory, not sure whether the offer was genuine.

"We're only getting fish and chips to take back to my place. Nothing fancy."

"Are you sure that's okay?"

"Yes." His gaze fell to the treasure in her hand. "It'll cost you, of course."

"Do you like chips?" Arran asked.

"I do," she told him. "And I'd like to have dinner with you."

"Good!" Arran grinned at her, revealing a perfect set of baby teeth.

"I suppose since you invited me for dinner, I should do something nice for you." She held her hand out. "Would you like the sea glass?"

"Thank you," he said, snatching it from her. "You are very clever at finding things."

"I think it was luck."

"No, he's right," Rory said. "You're very clever. You also drive a hard bargain."

They set off in the direction of the chip shop, following Arran, who walked briskly.

"I don't have to come for dinner," Jess said, feeling self-conscious again. "I was joking about the sea glass."

"Yeah, I know." He gave her a sidelong glance. "And I completely understand if you have something better to do on a Saturday night, but I'd be very happy for you to join us. Conversations with a four-year-old can get a little tedious."

"I can't promise to be a better conversationalist."

"I've always been a fan of your conversational skills," he said.

She did her best to rein in her smile. "In that case, I'd love to have dinner with you."

"I always have about three extra bottles of ketchup as backup," Rory said as they watched Arran smear yet more of the red stuff across his face. "I once ran out and it was quite the drama."

"You're a big fan of ketchup?" Jess asked Arran. She sat at the other side of the table from them and was happy she wasn't within his reach. Rory had a line of ketchup down his sleeve where Arran had used it as a napkin without warning.

"It's my favourite food," Arran replied with a mouthful of chips.

"I swear he'd happily eat it from a bowl like soup," Rory said.

Arran picked up another chip. "I like it best with chips. That's my favourite. What's your favourite?"

Jess mulled over the question while she chewed. "Chocolate."

"No!" Arran giggled. "Proper food."

"It is proper food. Sometimes I eat it for dinner so it must be proper food."

"It's sweets!" He looked to Rory for backup. "You're not allowed sweets for dinner."

"No, you're not." Rory shook his head. "I think Jess was joking."

"No …" She laughed when Rory glared at her. "Okay, I was joking. Of course you can't eat chocolate for dinner. I guess my favourite *proper* food is fish and chips. So it's very lucky that you were having that for dinner."

Arran grinned at Rory, then dived back into his dinner.

"Have you got anything planned for tomorrow?" Rory asked.

Jess briefly wondered if he was going to suggest they do something together, but from the way he continued eating she decided he was just making polite conversation.

"I need to finish putting a bookcase together. I started it this morning."

Rory's eyes widened. "I promised to help you with that. You should have said."

"It's fine. I thought I'd give it a go."

"If you get stuck, give me a shout." He grimaced slightly. "Not that you're likely to get stuck. Did I just sound like some macho chauvinist assuming women can't do DIY?"

"A little bit," she teased. "To be fair there's a good chance I'll mess it up, but it feels like a nice challenge."

"I'm sure you won't have any problems. But let me know if you need any help."

"Thank you."

Arran turned in his seat and raised his chin before sneezing loudly. Snot and ketchup sprayed over Rory.

"Bless you," he said flatly, looking down at the splatters over his T-shirt. "Did you really need to aim that at me?"

"My nose tickled," Arran said.

Rory smiled at Jess, who'd tried and failed to quash her laughter. "It's not that funny."

"Sorry," she said, with a hand over her mouth.

"If you think that's funny, you should hang out with us more often. This stuff happens all the time."

Arran wiped his nose on his sleeve, leaving a trail of ketchup and snot.

"I think you might need a bath," Rory said.

"I'm full up," Arran announced, then looked at his sleeve and laughed. The drips of ketchup down his front amused him too.

"I think I'll leave you two to clean yourselves up," Jess said.

"You're welcome to hang around," Rory said. "I just need to dunk him in the bath and put him to bed."

"Thanks, but I might go and get on with the bookcase." It had been a surprisingly lovely afternoon and she didn't want to ruin it by overstaying her welcome. "I can tidy up here, though," she said, standing when they did.

"Don't do that," Rory said. "Leave it, I'll sort it later."

"It's the least I can do. You did buy me dinner. Besides, putting a few dishes in the dishwasher isn't much effort."

"Thanks." He ruffled Arran's hair. "Can you say goodbye to Jess? Maybe you want to give her a hug?" His smile was full of mirth and Jess took a couple of quick steps backwards, eyeing the amount of ketchup down Arran's front.

"I don't think a hug is necessary," she said. "How about a wave?" She raised her hand and wiggled her fingers.

"Bye!" Arran said.

CHAPTER EIGHT

Leana was contemplating visiting Elspeth on Saturday afternoon when the doorbell forced her from the couch. Jet lag didn't agree with her and everything felt like a lot of effort. Flying home on her own hadn't been quite as bad as she'd anticipated, but she'd been absolutely exhausted when she'd arrived home the previous evening. She'd driven Alasdair's car back from Inverness airport and had been groggily hanging around the house ever since. Thankfully her mum had dropped supplies over for her that morning so she hadn't had to venture out in search of food. If it was Elspeth at the door, it would save her from leaving the house at all. She checked her watch as she trudged to the door. Elspeth probably wouldn't have closed the cafe yet.

The bell sounded again and Leana grumbled that she was coming as she reached the door.

"You're home!" Lexie said.

Leana felt a surge of energy at the sight of her best friend on the doorstep. "I missed you," she said.

"I missed you too," Lexie replied, stepping inside and hugging her tightly.

"Are you okay?" Leana asked when Lexie embraced her for longer than usual.

"Yes!" She smiled brightly. "Happy to have you home again. I messaged you earlier, but you didn't reply. I assumed you were sleeping so I thought I'd come and wake you up."

"I've been dozing on the couch," Leana admitted. "My family all kept messaging me so I stopped looking at the phone." As they reached the kitchen she plucked her phone from the counter and checked the screen, then swore under her breath.

"What's wrong?" Lexie asked.

"Alasdair called me this morning but I was half asleep. I promised I'd call him back. It's too late now. It's the middle of the night there. He sent a load of messages so he probably thinks I'm ignoring him."

"Why would he think that?" Lexie asked as they moved to the living room. Leana should probably have been a better hostess and offered her a drink, but she didn't have the energy.

"I think I *am* ignoring him. Or at least putting off speaking to him. I'm annoyed with him for staying in America but I'm not sure I'm thinking very rationally with the jet lag. I encouraged him to stay longer so it's definitely not rational to be annoyed with him about it."

"I'm surprised you didn't stay longer too. Six weeks travelling around California with Ghost Moon sounds incredible."

"I had to get back for work," Leana said.

"Mum and Dad could've found someone to fill in for you."

Leana frowned. "That's what Alasdair said too. I got annoyed with him."

"Why?"

"I don't like the way he talks about my job as though it's unimportant. He thinks I can take extra time off because I only work in a bar and anyone can do my job."

Lexie raised an eyebrow but didn't comment.

"What's that look for?" Leana asked. "Do you think my job is unimportant too?"

"No," Lexie said lightly. "But Alasdair's right that you could have asked for the extra time off. Not because anyone can do your job but because you've known your employers for your whole life and they think of you as a second daughter. Surely you know they'd have given you the time off?"

Leana didn't like the fact that Lexie was taking Alasdair's side, even if her argument was completely logical. "I always have the feeling that Alasdair doesn't think very much of my job. And if I'm honest, sometimes I think I should find a more fulfilling career path. Working at the pub was only supposed to be a stop gap after school. Do you remember when I wanted to be a nurse?"

"I remember you mentioning it a couple of times," Lexie said, looking puzzled. "Have you really been thinking about quitting the pub?"

"No." She sank further into the couch cushions. "Not seriously, but it's an idea."

"Wouldn't you have to go away to university and spend years studying to be a nurse?"

"Yes. Which isn't overly appealing, but I'm not sure I want to spend the rest of my life working in a pub. And I don't want Alasdair to be constantly embarrassed by my job. Maybe that's why he doesn't want to marry me – he's got an amazing career and he doesn't want a wife who works in a pub."

Lexie stared at her. "What are you talking about? Of course Alasdair wants to marry you."

As she opened her mouth to correct her, Leana realised she didn't have the energy for the conversation. She didn't want to think about it, never mind talk about it.

"I don't know what I'm talking about," she muttered, her eyes feeling heavier by the second. "I'm so tired."

Lexie smiled and patted a cushion at the end of the couch. "Why don't you lie down here and sleep for a little while?"

"I need to go and see how Elspeth is," she murmured as she lay down.

"Have a nap first." Lexie pulled a blanket over her. "Visit her later when you've had some sleep and are feeling a bit more yourself."

"Thanks," Leana said, giving in to the weight of her eyelids and letting sleep take over.

∿

Elspeth had just got home on Sunday afternoon when Leana arrived. The cafe had been busy over the weekend and she was ready to drop, but the sight of her sister gave her a boost.

"I missed you," Elspeth said, hugging her tightly in the hallway.

"You too," Leana replied. "I was going to come and see you yesterday but I fell asleep. Then I was awake most of the night and slept again for most of today. Jet lag is hell."

Elspeth walked to the kitchen. "I think you're supposed to force yourself to stay awake until bedtime."

"I was only going to have a quick nap. I feel horrible and groggy. Can you make me a coffee?"

"You'll be up all night again tonight," Elspeth said, pulling cups from the cupboard. "Tell me everything then. How was it? I'll try not to be insanely jealous."

"It was great. Lots of lazing around doing nothing, which was lovely. Oh, and the Grand Canyon was incredible. We hiked into it and my legs ached for days afterwards. Las Vegas was quite an experience too."

They were interrupted by the front door opening. Elspeth peered along the hallway to see Isla walking in.

"Easy to see who your favourite sister is!" she said to Leana. "You come to Elspeth first."

"Nice to see you too." Leana stood to hug her. "And I had to come to someone first."

Elspeth got another mug out. "She only picked me because she wanted to check I hadn't had a nervous breakdown while she was away." She paused and smiled. "Also because I'm nicer."

Isla dropped into a chair. "Thank goodness you're back. You can take over with looking out for Elspeth again. Being nice was wearing me out."

"*Were* you being nice?" Elspeth asked with a grin. It was good having both her sisters around again.

"How are you anyway?" Leana asked.

"Let's not talk about me," Elspeth said. "It's boring. Tell us about America."

"Why didn't Alasdair come back with you?" Isla asked.

"He was having too much fun." Leana looked thoughtful. "You know how he gets when he's with Josh."

Elspeth hadn't been at all surprised when Leana had messaged to say that Alasdair was staying in America for longer. It was exactly the sort of thing he'd do. And to be fair to him, he didn't have a work schedule that he needed to be back for. He could write songs anywhere.

"There's no news?" Isla asked, peering at Leana. "I thought you might have acquired a ring?"

Leana let out a short burst of laughter that startled Elspeth. She put coffees in front of her sisters and joined them at the table. "It's not *that* funny."

"Logan and I both thought you might come back engaged," Isla said.

"Really?" Leana asked. "Logan thought so? That at least makes me feel a bit better that it wasn't only me that missed it."

"Missed what?" Elspeth asked, blowing on her coffee.

Leana wrapped her hands around her mug. "Apparently Alasdair doesn't want to marry me."

"What?" Isla and Elspeth said at once.

"It turns out he's against the institution of marriage. He never wants to get married."

"Are you serious?" Elspeth asked, shocked.

"Yeah."

Isla looked puzzled. "I really thought he'd propose while you were away."

"Me too," Leana said sadly.

"You two are all right, though?" Elspeth asked. "You didn't break up?"

"We didn't break up. I'm also not sure if we're all right."

The front door opened again. A moment later, Arran burst into the kitchen and flung himself at Elspeth. At least he was happy to see her in the moment he arrived back. Pulling him onto her lap, she squeezed him hard.

"I missed you. Were you a good boy for Daddy?"

"Very good," Rory said, following him in. His gaze fell to Leana. "Hey! You're back. How was your holiday?"

"Great, thanks. I'm not a fan of jet lag, though."

"I'm happy to get my drinking buddy back," Rory said idly. He and Alasdair got on well, but apparently he was out of the loop about Alasdair's travel plans.

Leana gave him a teasing smile. "I missed you too. When would you like to go for drinks with me?"

"Oh … erm … I meant …" He looked slightly panicked and Elspeth felt sorry for him.

"Alasdair's still in America," Leana told him, giving up on her attempt at humour. She turned in her seat to look squarely at Rory. "Can I ask you a question?"

Elspeth was sure Rory was wishing he hadn't hung around to chat, but he gave a curt nod and Leana continued.

"Did you know that Alasdair had no intention of marrying me? Ever?"

Rory picked Arran up when he ran at his legs. "What?"

"I thought he was going to propose, but it turns out he doesn't want to marry me. He doesn't believe in marriage and he never thought that was worth mentioning."

"Seriously?" Rory looked as surprised as the rest of them. "What an …" He paused as he looked at Arran in his arms. "Idiot," he finally finished, then looked sympathetically at

Leana. "I had no idea. When I speak to him I'll tell him I think he's an idiot."

"Thanks," Leana said.

Elspeth felt an odd sense of pride for Rory sticking up for Leana. "How was your weekend?" she asked him.

"Good." His attention stayed on Arran, and Elspeth got the impression he was avoiding eye contact with her.

"Did you do anything fun?"

He hesitated, looking thoughtful. "Just hung around. The usual." His phone buzzed and he pulled it from his pocket. "I should get going," he said as he scanned the message. "See you all later."

Elspeth walked to the door with him. "Thanks for having him," she said, running a hand over Arran's hair as he hung around her legs.

"Please don't thank me," Rory said with a pained expression. "He's my son."

"Sorry." Elspeth shook her head; they'd had this conversation before, but she found the doorstep conversations difficult and tended to say the first thing that came to mind.

"See you on Wednesday," he said, crouching to Arran and giving him a big kiss on the cheek.

"Bye," Elspeth said as he walked away.

CHAPTER NINE

J ess was proud of her efforts with the bookcase. It had only taken her an hour to finish putting it together on Sunday afternoon. The only problem was the weight of it. Holding individual pieces of wood while she screwed them together was manageable, but once it was constructed it lay on its side in the middle of the room, too heavy for her to move into position. That wasn't such a bad thing. It meant she could take Rory up on his offer of help without feeling like a disgrace to women.

After spending some time composing a suitably breezy message before bravely pressing send, she then sat staring at her phone for ten minutes until he replied to say he'd just dropped Arran at home and would come straight over. Immediately, she went into a tailspin, tidying up the house and trying to find something casual yet sexy to wear. She felt completely flustered after changing her top for the third time. Checking the mirror, she wasn't overly happy with her choice, but she was comfortable in the skinny jeans and T-shirt. As she went back down to the living room, she dragged her fingers through her wavy, shoulder-length hair, ruffling it to try and infuse a little extra volume.

It was amazing how much tidying you could get done in

twenty minutes when you were against the clock. She'd even straightened out the bedroom, which was ridiculously optimistic. Scanning the living room, she panicked that she'd gone overboard. She didn't want him thinking she was a neat freak or that she was trying to impress him. Retrieving a jumper that she'd previously put away, she slung it back over the arm of the couch. She'd just moved a glass of water back from the kitchen to the coffee table when the doorbell rang.

Jess took a deep breath and wiped her hands on her jeans before she opened the door. "Thanks so much," she said on a long exhale. "You're a lifesaver."

"Always happy to help a damsel in distress." He held out a shopping bag. "I also brought beers. A bit of DIY and a couple of beers seems like a nice way to finish off the weekend."

"Perfect. Thanks." She led the way to the kitchen, feeling a little unsettled by his scrutiny of the house.

"Cute place," he remarked, looking around the kitchen.

"Thanks. It's just rented." She flipped the tops off two of the beer bottles and handed him one.

"You told Ava your place is tiny," he said as he clicked the bottle against hers.

She grimaced. "I'm not sure I want a housemate. I like living alone. And Ava seems lovely but I don't really know her very well and she …"

"Talks a lot?" Rory asked.

"Yeah." She tipped her head in the direction of the living room and he followed her through.

"Oh." He looked down at the bookcase. "It looks as though you managed pretty well yourself."

"Don't sound so surprised! I managed it fine. I just can't move it alone."

"Not such a damsel in distress after all." He set his beer on the coffee table then bent to lift the bookcase while Jess moved to take the other side. "Where do you want it?"

"In the corner." They shuffled across the room and got it in place, then Jess stepped back to look. "Finally, I have space to put my books."

Rory lifted the flap of the cardboard box on the floor and picked out a couple of books. "*Higher Chemistry*," he said, turning the book over. "*National 5 Chemistry, The Cradle of Chemistry*. I see you have eclectic reading tastes."

"Leave me alone." She took the books from him and deposited them on a shelf before nudging him away from her books.

"That's all you needed me for?" he asked, dropping onto the couch and reaching for his beer.

"Yes. I'm happy I managed to put it together myself. I feel very accomplished."

"You might want to wait and see if it holds up under the weight of all your textbooks before you congratulate yourself too much."

"It's sturdy," she insisted, taking the opposite end of the couch and sitting sideways with one leg bent up. Immediately, she began to panic about what to say. She hated gaps in conversation, and her brain worked like crazy to try and think of things to talk about.

"Why does Sunday night always come around so quickly?" she said in a rush. "It's always the same: it's Friday evening, then I blink and it's Sunday night. It doesn't help that I seem to spend half the weekend marking or planning lessons." She was blethering and was fairly sure she sounded nervous.

"That's a good thing about having Arran on the weekends. It forces me to be organised and get everything done during the week."

"I enjoyed meeting him yesterday. He's sweet."

"He's a little rascal. But he's so much fun."

She smiled, hoping she looked more relaxed than she felt. At least Arran was an easy topic of conversation. Once Rory started talking about him, he could go on for ages. Although, the conversation would probably lead to Elspeth, which she'd rather avoid.

"Are things easier with Arran now?" she asked. "Since you've settled into a routine for when he's with you and when he's with Elspeth." Mentally, she cursed herself. Why had *she* brought up Elspeth? This is exactly how she'd ended up in the friend-zone in the first place. She'd never get out of it if she carried on like this.

Rory pushed his head back into the couch, looking suddenly exhausted. "No," he said slowly. "I thought spending a lot of time with him over the Easter holidays would help, but most of the time when he's with me I feel as though I'm traumatising him."

"He definitely didn't look like a traumatised kid to me. He seemed perfectly content."

"Having you there helped distract him. Usually, he asks for Elspeth constantly." He stared up at the ceiling for a moment. "It's not so bad during the day – he asks when he's going home, but more like curiosity than anything. But at bedtime he cries for his mum. Practically every time he stays over. Sometimes I feel so bad that I want to put him in the car and take him home."

"Does Elspeth know that?" she asked, realising there was no escaping the conversation now. And maybe talking to him about his problems would bring them closer.

"No. I daren't tell her in case she suggests he doesn't stay over with me."

"Could she do that?"

He flicked his head to look at her. "What do you mean?"

"Does she have the right to say you can't see him, legally?"

"We agreed we'd figure things out between us and not get the courts involved. But she's his mum, if she thought it was better for him not to stay over at my place, I'm not sure I'd argue with her. Honestly, when he's so upset going to bed I'm almost tempted to suggest it myself."

"You're a great dad," she said. "And Arran obviously adores

you. Surely lots of kids get upset at bedtime, even if they live with both of their parents."

The smile spread slowly over Rory's face. "Thanks," he said quietly.

"What for?"

"For reminding me that bedtime was a battle even when we all lived together."

"See! There you go. I'm sure you're doing a great job. Change is always difficult."

"I knew it would be an adjustment, but there are so many things that didn't even occur to me when we split up."

"Like what?"

His brows knitted together. "Like today when I dropped Arran off. Elspeth asked what we'd done all weekend and I didn't know whether to mention that we'd hung out with you yesterday."

"So you didn't tell her?"

"No. I probably would have done if her sisters hadn't been there. Leana's having some problems with Alasdair, so I didn't want to say anything that would leave them complaining about me as well. Sorry, I'm blethering on. This must be really boring for you."

"It's like a soap opera," she said. "I feel as though I know them all. Seeing Isla and Logan in the pub felt like seeing celebrities."

He chuckled. "I'm sorry. I'll shut up."

"It's okay. It's probably good for you to get it all off your chest." Sadly, she seemed to have developed an odd fascination about his ex and her family. She was also keen to gauge how he felt about Elspeth now.

"It's all confusing. I don't think I need to tell Elspeth who I'm hanging out with, though, even if it is when Arran's with me."

"What about if it was the other way around? If she was hanging out with a male friend when Arran was there."

The twitch of his cheek didn't go unnoticed, and Jess began to wish she'd changed the subject when she'd had the chance. If he wasn't over Elspeth, did she really want to hear that?

"I'd never be concerned about Arran's welfare when he's with her. But at the same time, I probably wouldn't like it."

Her heart sank. "Not because of anything to do with Arran, but because you don't like the idea of her with someone else?"

"Yeah. It would bother me."

With great effort, Jess managed to keep her smile fixed. "Do you think you'll get back together?"

"No," he said firmly.

"But you're still in love with her?" She supposed she may as well know one way or another.

He took another swig of beer, then picked at the corner of the label. "Elspeth was my first love. She's the only person I've ever been in love with, and I think I'll always feel connected to her. Maybe that's because of Arran, I'm not sure. But I also don't want to spend the rest of my life wallowing and wishing things were different. She's not in love with me and I want to move on. I think that's better for everyone." He smiled gently. "You can just tell me to shut up. I won't be offended."

She shook her head, feeling a mixture of sadness and hope. The way he spoke about Elspeth made her think no one else would ever measure up. Whoever Rory ended up with would probably spend their life being second best. But when she looked at him, there was a part of her that thought second best might be enough.

"I'm sorry if I put you in an awkward situation," she said. "Do you think Arran will mention that I was with you yesterday?"

"This is what worries me. Not mentioning it was probably a bad move, but it all feels ridiculous anyway. If I was dating someone, I'd tell her. But it was just hanging out with a friend."

Jess swallowed hard. "Yeah."

"I'm probably worrying about nothing. Arran's got a

memory like a sieve. All he talks about are dinosaurs or random things. If I ask him what he's been doing at nursery or with Elspeth he can never remember."

"Fingers crossed he doesn't mention it then. But stop stressing about it now. Just drink your beer and chill out."

"Okay, I can do that. And then we're going to put all those books on the shelves."

"No. I don't need help with that. You'll only tease me about the number of textbooks I have."

"I think we should guess how many chemistry books you have. The winner buys the first round of drinks on Friday night?"

"Fine. As long as you don't tease me the whole time."

"I can't promise that," he said with a cheeky smile.

Jess grinned, not really caring about him teasing her. It was the closest she got to him being affectionate and she'd take all she could get.

CHAPTER TEN

A fter Rory left, Elspeth went back to join her sisters in the kitchen, happy they were there to take her mind off of the guilt she felt every time he left. It would be nice if that would go away sometime soon.

Arran climbed onto her lap when she sat back at the table, and she enjoyed the feel of his little body against hers. Even after one night away she missed him.

"What did you do with Daddy?" she asked, resting her cheek against his hair.

"Played," he replied.

She rolled her eyes at her sisters. Trying to find anything out from him was always impossible. Not just when he'd been with Rory, but when he'd been at nursery or with another member of the family.

"Did you go out somewhere or just stay at Daddy's house?" she asked.

"I don't know."

"I bet I can guess what you did," Leana said. "Did you build a rocket and fly to the moon?"

He giggled. "No!"

Isla looked thoughtful. "Did you go swimming in a pool filled with chocolate?"

"No! You're silly. I played with Daddy."

"And that's all I ever get out of him," Elspeth said on a sigh.

Arran twirled a section of Elspeth's hair around his finger. "Can I watch TV?"

"I suppose so." She kissed his head and set him on the floor.

He was almost out of the room when he stopped and turned to Isla. "I found sea glass for you."

"Ooh, brilliant. Did you find any good pieces?"

"Yes. Can you give me ten pounds for it?"

Elspeth's eyes widened and the three of them laughed.

"No, I can't," Isla replied.

"Oh." He stared at her for a moment. "You've got pretty hair."

"Thanks," she said with a frown. "Go and find my sea glass." She waited until he was out of the room before she spoke again. "What on earth was that?"

Elspeth affected a mock-stern look. "I'll have a word with him about lying. That's not acceptable."

"It was the extortion that worried me. When did he lie?"

"Saying you've got pretty hair."

"Ha-ha! I can't believe he asked for money for the sea glass."

Leana leaned onto the table. "What I can't believe is that none of the rest of us ever thought of that. You probably should pay us for it."

Arran came back in, carrying a Ziploc bag. He climbed onto a chair, kneeling as he opened the bag and poured the contents over the table. "I found sea glass for Isla and shells for Mummy."

"What about me?" Leana asked.

"How about you take the sand and bits of seaweed?" Elspeth suggested, frowning at the mess on the kitchen table.

Arran pushed the shells around until he found what he was looking for. "Here," he said, handing it to Isla.

Squinting, she brushed off the sand. "It's red. You found red sea glass! That's really pretty. Thank you." She went to the sink and rinsed the sand off, then held it up to the light. "It's gorgeous. Aren't you a clever boy?"

"Jess is clever," he said as he rifled through the assorted items on the table. He passed Elspeth a shell.

"Pardon?" Elspeth said.

"Jess found the sea glass. She's very clever. And she has pretty hair. Daddy said so."

Elspeth felt a dull pain in her chest. She glanced at her sisters, who both looked dumbstruck. "Who's Jess?" she asked, feeling as though she was picking a wound.

"Daddy's friend from work."

"And she was at the beach with you?"

"Yes." He kept his head down and continued to pass Elspeth shells. "Her favourite food is fish and chips so that's what we had for dinner."

"She had dinner with you?" Elspeth felt like a parrot but she needed clarification.

"Yes."

"At Daddy's house?"

"Yes."

Leana said her name in a tone that sounded like a warning, but Elspeth couldn't seem to stop herself.

"Did Jess stay after dinner too?" she asked. "When you went to bed?"

"Stop it," Isla said quietly, but Arran spoke over her.

"She cleaned the kitchen while Daddy put me in bed. Like you did when Daddy lived with us."

Elspeth felt sick and was only vaguely aware of Leana walking around the table.

"Was she there when you woke up?" Elspeth asked, forcing the words out.

"Stop it, *now*," Leana growled. Swiftly, she lifted Arran off the chair, kissing the top of his head before walking out of the room with him. A moment later, the sound of the TV drifted from the living room.

"You can't do that," Leana said when she walked back in and pulled the door closed behind her. "If you have questions, ask Rory, not Arran. He's four years old, for goodness' sake."

"You're right." Elspeth put her hands over her face as her chest felt as though it was being crushed. "I knew this would happen. I knew he'd find someone else. But it feels as though we only just broke up. How did he find someone else so quickly? He made out he was so upset when we split up, but he clearly doesn't care that much."

She heard the screech of a chair and felt a hand on her back before Leana's voice landed softly in her ear.

"You don't even know if he is seeing anyone. She's probably just a friend."

"He should tell me who Arran's spending time with. I'm his mother, I should know who's around my son."

Leana rubbed gentle circles on her back. "Do you feel you have to tell Rory who you spend time with?"

"No. But he knows everyone that I hang out with." She glanced up and caught Isla biting her nail. "Why do you look so nervous?"

"No reason. I mean, I'm not nervous."

Elspeth glared at her. "Oh my God! You know he's seeing someone, don't you?"

"No." She shook her head. "But we saw him in the pub on Friday."

"On a date?"

"With his colleagues. But there were a couple of women who he was spending most of his time with." She grimaced. "And now I feel awful. Like I was spying on him or something."

"Did he look as though he was with one of them?"

"Not really. I don't know. I shouldn't have mentioned it."

Tears spilled down Elspeth's cheeks and she leaned her head onto Leana's shoulder. "I can't believe this is happening," she said. Her throat felt so tight it was difficult to breath.

Isla moved around the table and pulled up a chair at the other side of her. Sandwiched in a hug from her sisters, Elspeth let herself cry softly for a few minutes. Eventually, Leana moved to get her a tissue.

"At the risk of making myself even more unpopular," Isla said, "why are you so upset at the idea of Rory seeing someone else? You split up with him. You can't not want him for yourself, but not want anyone else to have him."

Elspeth refused to respond. Mostly because she didn't have a good answer. She was the one who'd turned her and Rory's lives upside down. It was a bit rich to complain that he'd landed on his feet while she'd landed firmly on her head.

As much as she wished she could go back and undo the mess she'd made, that wasn't an option. Not after all she'd put Rory through. All she could do was try and make the best of things.

CHAPTER ELEVEN

Leana yawned as she let herself into the house on Sunday evening. The visit to Elspeth left her even more worried about her sister. If Rory was seeing someone else it was a bit of a slap in the face for Elspeth. They really hadn't been broken up for very long.

It was late enough that she could go to bed. Hopefully she'd actually manage a full night's sleep and feel better tomorrow. She had to work anyway, so that would help her to get back into a routine.

She was halfway up the stairs when her phone rang. At one time, seeing Alasdair's name on the screen would make her stomach flutter with butterflies, but now she only felt mild trepidation. Briefly, she even considered ignoring it.

"Finally!" he said when she answered. "I was worried I'd missed you again. The time difference is a pain. How are you?"

"Tired. The jet lag is still killing me."

"You'll feel better soon. How's everyone in Lannick?"

Walking into their bedroom, Leana sat on the edge of the bed. "Elspeth's not doing too well. She thinks Rory's seeing someone else."

"No way. Rory loves Elspeth. He definitely wouldn't start

seeing someone else so soon."

"Sometimes you just think you know someone," Leana said, "then it turns out that you don't."

There was a pause and she flopped back on the bed, wishing she hadn't said that.

"You're still angry with me?" he asked.

"Sorry. I'm tired. I was about to go to bed."

"I didn't do anything wrong," he said. "I didn't know there was a rule that I had to announce I didn't imagine us getting married. We never properly discussed marriage. You could have brought it up."

"I just assumed," she said.

"I realise that. But *I* assumed we were fine as we were. So I don't see why you're so angry with me."

"This conversation is pointless. I'm going to go to bed and we can talk about it another time."

There was a short pause. "Do you want me to call Rory and find out what's going on with him?"

"No." She sighed. "It's probably best not to get involved. If he is seeing someone, hopefully he has the decency to speak to Elspeth about it himself."

"I really can't imagine it. I got the impression he was still hoping Elspeth would change her mind and take him back."

"I kept thinking she might," Leana said, staring at the ceiling. "I really don't know what's going on in her head."

"I'm sure she'll be okay. You worry too much about everyone."

"My brain is foggy and I don't know if that's a compliment or an insult."

"It was more of an observation, but it's a good thing. I should let you get some sleep. Are you working tomorrow?"

"Yes. In the daytime."

"We're heading down to San Diego later today. I'll message you when I can."

"Okay."

"Oh, I almost forgot … I have a favour to ask you. I was supposed to rent the recording studio out to a couple of guys at the weekend. Will you be able to let them in? I feel bad cancelling on them."

"I guess so. I don't need to do anything, just let them in?"

"Yeah. I'll give them your number and tell them to call and arrange it with you. They're supposed to be there all day Saturday and Sunday, but you don't need to be in the house. I know them well enough and they're trustworthy. You met them once when we watched them playing a gig at the Isle's Inn. The band's called Bishop's Way. It's just the two guys: Conor and Patrick."

"It rings a bell." She actually wasn't sure she did remember them; Alasdair had been working to get more live music in the bars on Skye and they often went along to watch. "Just give them my number and I'll sort it out."

"You're the best." He paused. "I miss you."

"I miss you too," she said before ending the call.

On Monday morning, Jess scanned the staffroom but there was no sign of Rory. She lingered at the edge of a conversation with a couple of other teachers, nodding along as she sipped her coffee, but struggled to pay attention to their idle chat about their respective weekends. Eventually she muttered about getting to her classroom and wandered away.

Stepping into the hallway, she almost collided with Ava.

"I was just coming to find you," Ava said with a bright smile.

"The small talk in the staffroom is a bit much for a Monday morning," Jess said. "And I need to set up my classroom."

Ava raised her eyebrows. "You mean Rory's not in there so there's no need for you to hang around?"

"I really need to set up my classroom," Jess said, feeling her cheeks heating up.

"So you won't be interested to know I saw him heading down the hall a few minutes ago?" She tipped her head and Jess followed her gaze. The corridor was filling up with kids and a hum of chatter filled the air. "His classroom is along there, right?"

"Yes," Jess said.

"I'd say that's where he is then, if you were looking for him." Her eyes flashed with mischief.

"I wasn't looking for him," Jess said.

"You've gone bright red. And I already know you fancy him so it's a bit pointless trying to pretend otherwise. You should really make a move."

"I had dinner with him on Saturday," Jess said, lowering her voice. "I bumped into him with his son, and he invited me to eat with them."

"It doesn't exactly sound like a hot date," Ava said with a slight eye roll.

"He also came over to my place last night. I asked him to help me with the bookcase."

"That's more like it," Ava said, wiggling her eyebrows. "Did anything happen?"

"We had a good chat," Jess said. "It was really nice."

"You just *talked*?"

"Yeah. He's still getting over his ex. I don't want to rush things."

"I need more coffee for this conversation." Ava nodded towards the staffroom.

"I really have to get to my classroom. I'll talk to you later."

"Ask him out," Ava said, grinning. "On a proper date!"

"Maybe." Jess set off down the corridor. Her classroom was about as far away from Rory's as possible, but she had to pass his and slowed when she did. The door was closed, but she peeked in the window and saw him working away at his desk, a look of intense concentration on his face. Taking a step closer, she reached for the door handle, intent on saying a quick good morning. Then she hesitated. He looked to be in the middle of something, so she should probably leave him in peace. And she was slightly concerned about looking overly keen.

Before she had a chance to move away, he looked up at her. Inwardly, she groaned. Now she looked creepy, hanging around at his door, staring at him. Opening the door, she hoped it looked as though she'd been about to go in.

"Morning!" she said brightly.

He gave a weary smile. "Hi."

"I was just passing," she said, shifting her weight from foot to foot. "Looks like you're hard at work."

"Did you get the message about the staff meeting on Wednesday?" he asked.

She nodded slowly. "Yeah."

"I'm sure it's going to be a big waste of time." He rubbed at the back of his neck. "I could really do without it. Hopefully Elspeth doesn't mind me swapping things around this week. I usually go over and see Arran on Wednesdays. The meeting will throw my whole week off. Plus, I got roped into organising a fundraising raffle." He dragged his hands through his hair. "I can just about juggle everything, but then I get extra work and I'm not sure where to fit it in. I might have to give up Fridays in the pub for a while."

Jess's stomach lurched at the thought. Friday nights were the highlight of her week. "Maybe I can help you with the fundraiser," she suggested.

"Really?" He sat up straighter. "That would be amazing. I need to find local businesses to donate prizes."

"That's fine," she said, revelling in the warmth of his smile.

"Thank you."

"No problem." She took steps backwards towards the door. "Maybe we can get together one evening and discuss it?"

"That would be great. Thanks so much."

She told him she'd see him later and left him alone again, feeling pretty happy with herself.

CHAPTER TWELVE

E lspeth should have been relieved that Rory was moving on with his life. If he was seeing someone, it meant she didn't have to feel so guilty about hurting him. The trouble was that as the guilt faded, she was left feeling sad. And lonely. But if she was honest, she'd felt sad and lonely even when Rory was living with them.

The beginning of the week went slowly, and it was an effort for Elspeth to refrain from curling up in bed once Arran was at nursery and staying there until it was time to pick him up. She'd created her situation, and lying in bed feeling sorry for herself wouldn't get her anywhere. The numbness that she'd felt for so long had only recently started to ease and she refused to go back to it.

What she needed to do was keep busy. Work had always been her saviour. When everything felt too much, she could throw herself into work and forget everything else. Her idea to cut her working hours was ridiculous. She should be working more, not less. Time off was the last thing she needed.

So on Tuesday she opened the cafe again, forcing herself to chat politely with the few customers who came in and ignoring the feeling that her heart wasn't in it.

Rory couldn't come over on Wednesday as he usually did and had said he'd come on Thursday instead. Elspeth had told him it made no difference to her. What she hadn't considered was how Arran would react. By the time she took him up to bed on Wednesday, he was practically hysterical. Elspeth ended up in tears herself and was emotionally exhausted by the time he finally drifted off.

With the feeling that she'd probably scarred him for life by breaking up with Rory, she tossed and turned throughout the night. As her mind tortured her with thoughts of the mess she'd made of their lives, she was finally hit by an idea of how to make things better for Arran. When the sun came up, she was certain she knew what she should do. The sense of purpose was invigorating.

While Arran was eating his breakfast she made a quick phone call and felt a sense of relief as soon as she hung up. After dropping Arran at nursery, she hurried to her parents' place.

Walking into the kitchen, she was struck by memories of baking there: as a child when it was all for fun, and later when she'd done the prep for the cafe while her family members came and went. She'd always enjoyed the bustle, but in the last six months she'd taken to doing all the baking in her own kitchen or in the cafe. It was a while since she'd done anything in her parents' kitchen. She and Arran had stopped having dinner there too. It had seemed like a natural progression when Rory had moved in with them, but she felt a pang of sadness over it.

"Morning," her dad said. He was sitting at the kitchen table across from her mum. "Everything okay?"

"Yes."

"You look pale," Christine said. "You're not coming down with something, are you?"

"No. I'm fine. Are you working this afternoon?" Her mum worked part-time in the office of the local primary school and usually had Thursday afternoons off.

"No, I've got the day off. I'm going out with Isla – delivering a painting on the mainland and getting lunch on the way."

"Lovely," Elspeth said quietly, then turned her attention to her dad. "I don't suppose you're free this afternoon? I need someone to watch the cafe for an hour or so."

He shook his head. "I'm taking two distillery tours this afternoon."

"Is everything okay?" Christine asked.

"I have a doctor's appointment. I guess I can close for an hour. Or maybe Leana's free."

"She's working in the pub today," Christine said while Keith moved to put his mug by the sink.

He kissed the top of Christine's head. "I need to get to work. I'll see you later."

"You're not ill, are you?" Christine asked once he'd gone.

"No." Elspeth touched her cheek. "Do I look that bad?"

"I meant the doctor's appointment."

"It's not really for me," she said, pulling out a chair and taking a seat. "I want to get some advice about Arran. I'm worried about him." Making the appointment with the GP felt wonderfully proactive. Hopefully the doctor would put Elspeth's mind at ease that she was worrying about nothing. But if she thought Arran was having a problem dealing with things, she'd be able to suggest ways to help him. Asking for advice felt like responsible parenting.

"What's wrong with Arran?" Christine asked.

"Nothing, physically. But I think he's very confused about the situation between Rory and me. It's hard to know what's going on in his head. I wonder if he needs to see a child psychologist or something."

"I'm sure he's fine," Christine said. "Good to get professional advice though if you're concerned. Are you seeing Tricia Andrews?"

"Yes." Dr Andrews had been their family doctor for years. She'd been the first port of call when Elspeth had found out she was pregnant and had been a lovely, soothing presence in a stressful time.

"Maybe you can mention how stressed you've been," Christine said hesitantly. It wasn't the first time she'd suggested Elspeth speak to the doctor. She also wasn't the only one. Rory had raised the subject too, and Elspeth had torn strips off him in response – accusing him of suggesting she must be ill to want to split up with him. Remembering how hostile she'd been towards him gave her a flutter of anxiety deep in her stomach.

"I'm fine," she said forcefully. "I only want to make sure Arran is okay."

"Whatever you think," Christine said. "I better get ready. Isla will be waiting for me."

"Have a good day," Elspeth said, then left the warmth of the kitchen and walked back to the cottage to get on with some baking.

A few hikers stopped into the cafe for lunch, making Elspeth panic that she might actually be busy on the one day that she needed it to be quiet. Thankfully the place was empty again after lunch, and Elspeth put the closed sign on the door, hoping that she wouldn't have too many unhappy customers arriving to find the cafe closed. With any luck, the appointment would be on time and she'd be back in an hour to open up again. She'd probably pick Arran up straight after the doctor's appointment so she didn't have to go out again.

As she stood at the reception desk at the doctor's surgery, her phone vibrated in her bag. She ignored it and continued chatting to the receptionist as she filled out the latest data protection form, signing it without bothering to read it.

She smiled at a grey-haired lady as she took a seat in the waiting room. The quiet made her nervous and a bout of nerves hit her. What if Dr Andrews told her that Arran's bedtime tears were a sign of irreparable psychological damage and that she'd traumatised him for life? Maybe she'd be better keeping her concerns to herself rather than risking a lecture about what a terrible parent she was.

Telling herself to get a grip, she focused on the fish swimming around a large tank at the side of the room. Arran always loved to watch them whenever he was there.

Her phone vibrated again ten minutes later, reminding her of the previous missed call. She pulled the phone out, fully intending to cancel the call and turn her phone off. Until she saw it was Rory. He should be at work.

"Are you okay?" she asked as she answered it, half expecting it to be a pocket dial.

"The nursery rang me," he said. "Apparently they tried you but got no answer. Arran fell and needs to be picked up."

"Is he all right?"

"Yeah. They didn't seem worried. But he bumped his head and they have that policy about head injuries."

She sighed heavily.

"Can you get him?" Rory asked. "I was in the middle of a lesson. When I didn't answer my mobile they called the school office."

"Sorry. I'm at an appointment." Quickly she ran through a brief mental list of people she could ask to pick him up.

"Can you ask Isla?" Rory suggested, clearly going through the same thought process as she was.

"She's on the mainland for the day with Mum. Dad's taking tour groups around the distillery, and Leana's at work. Maybe I could try Logan, or Leana might be able to nip out from the pub and get him." She shook her head. "Never mind, I'll go and get him myself."

"Where are you?"

"I'm at the doctor. I'm waiting for my appointment but I can rearrange it."

"Are you okay?"

"Yes." She picked up her bag from beside the chair, preparing to leave. "It's not urgent. I can come back another day." Or maybe never, considering she wasn't entirely sure telling the doctor that she'd messed up her kid's life was really a great idea.

"Hang on a sec," Rory said. There was a muffled conversation in the background before he spoke to Elspeth again. "I can get him."

"I thought you were in the middle of a lesson?"

"There's only half an hour left. I can get someone to cover for me. It's fine. I'm leaving now. I'll see you at home."

She barely had time to thank him before the line went dead. Returning her phone to her bag, her mind got stuck on Rory's voice referring to the cottage as home. He always did that, and she wondered how long it would be before he started calling it "her house" instead.

When her name was called she looked up to see Dr Andrews smiling at her across the room. She followed her silently and took a seat across her desk with a feeling of dread.

"I'm worried about Arran." As she forced the words out, her chin quivered and she burst into tears.

CHAPTER THIRTEEN

Arran and Rory were side by side on the couch when Elspeth arrived home.

"I'm really sorry." She avoided eye contact with Rory in the hopes he wouldn't notice she'd been crying. It was like a dam had broken when she'd started talking to Dr Andrews, and she'd sniffed and sobbed her way through the conversation with the kind and patient doctor.

"How are you?" she asked Arran, gently pushing the hair off his forehead as she searched for a bump. There was a small bruise above his right eye.

"He seems fine," Rory said.

Arran dragged his gaze from the TV for a moment. "Daddy said I can watch TV even though it's not the weekend!"

"I think TV is fine if you're poorly or injured." She ruffled his hair. "I'll find you some dinner."

"Is everything okay?" Rory asked.

Nodding, Elspeth walked away, feeling his eyes on her the whole time. She was staring into the kitchen cupboards, trying to concentrate for long enough to come up with an idea for what to have for dinner when she heard Rory come in. "I'm really sorry you had to leave work," she said, without turning around. "You won't get into trouble or anything, will you?"

"No. I got someone from the office to keep an eye on the class for the last half hour. She'll no doubt make me pay for all her drinks tomorrow night, but it's fine."

"You still go out for work drinks on Fridays?" she asked.

"Yeah." His tone changed. "But if you ever want me to have Arran from Friday night instead of Saturday, that's fine."

That wasn't actually what Elspeth had been thinking about. She'd been wondering if his Friday nights involved the woman he was seeing. More tears stung her eyes and she continue to keep her attention fixed on the contents of the cupboard.

"Do you want a cup of tea?" she asked. "I can bring it through."

"No, thanks."

Elspeth waited for the sound of him going back to the living room, but he stayed where he was. The silence was uncomfortable, and Elspeth randomly moved a packet of pasta and then a box of rice.

"Are you sure you're okay?" Rory asked.

"Yes. Fine. Maybe you ought to keep an eye on Arran."

He sighed heavily. "Can you turn around and look at me?"

Squeezing her eyes shut made the tears spill down her cheeks.

"I'm fine," she said as she turned to him.

"You're obviously not. I realise it's probably none of my business, but you had a doctor's appointment and then you come home in tears. Can you tell me what's going on so I don't assume it's something terrible?"

"There's nothing wrong," she sniffed. "I'm fine."

"Why were you at the doctor?"

She brushed tears from her cheeks and leaned against the counter. "I wanted to ask about Arran. I was worried that he wasn't coping with you moving out and the whole situation with us so I wanted to check he shouldn't have some sort of counselling or something."

"What did the doctor say?"

More tears came. "She said from what I described he sounds like a happy, healthy kid. She thought we'd handled everything perfectly and it didn't sound as though there was anything to worry about with Arran."

Rory bit his lip and took a few steps towards her. "So why are you so upset?"

"I'm not. Just ignore me." Her vision blurred with yet more tears and she covered her face with her hands. The feel of Rory's arms folding around her made her cry even more and she buried her face in his chest. It was the first time she'd had physical contact with him since he'd moved out, and it felt safe and comforting. She clung to him, savouring the feel of his muscles beneath his shirt and the heady scent of him that was so familiar. "Sorry," she said when she finally pulled away.

"You don't need to apologise." He led her to the table and pulled out a chair for her before fetching a box of tissues and setting them on the table. She wiped her eyes and blew her nose. "What else did the doctor say?" Rory asked softly.

She took a deep, shuddering breath and did her best to keep her voice even. "She thinks that maybe I should have counselling." Her chin trembled and she paused to compose herself. "She said that having Arran when I was so young was traumatic and that I probably didn't process all the emotions around it properly."

"That makes sense," Rory said. "You went through a lot."

Elspeth was thankful that he refrained from mentioning that he'd said all of this to her when they'd been trying to fix their relationship before he moved out. He'd suggested she should talk to a therapist and even asked if she was depressed. She'd been adamant she wasn't, but now she wasn't so sure.

"She says I work too much and that I probably have burnout and that I should stop working completely for a while." She searched Rory's features, wondering if he'd find the suggestion as ludicrous as she did, but he barely reacted. "I can't stop working," she said fiercely.

"A break might do you good." He moved his chair closer and put a hand over hers.

"I couldn't, even if I wanted to. Dad was shocked at the idea of me taking two days a week off. If I tell him I want to close for a month he'll go crazy."

"No, he wouldn't," Rory said confidently. "Keith wouldn't care."

"You don't get it," she said, pulling her hand from his. "It was so much stress for Mum and Dad to set up the cafe for me. They had to borrow money from Logan and then spent years paying him back. I can't just close up. They'll think I'm completely ungrateful."

Rory swallowed hard. "No, they wouldn't. I promise you that if you talk to them they'd be okay with it. They'd probably be happy about it."

"I don't even know what I'd do if I took time off." She reached for another tissue. "But Dr Andrews said that might be part of the problem. She said I've got into the habit of using work as an escape from my problems, and that it was probably a good coping mechanism for a while but it's clearly not working any more. She suggested I find something to do for myself that isn't working or looking after Arran."

"Why don't you give it a try? Take a month off and have a proper break."

"It's not realistic. I need the money apart from anything else."

"You can manage for a month. And what if I start paying child support? That would help."

"No," she said, raising her voice. They'd had that conversation a few times and she always refused him. "You shouldn't have to pay child support when I'm the one who asked you to move out. It's already unfair that you and Arran are being punished for my choices."

"What's that supposed to mean?"

"It means I was the one who split our family up, and now you and Arran only get to see each other a couple of times a week. So, there's no way I'd ever take money from you. It's not as though you can afford it either."

"I'd manage," he said, looking at her in confusion. "And you don't have to keep feeling guilty. We both decided I should move out."

"But you didn't want to."

"No, but I agreed it was for the best in the circumstances."

The circumstances being that she didn't want to live with him any more. Sometimes, she thought it might be easier if he wasn't quite so lovely about it all. If he'd shout at her it might ease her guilt. She stayed where she was while Rory moved to fill the kettle. She felt utterly drained and all she wanted to do was sleep.

"Go and sit with Arran," Rory said, putting a cup of tea in front of her. "I'll find some dinner."

She thanked him and wandered to the living room, too exhausted to protest the offer.

On the couch, Arran snuggled up to her and she stared blankly at the cartoons on the screen. Her mind whirred over everything – trying to figure out if she really could close the cafe for a little while, and if it would even help. She wasn't at all convinced it was what she needed. Without her routines she'd probably fall apart altogether.

Rory called through to them after half an hour, telling them dinner was ready. Surprisingly, Arran made no complaint about having to move away from the TV and went happily into the kitchen.

"Sausages and mash," Rory announced.

"Can I have ketchup?" Arran asked.

"Yes." Rory got it from the fridge and set it in the middle of the table. "But try and get most of it in your mouth today instead of over your face and down your top."

"It drips!" Arran said with a grin.

Elspeth had no appetite but managed a few mouthfuls while Rory and Arran kept up a constant stream of chatter. She insisted on tidying up when they'd all finished and shooed them away to the living room. The sound of them playing together while she loaded the dishwasher alternately filled her with joy and self-loathing. In some ways it was so easy having Rory around, and in some ways it felt impossible.

They were wrestling on the floor when she went into them.

"I think it might be bedtime," she said.

Rory ran a hand through his hair when he stood up. "Which story are we having tonight? I'd like *The Cat in the Hat*."

"I want Mummy to read," Arran said.

"Oh." Rory looked surprised and possibly offended. "Okay."

"It's Daddy's turn to put you to bed," Elspeth said, hiding her shock that he wanted her for once.

Arran bounded up onto the couch before flinging himself into Rory's arms. "Daddy can help me get ready and Mummy can read the story."

"You are one spoilt kid," Rory said. "But I guess that's fine." He looked to Elspeth for confirmation and she nodded her approval.

She gave them five minutes before following them up. Arran was already tucked up in bed and Rory lay beside him as they chatted.

"Are you sure you want me to read?" Elspeth asked, expecting that Arran might have changed his mind by now.

"Yes." He rolled onto his side and kissed Rory's cheek. "Goodnight, Daddy."

"Goodnight," Rory replied. "Try not to injure yourself at nursery tomorrow!"

Arran giggled. "Okay."

"Thank you for collecting him today," Elspeth said stepping onto the landing with Rory. "And for putting up with me."

His brows twitched together. "Will you take some time off like the doctor said?"

"I don't think it's a good idea. And I don't see how it will help. If anything, it's likely to cause tension with Dad. I can't deal with that."

"Talk to your parents at least. Please."

"I'll think about it," she said. "You don't have to worry about me you know."

"I might not have to," he said, moving away from her. "But I do."

She watched over the bannister as he walked downstairs, then she went back to Arran. She read the story and lay with him until he was asleep. On the landing, she contemplated going to bed herself when a noise downstairs drew her attention. Her mum smiled up at her from the bottom of the stairs and whispered hello. Keith was just closing the front door behind them.

"What are you doing here?" Elspeth asked, walking down. Her dad's features were scrunched in a frown and Christine looked as though she'd been crying. "Has something happened?" she asked, a feeling of dread fluttering in her chest.

"No," Christine said. "We just want to have a chat with you."

Elspeth led the way into the living room, then turned back to them. "You're freaking me out. You look so serious. Everything's okay, isn't it?" Her mind raced back to leaving the cafe that afternoon. "I didn't leave the water running in the cafe or the oven on or something?"

"No." Christine sat beside her and patted her knee while Keith lowered himself into the armchair. "Everything's fine."

"We were just talking to Rory," Keith said.

"He spoke to you?" Her jaw tensed along with every muscle in her body. "Of course he did."

"He's worried about you," Christine said. "We all are."

"There's no need." Elspeth folded her arms across her chest. "I'm fine."

"Do you want to close the cafe for a month?" Keith asked.

"No, I don't."

"But the doctor advised you to take some time off?" he asked.

Elspeth rolled her eyes. "I told Rory that in confidence. He has no right to go around telling everyone."

"Don't be silly," Christine said, shaking her head. "You know he wouldn't do that. But he thinks you won't close the cafe unless you're forced to."

"No one can force me to close the cafe," she said indignantly.

Keith rubbed his hands over his face, then looked at her sadly. "You *run* the cafe," he said in a gentle tone. "You don't *own* it."

Elspeth let out a humourless laugh. "So you're going to close the cafe to force me to stop working?"

"Aye," Keith said. "For a month to start with and then we'll talk about what happens after that."

"You can't decide that for me," Elspeth said, sounding slightly hysterical. "I need the money, and I don't want to stop working. I don't need to. I'm not ill. There's nothing wrong with me."

"Money isn't an issue," Keith said. "While you're not working, you don't have to pay us rent. And if you're hungry, you know what time we eat dinner. Our kitchen's been bloody quiet recently anyway. There's only Logan who eats with us these days."

"I don't want to close the cafe." Elspeth adopted a calmer tone, suspecting that hysterical outbursts would only confirm the idea that she needed a break.

"It's not a discussion." Keith stood up. "The cafe's closing for a month and that's the end of it."

"Dad!" she snapped, but he walked out without looking

back. The front door banged behind him a moment later. Elspeth turned to her mum. "What's his problem?"

"He's worried about you. And he's angry with himself for not insisting you take time off ages ago."

"I'm going to kill Rory," Elspeth said. "He had no right to go behind my back and speak to you. It's none of his business."

"It *is* his business," Christine said. "Surely you can see that."

"Why? Because I'm the mother of his child and he thinks I'm being a terrible mother?"

Christine raised an eyebrow. "No. Because he loves you and he's concerned about you."

"No." Elspeth bit her lip, thinking of his clever new friend with the pretty hair.

"He only came to talk to us because he was worried," her mum went on. "And it wasn't his idea to insist on closing the cafe. That was all your dad. But, really, what's the harm in it?"

"Probably nothing. But there's also no point to it. I'm fine."

"You might get better quicker if you stop telling yourself that."

Elspeth's chin twitched. "I don't know what's wrong with me," she murmured.

Her mum's arms circled around her and her forehead touched hers. "You've been doing too much for too long. Now you need a rest."

CHAPTER FOURTEEN

Closing the cafe made Elspeth decidedly uneasy. She loved her job, and the thought of having it taken away from her, even temporarily, didn't sit well. Being idle for a month might sound like bliss to some people, but to Elspeth it sounded like torture. She liked being busy.

On Friday morning she put an announcement on the website and the social media sites saying that they would be closing temporarily. Once Arran was at nursery she went over to the cafe and made a list of things she needed to do, then got to work. She hadn't been there long when her dad walked in with a face like thunder.

"For once in your life will you do as you're told," he snapped. "I told you the cafe isn't going to open for a month. Which part of that don't you understand?"

Walking out of the kitchen, Elspeth met his gaze with a steely one of her own. "I understood completely. You made it pretty clear."

"So why are you here?"

She put her hands on her hips. "Do you actually think I can just flip the sign on the door and walk away for a month?"

"Yes! That's exactly what I want you to do."

"What about the food in the fridge?" she asked calmly. "And the dishes in the dishwasher? The crumbs on the floor which will likely attract mice if I don't sweep them up?"

"Oh." His features relaxed and he looked fairly sheepish.

Pulling out her phone, Elspeth brought up the homepage of the website and held it out to show him the announcement that they were closed. "See! I'm doing as I'm told so you can stop throwing your weight around. As soon as I've cleaned and sorted out the kitchen I won't be back here again for a month." Sadness settled in the pit of her stomach and she scanned the room that had been her refuge for the last four years. Her gaze landed on Isla's paintings hanging on the wall. "What about those?" she asked.

"What about them?"

"Isla's not going to be happy. Closing the cafe affects her income too."

"She's a big girl, she can figure it out. If she wants to open up to sell her paintings she's welcome to."

"You know there's no way she'll do that."

"That's up to her," he said.

"See you later," Elspeth said, heading back to the kitchen.

"I'm not trying to punish you, you know?" Keith said.

She nodded and didn't look back.

"I love you," he said quietly.

"I know." She was too angry to tell him she loved him too. Continuing to the kitchen, she took a deep breath and tried to remember what she'd been doing before the interruption.

She spent all day expecting a visit or phone call from Isla. The lack of contact made her think the news of the cafe closing hadn't reached her yet. Twice, customers had knocked on the door and asked if she was open, despite the sign on the door stating otherwise. Each time she'd fought the urge to let them in and ask what they wanted.

By the middle of the afternoon, the place was spotless. Stepping outside and locking the door filled her with a sense of loss and she had to remind herself it was only temporary.

She contemplated having dinner at her parents' house that evening, but instead made pasta for her and Arran. They ate it in front of the TV, Elspeth having steered the decision of what to watch to a Disney film that reminded her of her childhood and felt familiar and comforting. When Rory called, anger coursed through her and she didn't answer the phone. He called again later in the evening, then followed up with a message asking why she was ignoring him.

Frowning, she set the phone aside, ignoring him again.

On Friday afternoon, Jess rushed along the corridor and burst out through the main school doors. Rory had just left and she was keen to catch him before he drove away. She'd parked her car beside his that morning, so she slowed her pace and tried to look casual when she saw him standing between their cars, staring down at his phone.

"I'm so ready for a drink," she said, making his head shoot up.

"Me too," he muttered.

"I've also been thinking about the raffle. We should get together sometime and you can let me know what you want me to do."

He looked at her with a puzzled expression.

"I said I'd help you organise the raffle." After not finding a chance to speak to him all week she was feeling bold about engineering a way to spend time with him. "I just need you to tell me what I should do."

"Yes." He scratched the back of his head, seeming distracted. "That would be great."

"What are you doing for dinner?" she asked, sounding way more confident than she felt.

He shook his head vaguely. "Frozen pizza."

"Sounds good. I could bring salad, and a bottle of wine. We can have dinner together before we go up to the pub. That'll give us chance to discuss the fundraiser."

He opened and closed his mouth, then glanced at his phone again.

"You seem miles away," Jess said.

"Sorry. I think Elspeth is annoyed with me. I tried to call but she didn't answer."

Jess forced her lips to stay fixed in a smile. "Why would she be annoyed with you?"

"Long story," he said on a sigh.

"I'm going to nip home and get changed. Then I'll call at the shop and pick up salad and wine. You can tell me all about it over dinner. Okay?"

His brow wrinkled and he looked thoughtful for a moment. "Yeah," he finally said. "Thanks."

"See you soon."

As she drove away, she let out a long breath. It would be nice if she didn't feel as though she was chasing him so much, but it didn't matter; she got to have dinner with him. The more time she spent alone with him the better. Whenever he was ready to move on from Elspeth, she'd be there, waiting.

An hour later, she stood on his doorstep and smoothed down her grey shirt dress, which was cinched at the waist with a thin belt. It was a little chilly for sheer tights but it wasn't as though she'd be outside much.

"Hi," Rory said, when he answered the door. He'd changed into jeans and T-shirt and looked much more relaxed than he had done outside the school.

"Are you okay?" Jess asked, brushing past him as she stepped inside. "You seemed stressed earlier."

"It's been an eventful week," he said, leading the way to the kitchen.

"Did you have an argument with Elspeth or something?" Jess cursed herself for immediately bringing the conversation around to Elspeth, but if they'd had an argument she was keen to know.

"Not really." He rooted in a drawer for a corkscrew when she passed him the bottle of wine. "I can't explain it all but I was trying to help. She's not in a good place at the moment and I was worried so I spoke to her parents."

Jess winced.

"That sounds bad, doesn't it?" he said. "But I know her parents well and they're really lovely and supportive. Except they can't support her if they don't know what's going on."

"I suppose," Jess half-heartedly agreed.

He handed her a glass of wine, then turned the oven on. "It was probably a bad move. But I meant well."

"She should at least appreciate your concern," Jess said, sitting at the table when he did.

"I suspect Elspeth would argue that I have no right to interfere in her life, even if it's because I'm concerned."

"She's the mother of your child, and Arran spends most of his time with her so—"

"I'm not concerned about Arran," Rory said sharply. "I'm worried about Elspeth, but I've never once questioned her ability to care for Arran. So I really don't have any right to interfere in her life." He stood and paced to the window which looked out over a tiny back garden.

"Sorry," Jess said automatically. "I shouldn't have commented."

He shook his head and leaned heavily against the sideboard. "No, I'm sorry. I shouldn't be dumping all this on you." When his phone buzzed he took it from his pocket and read a message. "Tom says he'll be in the pub at seven. The rest of them should be there about then too." He sighed. "I'm not sure I'm feeling sociable enough for a night in the pub."

"We could always stay here, if you want."

His lips twitched upwards. "You're a glutton for punishment. I definitely can't subject you to an evening listening to me complaining. Let's have dinner and wander up to the pub. I'll probably feel better after a couple of drinks."

Jess did her best to hide her disappointment. Sadly, she'd be more than happy to listen to him complain for the evening as long as she had him all to herself. "I brought stuff for a salad," she said, moving to the shopping bag which she'd set on the counter.

"Thanks," he said before his phone began to vibrate with a call. He stared at it dumbly.

"Is that Elspeth calling you back?" Jess asked, busying herself with the salad.

"No. It's some random number." He answered it hesitantly. His features relaxed and he greeted whoever it was cheerfully, then walked out of the kitchen as he chatted. Jess strained to hear, but listening to one side of a conversation wasn't overly informative.

"That was slightly bizarre," Rory said, walking back in a few minutes later.

"Who was it?"

"Mary, the landlady of the pub in Lannick." He reached around her and stole a cherry tomato from the chopping board.

"Does the pub landlady often call you?"

"No." He chuckled. "When I moved to Lannick I was really shocked that everyone seemed to know everything about each other. Nothing ever stays a secret for long. I kind of hated how gossipy it felt at first, but they all seem to really care about each other so it doesn't feel malicious or anything."

"So why was the landlady calling you?"

"Oh, she wanted to tell me about something she'd heard."

Jess laughed. "She called you to gossip?"

"Not gossip," he insisted. "Pass on information."

"Spoken like a true gossip!" She rolled her eyes. "So what was the information she was passing on?"

His eyes sparkled with amusement. "I could tell you but then I'd have to kill you."

"Very coy," she said, as she sliced the cucumber. "Now I'm even more intrigued."

"It was nothing." Whatever it was, he clearly wasn't willing to share it. Presumably it involved Elspeth. "This kitchen isn't very well equipped," he said, changing the subject. "But there's a salad bowl around here somewhere." Placing his hands on her hips, he moved her gently to the side, then retrieved the bowl from the cupboard by her legs.

After putting the pizza in the oven, he took a couple of papers from the sideboard. "You wanted to help me with this raffle, right?"

"I'm not sure *wanted* is the right word," she said, joining him at the table again.

"You volunteered. You can't back out now."

"What do you want me to do?"

"I made a list of local businesses to approach about donating prizes. Can I give you half of them?"

Jess scanned the list in a bid to avoid eye contact with him. He was right that she'd volunteered and it would be rude to change her mind now, but she hadn't fully considered what she'd be doing. Cold calling local businesses really wasn't her idea of fun.

"No problem," she said.

"They can donate services or goods or vouchers depending on what kind of business it is," Rory said. Taking a pen, he drew a line to divide the list in two. "You take the top half. I need to have a list of prizes in three weeks so we can announce the raffle in the next school newsletter. The money raised will be used for new books for the library."

"Okay." She sipped her drink and forced a smile.

"Thanks. You're a lifesaver. I really can't wait for the

summer break. I feel as though I'm drowning in work at the moment."

"I'm happy to help," she said, feeling much more willing when she saw how stressed he was.

When the oven timer beeped, Rory set the table. They chatted about work as they ate, then Rory insisted they go up to the pub after they'd finished dinner.

He lingered at the doorway of the Merchant Bar when they arrived. "I'll see you inside. I want to try and call Elspeth quickly."

Jess nodded and ignored the heaviness in her chest as she walked inside. She got herself and Rory a drink at the bar, then joined their colleagues. There were only a few of them, and she felt awkward as she sat with them. Ava had needed to go straight back home after work so Jess was back to feeling like an outsider as the rest of them chatted easily.

More colleagues arrived over the next hour and Rory flitted between them as he usually did, chatting with everyone. When he slipped outside, Jess presumed he was calling Elspeth again, then assumed from the look on his face when he returned that she still wasn't answering.

She tried to get his attention but he swiped his jacket from the back of a chair, and said goodnight to the group as a whole before leaving abruptly.

He hadn't even looked at Jess.

∼

"Is Daddy coming today?" Arran asked over breakfast on Saturday morning.

"Yes." Elspeth checked the clock. "He'll be here to pick you up in a wee while. Shall we go for a walk before he gets here?"

"No. I don't like walks."

"It'll be a fun walk," Elspeth said. "Finish your breakfast and let's go."

She had to jolly Arran along at first, but soon he was happily scaring seagulls away from the rocks at the shore and throwing stones into the water when they stopped sporadically on the path around the loch.

"Can we go and see Leana?" Arran asked when they got near to her house.

"No. Daddy will be waiting." Even though the whole point of the walk was to make him wait, she didn't want to keep him waiting too long. Just long enough to make a point.

Rory's car was outside the cottage when they arrived back. They found him in the kitchen, sitting at the table with a cup of coffee.

"Sorry we're late," Elspeth said.

He looked pointedly at her phone on the sideboard. "I tried calling you."

"Forgot my phone," she said innocently. "We went for a walk and I lost track of time. I should probably get used to that considering I'll have a lot of time on my hands for the next month."

"So you're taking time off?"

"Yes. I didn't have any choice, thanks to you."

"What are you talking about?"

Elspeth smiled at Arran, whose eyes were flicking back and forth between them. "Do you want to go upstairs and choose some toys to take to Daddy's house?"

He nodded and ran out of the room.

"You spoke to my parents behind my back," she hissed as Arran thudded up the stairs. "Dad said I had to close the cafe. He didn't give me any choice."

Rory's expression made it clear that Christine had been right about that not being his idea. Clearly he didn't know anything about it, but it didn't stop Elspeth from being furious with him.

"I confided in you," she snapped. "And you immediately went and told my parents. I feel like a child who has no control over my life. I just have to do what other people tell me to."

"I'm sorry." Rory rubbed his temples. "I didn't know Keith would do that. I just thought it would help if I got them to speak to you so you knew it was fine with them for you to close the cafe."

"I didn't want to close the cafe."

"But I thought if they spoke to you you might change your mind. If the doctor thinks you should take time off you probably should."

"Well, I am. So you get your wish."

"Don't be like that," he said. "Is this why you wouldn't answer the phone to me last night? Because you're angry with me?"

"Yes," she said curtly.

The chair legs screeched across the tiles as he stood up. "We have a child together. You can't decide to ignore my calls. How would you feel if you tried to call me when I have Arran and I ignored you?"

She didn't have an answer for that, not one she was prepared to admit out loud anyway, because if it was the other way around she'd be furious. She knew it was petty to ignore his calls. But she was feeling fairly petty.

Arran pounded back down the stairs and barrelled into the kitchen. "Can I take Bumblebee?" he asked, holding up the bright yellow car that transformed into a robot.

"Yes," they replied in unison.

"Have you got anything planned for the weekend?" Elspeth asked, trying to lighten the atmosphere around Arran when she followed them to the door.

"I don't know what we're doing," Rory said frostily.

"I'll see you tomorrow." She gave Arran a quick hug before he shot off outside. "Bye," she said to Rory.

He picked up Arran's bag and stepped outside, then turned back to her. "I'll have him back at the usual time tomorrow. Unless I lose track of time, then we'll be late."

Her shoulders slumped as she watched him walk away. She'd been asking for that, but it hurt nonetheless.

After about half an hour of moping around the house, she sent Rory a quick message that simply said she was sorry.

A reply came immediately.

"Me too."

CHAPTER FIFTEEN

Leana thoroughly enjoyed her random conversations with Lexie as they worked in the pub together on Friday night. She waited until the end of the evening when the customers had left and they were tidying up before she filled Lexie in on her argument with Alasdair in America. Lexie also seemed surprised that he didn't want to get married.

"You're not going to break up with him, are you?" she asked.

"No. At least I don't want to. But the more I think about it, the more I feel kind of free now."

"What does that mean?" Lexie asked as she lifted stools up onto the tables.

"It means I could go away to uni and not feel bad."

Lexie paused and stared at her. "Alasdair would flip out. You can't move away and leave him."

"I always thought we'd get married and have kids, but now I feel as though I can do anything I want."

"You could do anything you wanted before. If you'd wanted to study, Alasdair would've supported you. Now it sounds as though you're trying to find a way to get your own back at him."

"I'm not," Leana said, not entirely sure whether that was true.

"So you really want to train to be a nurse?"

"Maybe," Leana said. "I always liked the idea of helping people."

"You already help people," Lexie said cheekily. "You help thirsty people!"

"I also have another idea for a new career path. I could rent out Alasdair's recording studio. That would be an easy way to branch out and have my own little business. He always talks about doing it, but he's not great at organising things."

"That's a better idea," Lexie said. "You could still work in the pub and you wouldn't be abandoning me to go off and study."

"I actually have musicians coming in this weekend." Leana pulled her phone from her pocket. "Which reminds me, I need to set an alarm. They're coming over at eight o'clock tomorrow. That's not very rock and roll, is it? I thought musicians slept until midday."

"You should know," Lexie said.

"Alasdair's not very rock and roll either," Leana mused.

"So are you really going to be renting out the studio regularly?"

"I don't know. We talked about it when we first moved in but Alasdair never did anything about it. I don't know if it's his bad organisational skills or because he's a bit precious about the studio. I'm not sure he's keen on having random people use it. He knows the guys who are coming this weekend. I think it's more of a favour than anything."

"You should get going if you have to be up early," Lexie said. "I'm going to nip up and say goodnight to Mum and Dad, then I'm going home too."

"I'll see you soon," Leana called as she grabbed her coat and headed for the door. She was almost at her car when a voice called out to her. With a hand over her racing heart she growled at Nick. "Are you trying to give me a heart attack?"

"No. Sorry. I was heading over to see where Lexie was. Didn't mean to scare you."

"I'm not used to going home in the dark on my own. Alasdair knows I find it creepy, so he usually meets me if I'm working late."

"How long is he staying in the States for?"

"Six weeks, so I better get a bit braver." She said goodnight and got into her car. It wasn't just driving home alone that gave her the creeps; their lovely, secluded house suddenly seemed foreboding when she pulled up outside to find it all in darkness. Thankfully the security light turned on as she hurried to the door.

In the kitchen, she calculated the time difference before calling Alasdair. "Did I wake you?" she asked.

"No," he said through a yawn.

"That sounds like a lie. How's everything in San Diego?"

"Great. We played a gig at an underground bar last night."

"Sounds like fun. I just got home from work."

"How was it?"

"Good. I was working with Lexie. It was nice to have a proper catch-up with her."

"That's good," he said, yawning again.

"I'll leave you to go back to sleep. I'm going to bed now too."

They told each other they loved each other before ending the call. Leana put the phone on the counter while she got a glass of water. It was only when she was snuggled up in bed that she realised she'd left her phone downstairs. But she was already falling asleep and she was sure no one would be desperate to contact her overnight.

The sound of the doorbell pulled Leana from a deep sleep the following morning. Ignoring it, she pulled a pillow over her head and began to drift off again. When it rang again, she groaned and got out of bed, irritated at leaving the warmth of it behind.

As her bare feet padded down the wooden stairs, she cursed whoever was at the door.

"I was working last night," she grumbled loudly, assuming it was one of her family members, come around for some inane reason, or no reason at all. "I actually like to sleep sometimes you know?"

Snatching the door handle she pulled roughly at the door and came face to face with three strangers. She blinked a few times, feeling suddenly self-conscious in her pyjamas. The young men all stared at her.

"Would it be better if we came back later?" the one closest to her asked.

She squinted at him, one hand still gripping the door handle. "What for? Who are you?"

"I think we spoke on the phone." He scratched at his ear. "You're Leana, right?"

"Yes," she said suspiciously.

"I'm Conor. We're here to use the recording studio."

Leana cringed. "I'm sorry. I definitely set my alarm. I don't know what happened." She remembered leaving her phone in the kitchen and inwardly cursed.

"We could come back in a wee while if now isn't a good time," Conor said.

"No. It's fine. I'm sorry." She opened the door wider. "Come in."

Conor gave her a brief smile and stepped inside while the other two stepped forward, looking slightly sheepish.

"Patrick," the taller of them said, offering his hand.

She shook it, wishing she wasn't greeting them in her pyjamas. At least they were the comfy, practical kind and she didn't have to worry about having too much bare skin on show. Glancing down, she realised they were probably her oldest pair of pyjamas. The matching grey set were dotted with pink hearts and she'd had them since she was a teenager. Maybe something slinky and exposing would have been preferable.

"We've met before," the third guy said as he wiped his shoes on the mat. "I'm Jake."

"The sound guy!" She nodded her head. "Yes. I remember you."

"Sound engineer," he said, an amused smile playing at his lips.

"Yes. That's what I meant." She looked around at them in the hallway. "Do you want to go straight upstairs?" Again, she glanced down at her threadbare pyjamas and winced. "I mean, should I show you up to the studio?"

"That would be great," Conor said.

"After you." She gestured to the stairs, not relishing the thought of going first. There was definitely a hole somewhere in her pyjama bottoms, and she didn't want to chance anyone walking behind her.

Jake led the way. He'd worked with Alasdair before and had been to the house a few times.

"You know the setup, don't you?" she asked, following them into the recording studio.

"It'd be great if you could give us a quick run through," Patrick said, parking himself at the office chair by the desk.

"Right." She panicked as she looked around. "So there's the isolation booth over there," she said hesitantly.

Conor looked at her with a pained expression and shook his head. "He was just messing with you. Ignore him."

"Sorry," Patrick said, grinning at her. "Couldn't resist."

"I know the setup," Jake said. "We're fine, thanks."

"Okay." Leana backed away. "I'll leave you to it. I'll be out most of the day, so you don't need to worry about disturbing me. Not that you would." Her eyes darted around. "It's soundproof. Obviously. It's a recording studio." She backed into the doorframe and her cheeks flooded with heat. "I can leave tea and coffee out in the kitchen," she blethered on.

"Help yourselves." They all stared at her and she felt like a prize idiot. She'd almost made her getaway when Jake called out to her.

"If you're not going to be around, is there a spare key we could have?" he asked. "We might nip out for lunch later."

"Yes. Sure. I'll leave it in the kitchen." She closed the door and scurried to her bedroom, breathing a sigh of relief when she was alone. All she'd had to do was let them in; somehow she hadn't foreseen just how much she could embarrass herself in that scenario.

She'd told them she'd be out most of the day, but she didn't start her shift at the pub until the afternoon and she didn't have anything else planned. It felt uncomfortable to be at home when there were strangers there. Elspeth would probably be happy to have help with the cafe, or just company if it wasn't busy.

When she arrived at the cafe she was confused by a sign on the door that said they were closed until further notice. That couldn't be right. If her whole morning turned out to be a bad dream, she'd be thrilled. All the embarrassment of the morning erased in a second.

"What's going on?" she asked, letting herself into her parents' kitchen.

"Good morning to you too!" her mum said.

"Sorry. Good morning! What's happening with the cafe? Where's Elspeth?"

"Didn't she message you?" Christine was busy chopping vegetables and only glanced at Leana.

"I haven't heard from her for a few days."

Christine tutted. "I thought she'd have been in touch with you. The doctor recommended she take some time off. She didn't want to, but your dad insisted. So the cafe's closed for a month or so."

Leana dropped into a chair. "And Elspeth's okay with that?"

"No. But your dad put his foot down. I think it's probably for the best."

"She did seem to be headed for a nervous breakdown," Leana mused. "Or was in the midst of one. Is she at home?"

"No. She borrowed my car. Didn't say where she was going. Just said she felt like a drive."

"Arran's with Rory?"

"Yes. It was Rory who told us what the doctor had said, so I think he's in Elspeth's bad books too."

"What a lot of drama. Hopefully the time off will do her good though."

"I really hope so." Christine paused in what she was doing. "I'm worried about her."

As her mum's chin twitched, Leana went and put an arm around her shoulders and gave a quick squeeze. "She'll be all right."

"I don't know what to do to help," Christine said, dabbing at the corner of her eye with her sleeve.

"I don't think there's much you can do. Just be here when she needs you, like you always are." She smiled sadly. "What are you cooking?"

"A stew. I thought I could take some over to Elspeth. At least make sure she's eating properly. They hardly ever come over for dinner any more."

"Can I help?" Leana asked.

"Yes." Christine handed her the knife and Leana took over chopping the carrots on the board. "Are you working today?"

"Yeah. This afternoon. I'm avoiding being home until then." She explained the situation with the recording studio and they had a good laugh about her answering the door in her pyjamas. After a relaxed morning at her parents' house she ate lunch with her mum and dad, then headed home again.

She'd just walked into the kitchen when the creak of the stairs put her on high alert.

"I thought I heard you come in," Conor said cheerfully. "We were wondering about the food situation around here."

Leana's eyebrows shot together. "Alasdair only said I should let you in, he didn't say anything about providing food. I have to go to work soon."

"That's not what I meant," Conor said in a rush. "I just thought maybe you could recommend somewhere for lunch." He checked his watch. "Late lunch."

"Yes, of course. Sorry." She shook her head. "There's only really the pub locally." She thought about the cafe and felt a pang of sadness at it being closed. Over lunch with her parents, she'd suggested the rest of the family could pitch in to keep it running while Elspeth had a break, but her dad vetoed the idea, saying it would be too hard for Elspeth to keep away.

"The Old Inn?" Conor asked. "Is the food any good?"

"It's great. But I work there so I might be biased."

He smiled warmly. "That's where you were working last night. If I'd have known you work late we could have arranged to come over later. I feel bad that we woke you up."

"It was my own fault. I'm sorry. I'm really embarrassed. I must have looked a complete state answering the door half asleep."

"Don't worry about it. You looked fine." His eyes sparkled with amusement and he held her gaze until she felt uncomfortable and had to look away. "We're going to head out and find something to eat." He smiled at her again, then walked out.

She got herself a coffee and waited until she heard them leaving, then went upstairs to get ready for work. All the while she felt a vague annoyance at Alasdair for staying in America. If he'd have come back with her like he was supposed to, he could have dealt with them, and she wouldn't have felt uncomfortable in her own home.

CHAPTER SIXTEEN

Once again, Leana thought of Alasdair on the drive home from work, wishing he was there to keep her company. The big house had been his idea and while she generally loved it, she realised it was more to do with the occupant than the building. Arriving back to an empty house was depressing.

Except as she pulled the car down the drive, she realised it wasn't empty at all. Lights were on and a car sat at the front of the house. She'd fully expected the band would have finished their recording session, but apparently not. In the kitchen, pizza boxes were piled on the counter.

Leana took her phone out and called Alasdair, all thoughts of missing him replaced by a wave of anger. She didn't even manage a greeting.

"How long did you tell them they could be here for?" she asked, her voice raised and fuelled by tiredness and irritation.

"Who? What are you talking about?"

"Your musician friends," she snapped. "First, I had to wake up stupidly early to let them in. Now, I get home from work and they're still here. I'm tired and I can't go to bed because there are strange men in the house."

"You can go to bed," Alasdair said. "It's fine."

"It's not fine! Do you really not see that I'm in a vulnerable situation here? There's no way I can go to bed until they leave. They also have the spare key," she said, noticing it wasn't back in the place where she'd left it.

"You gave them a key?"

"Yes. I wasn't planning on being home all day, so they asked for a key for when they went out for lunch. I don't know if they're planning on keeping it and letting themselves in again in the morning. I'll never sleep knowing that someone else has a key and could wander in at any time. Especially since they know I'm here alone."

"They're nice guys," Alasdair said on a sigh. "Go up and ask how long they're going to be. They'll take the hint and leave. You can ask them for the key too. I'm sure they weren't intending to let themselves in tomorrow."

She tapped her fingers on the counter. The idea of going up and asking them when they'd be leaving didn't fill her with joy, but she supposed it was a sensible approach to the situation.

When she turned, she almost dropped her phone at the sight of the figure in the doorway.

"Sorry," Conor said as she gasped. "I didn't mean to scare you."

Alasdair's voice in her ear asked if she was okay. She muttered that she was fine and would call him back, then ended the call.

"I'm really sorry," Conor said, not moving from the doorway. "We lost track of time but Patrick and Jake are just packing things up and then we'll get going. I'm sorry if we made you uncomfortable."

"It's fine," she said, catching her breath. "I just wasn't expecting you to still be here." His gentle smile put her at ease and she felt herself relax. "I feel as though I manage to embarrass myself whenever you're around."

"There's nothing to be embarrassed about."

"So you didn't hear me on the phone?"

The corners of his mouth twitched upwards. "You were quite loud. But you're right – it must be weird for you having strangers in your house. When we arranged it I thought Alasdair would be here. I can see why you're annoyed."

"Only with him," Leana said lightly. "It's nothing against you."

"Thanks for letting us use the studio anyway. If you'd rather we didn't come tomorrow, just say so."

"It's fine," she said.

He took a few steps into the room and set the spare key on the island in the centre of the kitchen. "I'll leave that for you. And we can come later tomorrow so you don't have to get up so early."

Leana felt herself flush at the realisation that he'd heard what she said about them having the spare key and her being vulnerable in the house alone. "I'm working earlier tomorrow so I'll need to leave around ten."

"Shall we come just before ten then?" he asked.

She told him that would be fine, then heard footsteps on the stairs before Jake and Patrick appeared.

"How was work?" Jake asked.

"Good, thanks," she murmured, feeling far too tired for small talk.

"We'll see you tomorrow," Conor said as they headed for the door.

Leana called goodbye to them, happy to have the house to herself again. Picking up her phone, she sent a quick message to Alasdair reassuring him everything was fine, then set an alarm for the morning and made sure to take the phone upstairs with her.

Thankfully, she was looking much more respectable when she let Conor, Patrick and Jake in the following morning and managed a short interaction without embarrassing herself before she left for work.

Lexie arrived for her shift late in the afternoon and they

worked alongside Angus over the hectic dinner period. "How was your weekend?" Leana asked Lexie when things slowed down and they stood together behind the bar.

"Fine," she said with a shrug. "How was yours? You've been working all weekend, haven't you?"

"Pretty much. I had that band in the recording studio yesterday so I hid out at Mum's before work."

"Were you at the cafe? That's so typical of you to spend your time off helping Elspeth."

"No," Leana said, then faltered. "The cafe wasn't open."

"On a Saturday?" Lexie raised her eyebrows. "Why not?"

Leana glanced at the regulars sitting along the bar. No doubt tongues would start wagging soon enough, but she didn't want to be the one to start a load of rumours.

"Elspeth's a bit under the weather," she said. "She closed the cafe for a wee while."

"Is she okay?"

"Yes. Just needs a break. She works too hard."

"It's a Mackenzie family trait," Lexie said lightly.

Leana smiled. "That's a bit rich, coming from you."

Angus walked out from the kitchen and told Leana she could go home. She got her coat then lingered at the bar by Lexie.

"It doesn't seem as though I'm going to follow up on my idea of renting out the recording studio, anyway. It's been a bit of a disaster." She gave a brief rundown of her embarrassing encounters, much to Lexie's amusement.

"Will you message me later and let me know what you do to make a fool of yourself when you get back home?"

"I'm glad I keep you entertained," Leana said. "You won't be laughing when I leave you to go off to train to be a nurse."

"No, I won't," Lexie said sternly. "You're not serious about that, are you?"

"I don't know. It keeps niggling at me. I might look into it."

She said goodbye to Lexie and Angus, then almost collided with Nick when she walked out of the pub.

"We need to stop running into each other like this," she said lightly.

"What?" He looked miles away.

"I saw you after my shift on Friday too. Some people might think you have a drinking problem, but I guess it's actually a Lexie problem."

His eyes roamed around and he looked slightly confused, as though he wasn't quite sure what he was doing there. "You're right. She only left a couple of hours ago. I should leave her alone."

"I was joking," Leana said. "What's going on?"

"Nothing." He swallowed hard. "Did Lexie seem okay to you?"

"Yes. Fine. Why?"

"No reason. I think she missed you while you were away. She'll be glad to have you back." His cheek twitched and he smiled nervously. "I'll probably just have a quick pint and then head home again."

"I was only joking about you being here a lot," Leana said, putting a hand on his arm. "Is everything okay?"

"Yes. Why?"

"You seem a bit jumpy."

"I'm fine. I'll see you around." He pushed the door and walked inside before Leana could say anything else. Nick could always be a little awkward but the exchange was strange even for him.

Back at home, she found the place deserted. A message from Conor lit up her phone, thanking her again and telling her they'd left the spare key in the kitchen. Hopefully she'd never run into him again and her embarrassing weekend would soon be forgotten about.

CHAPTER SEVENTEEN

As the days went by, closing the cafe felt more and more ridiculous to Elspeth. She wasn't ill, so hanging around doing nothing made no sense. Her family were all bustling around with their usual routines and she didn't see why she shouldn't do the same. To make things worse, everyone was treating her like she was delicate. She'd taken to trying to start arguments just to see if she could, but even Isla wouldn't take the bait. Her prickly sister was usually so easy to wind up, but she'd been nothing but kind and patient. It annoyed Elspeth immensely.

The cottage had never been cleaner and as she stared into her coffee mug on Wednesday morning, she contemplated sneaking over and opening the cafe. Insistent knocking at the front door put a stop to the thought.

Lexie's cheeks were pink as she stood on the doorstep, and her hair was pulled into a messy ponytail. Behind her, Elspeth caught sight of the minibus with the activity centre's logo.

"Where is it?" Lexie said in a rush. "I'm having a nightmare of a morning and if I don't leave again in about five seconds I'm going to be late."

"Where's what?" Elspeth asked in confusion.

"The food! I thought you'd be at the cafe. Please tell me the lunches are ready?"

Elspeth swore loudly, then slapped a hand over her mouth. Lexie took a group out hiking on Wednesday mornings and Elspeth made the lunches for them.

"I'm sorry," she said, peeling her hand from her mouth. "I forgot."

"Ha-bloody-ha! You're hilarious, but I really am late now so stop messing around and give me the lunches."

"I don't have them," Elspeth said, her mind whirring as she tried to figure out if there was any way for her to whip something up quickly. "I could bake some biscuits, but I don't think I have anything for the sandwiches."

"I don't have time for you to bake biscuits!" Lexie paced outside of the door. "How the hell did you forget?"

"I'm sorry."

"I don't care if you're sorry." Lexie's face was bright red and her hands were clenched by her sides. "What am I supposed to do about lunch? I don't have time to organise something else, and I can't turn up with no food. I trusted you with a job and you're making me look unprofessional. The other catering company might not do the best food, but at least they never forget!"

"What can I do?" Elspeth asked.

"Nothing," Lexie snapped. "I'll have to stop at a shop and see if I can at least get some snacks."

"I can go shopping," Elspeth said, desperate to make amends. "You need to pick up the group, right? So I can go and buy lunch and meet you at the start of your walk. Just send me a message with the location."

Lexie got her phone out and began tapping away. "I'm sending it now. Get there as fast as you can. I can't believe you forgot. How am I supposed to trust you to do your job if you just forget?"

Elspeth thought Lexie was overreacting, especially given

that she'd already found a solution. "I'll meet you there with lunch," she said, checking that the location had come through on her phone. "You go and collect the hiking group. Don't worry about the food."

"You better be there," Lexie growled and turned towards the minibus.

After a mad dash to buy sandwiches and snacks, Elspeth made her way to Ullinish, parking in a lay-by in the spot that Lexie had indicated. Or so she thought. There was no sign of the minibus or hiking group, so she went into her phone to make sure she was at the right place. She'd hardly had a chance to check when the minibus pulled up a little way in front of her, and she watched Lexie jump out and walk towards her.

"I'm really sorry," Elspeth said, stepping out of the car and holding out the paper bag with the food.

"I'm sorry," Lexie said. "I completely flipped out at you. Everything seemed to be going wrong this morning and I took it out on you."

"Don't worry about it."

Lexie glanced back at the group, who were exiting the minibus and chatting amongst themselves. "How on earth did you forget?" she asked lightly.

Elspeth smiled. "I presume you haven't heard about my breakdown. My parents and Rory ganged up on me and now I'm not allowed to open the cafe for a month. The hiking group slipped my mind."

"Are you serious?"

She nodded. "The doctor said I'm stressed and burnt out, so my family have all freaked out and are insisting on treating me like a child."

"Shit." Lexie glanced behind her again. "I'm sorry. I feel like the worst friend in the world. For one thing, I had no idea things were that bad, and for another I've just bitten your head off for no reason."

"There *was* a reason," Elspeth corrected her. "I forgot the sandwiches."

"Even so, I overreacted quite dramatically."

"It was actually nice to have someone treating me normally. And I'm kind of glad you didn't know. I'd expected it to be the hot topic in Lannick by now."

"Leana mentioned you'd closed because you weren't feeling well, but I thought she meant for the weekend. I didn't realise what was going on. She probably didn't want to discuss it in the pub."

"You should get going," Elspeth said. The group didn't seem to be getting impatient, but she didn't want to hold Lexie up.

"Let's get together soon."

"Anytime! I don't have a lot going on in the next few weeks."

"You should join some of my groups at the activity centre. It'd be a laugh."

"That's not a bad idea. I'm already bored out of my mind. I need to find something to keep me occupied."

Lexie's eyes sparkled. "Do you want to come on the hike with us?"

"What?"

"Come with us now. They'll love to meet you. They're always raving about your baking."

"Perhaps not the best day to meet them considering I forgot to bake anything."

"They won't care. They're really lovely. I'll tell them there was a mix-up today."

"Okay." Elspeth locked her car and set off towards the group with Lexie. "Can we not say I forgot because I've been busy having a nervous breakdown?"

Lexie screwed her nose up. "Good plan. Let's not say that."

After having heard so much about the hiking group, Elspeth enjoyed meeting them. They were more than happy for her to join their hike, and each of them made an effort to chat to her as they ambled along behind Lexie. It was fun to see her being a tour guide, and Elspeth was impressed by her knowledge of the area.

When they reached Ullinish Point, the group crossed the rocky tidal causeway to the tiny uninhabited island of Oronsay. There, they stopped for a rest and to admire the view over Loch Bracadale. Lexie and Elspeth wandered a little away from the group.

"So, are you okay?" Lexie asked, looking at Elspeth with concern.

"Yes. Please don't start looking at me sympathetically. I'm sick of all the head tilts and soft tones. I understand that everyone's worried about me, but they're all driving me crazy."

She smiled widely. "I'll try not to be too nice! Honestly, I've been worried about you since you split up with Rory but you never seemed to want to talk about it so I stopped asking."

"Sometimes I think I made the biggest mistake of my life," she said, taking a seat on a large rock.

"Breaking up with Rory?"

"Aye. It all feels such a mess."

"Do you want to get back with him?"

"I don't even think that's an option now."

"Talk to him. Tell him how you feel."

"I'm not sure how I feel," Elspeth said. "And after all I put him through, I don't want to mess him about. You're not supposed to give me sympathetic looks, remember?"

"Sorry," she said lightly.

"I spoke to Dr Andrews again this week. She wants me to have counselling."

"That's probably a good idea."

"I hate the thought of it, but I guess I'll give it a go. There's a waiting list but Dr Andrews is trying to find someone who can do it over videocalls. I should be able to see someone sooner that way."

"It can't do any harm. And hopefully the time off work will help. Maybe everything will feel clearer after a break from running around."

"I feel lazy."

"Oh my God! You've been a single parent working full time since you were seventeen. You don't take weekends off and you never have a holiday. I don't think anyone can accuse you of being lazy. You've earned some time off. Relax and enjoy it."

"I'll try," she said, reassured by Lexie's assessment. Elspeth never really thought of it like that. "Why were you having such a bad morning anyway? You were pretty stressed yourself when you shouted at me on the doorstep. Maybe you need a break too?"

"I'm really embarrassed now. It was just one of those mornings. I couldn't find the keys for the minibus, then when I finally found them there was no diesel in it so I had to go and fill up. Plus I got my period and had cramps and was feeling generally crappy."

"Poor Nick. Does he have to go into hiding once a month?"

"I'm not usually that bad." Her smile slipped. "Do you know the feeling when it's like you're holding yourself together by a thread and it feels as though the thread might snap at any moment?"

"Yeah. I know it well. What's going on?"

Lexie shook her head. "Nothing. Sorry, you've got enough to deal with without listening to me complain."

"You can still talk to me," Elspeth said.

"I'm being dramatic," Lexie said with a smile which didn't come close to reaching her eyes. "Ignore me."

"Lexie!" one of the women called. "Can you come and help us settle an argument, please?"

She rolled her eyes at Elspeth and set off back to join the group.

Having Elspeth tag along on the hike was exactly the distraction Lexie needed. It gave her a boost to get through the morning. She got the feeling Elspeth enjoyed it too, which meant that Lexie didn't feel quite so bad about the way she'd shouted at her. Even so, she was still embarrassed by her outburst – all over packed lunches. Her nerves had felt fairly frayed for the past couple of months, and she was glad it was only Elspeth she'd snapped at and not customers.

The afternoon seemed to go at a snail's pace, and it was an effort to muster enthusiasm with the group she took out kayaking.

After struggling through the day, she was about ready to collapse when she got home.

"I cooked," Nick announced as she walked into the kitchen.

"It smells good." She only wished she had an appetite.

"Shepherd's pie. I got home early and I know Wednesdays are busy for you, so I thought I'd make your favourite. It's probably not as good as when you make it though."

"Thank you." She kissed his cheek. "I might jump in the shower quickly."

He smiled at her. "It'll be ready in ten minutes or so."

"Perfect," she whispered.

After her shower, she decided she may as well get into her pyjamas. She often changed into her pyjamas straight after work. It was much more comfortable. At the top of the stairs she caught a whiff of the shepherd's pie and heard the gentle hum of the radio drifting from the kitchen.

Needing a moment to compose herself, she backtracked to the bedroom and lay down on the bed. Curling up on her side, she kept telling herself to get up and go downstairs, but her body didn't want to comply so she lay quietly, waiting for Nick to inevitably get impatient and shout up to her.

She was starting to nod off when she heard footsteps on the

stairs. "I was about to come down," she said when Nick sat on the edge of the bed.

"What's going on?" he asked, rubbing her leg.

She shook her head as a lump formed in her throat. Sitting up, she wrapped her arms around Nick's waist and managed to bury her face in his shoulder before she started crying. He held her tightly. The fact that he didn't seem too surprised by her sobbing made her think he knew exactly why she was upset.

The first months of trying to get pregnant had been exciting. She hadn't worried at all in those first months. But the last few months had her feeling increasingly uneasy. Each time she got her period she was disappointed. Each time was harder. They hadn't discussed the fact that it hadn't happened yet, and it had become the proverbial elephant in the room. Lexie avoided bringing it up because it felt like once they talked about it, it made it a real problem. And she wasn't sure she was ready to admit that yet.

"I got my period," she finally said, pulling away from Nick and wiping at her eyes. "Sorry." She wasn't sure whether she was apologising for soaking his T-shirt with her tears or for not being pregnant.

"It's okay," he said. "We haven't been trying for that long."

"It's been six months. I thought I'd be pregnant by now."

"We'll keep trying," he said, brushing tears from her cheek with his thumb. "We just need to be patient. It'll happen."

"I know." She puffed out a breath. "But I keep thinking, what if it doesn't happen?"

"It will. It's perfectly normal to take up to a year. Or even two years. So we definitely shouldn't start panicking yet."

She sniffed. "Have you looked it up?"

"Yes." He gave her a crooked smile. "You know I like to be well-informed."

"I researched it too," she said. "So I know that we just have to keep trying, but it's so disappointing every time I get my period."

"I know. I'm sorry."

She put a hand on his cheek. Another reason she'd been avoiding the conversation was because she didn't want Nick to worry. "I feel as though it's my fault," she said.

"Of course it's not."

"It's my body," she said.

He scrunched his features up. "It's my sperm."

They both chuckled, though she wasn't sure why. It wasn't funny really.

"I keep thinking about the abortion," she said sadly. "It seems unfair that I could get pregnant when I didn't want to, but now that I want it, it's not happening. Do you think it's karma or something?"

"No. It's just life." He kissed her briefly. "And at least trying to get pregnant is fun."

"That's true." She dragged her fingers through his hair. "I love you."

"Love you too. Do you want to come down and eat?"

She nodded and let him pull her up from the bed. Talking to Nick about it felt like unscrewing a pressure valve. The feeling that she was about to explode faded and she could breathe easier.

She should have known he'd make her feel better. He always did.

CHAPTER EIGHTEEN

Arran was waiting by the window for Rory on Wednesday afternoon and ran to the door as soon as he saw the car. "Daddy's here!" he shouted, though Elspeth had already gathered that.

She'd made spaghetti bolognese and caught Rory's appreciative sigh as he inhaled the aroma from the hallway. Usually, she made something quick and easy, and left the two of them to eat alone while she found something else to do, either upstairs or at the cafe. If she ate with them it was usually a casual dinner from their laps in the living room. That felt less intense, but having dinner around the table the previous week had been pleasant, and it was probably good for Arran if they sat down to dinner together from time to time.

"Something smells amazing," Rory said as he walked into the kitchen with Arran swinging on his arm.

"It's spaghetti," Arran told him. "And garlic bread."

"Perfect. I'm so hungry."

"It's ready now," Elspeth said.

"How's your week been?" Rory asked once they were tucking into the food.

"Good," Arran said, sucking spaghetti through his teeth.

"I'm glad," Rory replied. "But I wasn't actually talking to you!"

Elspeth smiled as she wound spaghetti onto her fork. "I was tearing my hair out on Monday and Tuesday, but today was much better."

"What did you do?"

"Well, Lexie arrived and shouted at me this morning. I'd forgotten about the lunches for the hiking group and she wasn't happy with me. Totally flipped out."

"It's only sandwiches. Couldn't you make some quickly? It's not such a big deal is it?"

"I think she was having a bad morning. But I went to the shop for sandwiches and then I ended up going on the hike with them. I had a good time." It had made the day go quickly too. By the time she'd got home, it was almost time to pick Arran up. She'd told Lexie she could continue making the lunches for the hiking group while the cafe was closed, but Lexie had insisted she'd go back to using the other catering company for a few weeks so Elspeth could have a complete break. "I guess I need to find more things to keep me busy."

"Can you find a hobby? What about drawing? You were really good at drawing sketches when you were designing cakes."

"Maybe." The conversation made Elspeth uncomfortable – as though they were finding ways to fix her. "How's work?" she asked in a bid to change the subject.

"It's fine. Busy, as always. The constant stream of marking and planning doesn't change. I seem to keep getting roped into extra work too."

He'd often spent his evenings with papers strewn across the kitchen table when he'd lived with them. Elspeth was struck by an image of him chewing his lip as he worked. He always looked so serious when he was concentrating. Arran had the same intense look when focusing on a task.

"Spaghetti is like worms," Arran said, dragging Elspeth from her thoughts.

Rory nodded solemnly. "And the sauce is brown like mud, so it's like worms wriggling through mud."

"Thanks for that lovely visual." Elspeth pulled a face at Arran. "You two are disgusting."

"You're eating worms in mud too," Rory said. "So you're just as disgusting as us. And you're the one who made us muddy worms for dinner, so I think you're the most disgusting of all. Why are you making us eat this?"

Elspeth couldn't help but smile as Arran erupted in a fit of giggles. "I thought it would make a change from fish fingers," she said. "Those poor fish."

"That's true." Rory turned to Arran. "You're mean, always wanting to eat fingers from poor little fish."

"Fish don't have fingers," Arran said.

"Well, not any more," Rory said. "You've eaten them all. They're all swimming around the sea, looking for their fingers!"

The conversation continued to be silly, and they were all laughing as they tried to think up the most disgusting things to eat. Elspeth's cheeks were aching from smiling so much when Rory's phone began buzzing in his pocket.

"Who is it?" Arran asked, as Rory looked at the screen.

"Just a friend." He silenced the phone and shoved it back into his pocket. "I'll call back later."

"Is it Jess?" Arran asked. Elspeth watched Rory's reaction. He looked decidedly nervous. Before he had a chance to answer, Arran piped up again. "Can we play with Jess again one day? She's nice."

"Maybe," Rory said. "We bumped into a colleague of mine in Portree one day," he explained to Elspeth.

"That's nice."

"She helped us find sea glass," Arran said, laying his cutlery haphazardly beside his plate. "She's very clever."

Elspeth managed to keep smiling as she moved to clear the table.

"Are we going to play for a while before bed?" Rory asked Arran. "We could go outside and kick the ball around for a bit if you want?"

"Yes," Arran replied, sliding off his chair and heading for the door.

As Elspeth cleaned up the dinner things, she kept thinking about the look on Rory's face when Jess had come into the conversation. He'd looked guilty, and Elspeth was once again left contemplating the fact that he was possibly seeing someone else. What really annoyed her was that they'd promised to be open and honest with each other. If he was in a relationship, she wished he'd tell her. Although maybe she'd rather not know. If he outright told her he was involved with someone she wasn't sure how she'd cope with the news.

Stepping outside, she shook the tablecloth to get the crumbs off it, then walked to the side of the house, following the sound of Arran shouting for the ball. Rory kicked it to him. He had his phone to his ear and smiled as he chatted.

Elspeth's stomach churned, and she slipped away before he caught sight of her watching him.

As motivation to start calling local businesses, Jess told herself it would give her a good excuse to speak to Rory and tell him about any prizes she managed to rustle up. Unfortunately, the first three people she called thought she was selling something and ended the calls abruptly. On the fourth try, she had a lovely chat with a woman at the local beauty salon, who said she was happy to donate a gift voucher for a manicure.

The call left her on such a high that she immediately scrolled to Rory's number and pressed dial. It was only when it began to ring that she panicked about what she'd say. When it went to voicemail, she floundered over whether to leave a message. After opening her mouth to speak, she thought better of it and hung up. Pulling her legs under her on the couch, she stared at the phone in her hand. Maybe she should have left a message. It was annoying when someone called and didn't leave a message. But even with time to think about it, she wasn't sure what she'd have said. Securing one prize for the raffle felt a bit pathetic all of a sudden. It hardly warranted calling Rory to tell him.

Since she hadn't left a message, she didn't really expect him to call back, so she was pleasantly surprised when the phone rang ten minutes later.

"Sorry I missed your call," he said casually. "Everything okay?"

"Yes." She swallowed and adopted her breeziest tone. "I was only calling to complain about the raffle. Cold-calling people is awful. Have you had people hang up on you as well or is it just me?"

"Erm ..."

She laughed. "You haven't even tried, have you?"

"There's still loads of time. And I don't see how difficult it can be to get people to donate prizes. It's for a good cause. Did you mention that when you called people?"

"Of course I did! But raising money for the school library doesn't really tug on people's heart strings."

"You need to invoke a sense of community," he said, puffing as though he was out of breath. "The school's the heart of the community, and supporting local youths is an investment in the future."

"Maybe when you've actually tried calling someone, you might be better placed to give me advice on how to go about it."

"Good point." His voice became muffled, and it sounded as though he was moving around. "Did you manage to get any prizes?"

"The beauty salon in Portree pledged a voucher for a manicure."

"You need to work harder," he said lightly. "A manicure definitely wouldn't entice me to buy a raffle ticket."

"Maybe you can work on getting some more interesting prizes," she suggested. "Where are you, by the way? It sounds like you're running."

"I'm having a kick around with Arran. And realising I'm pretty unfit."

"You're at Elspeth's?"

"Yes. I always come over for dinner on Wednesdays and put Arran to bed."

She nodded. "I know. I forgot what day it was." She'd never have called him if she'd realised. "I should let you get on. It doesn't sound as though you can manage running and talking at the same time."

"Hey!" His breaths sounded even more ragged as he laughed. "I'm not that unfit. Did you just call to tease me or what?"

"No." She smiled brightly. "I called to complain at you for roping me into helping with the fundraiser. The teasing's a bonus!"

"Thanks a lot."

"You're welcome. I'll see you at school."

After ending the call, Jess sank back into the couch cushions. The ease of the conversation left her with a warm glow of happiness. She'd even managed a bit of flirting, so she was definitely making progress.

CHAPTER NINETEEN

Leana was getting ready for work on Wednesday afternoon when her phone buzzed with an incoming call. Smiling, she answered the phone to Kyle. Even though he was one of her closest friends, they often went for weeks or even months without speaking. When they did speak, it was always as though no time had passed since their last conversation.

"What on earth has happened?" he asked, in his usual dramatic tone.

"What do you mean?" She settled herself on one of the stools at the kitchen island.

"I mean, Alasdair is in America and you're at home! What's going on?"

"Long story," she said.

"Well, I'm not working until this evening. Start talking."

Leana checked her watch. "I have to be at work in half an hour. But I can give you the short version. Josh invited us to travel around California with them. I said no, Alasdair said yes. I had to get back for work."

"So everything's fine between you two? I was panicking that you'd fallen out."

"Things aren't great. He told me he doesn't want to marry me, which caused some heated discussion."

"I can imagine," he said flatly.

"Why don't you sound surprised? Everyone else has been shocked that he doesn't want to get married. I thought you would be too."

"I'm sort of surprised."

"I know how high-pitched you go when something catches you off guard. You're not at all high-pitched."

"Justin said something at Isla's wedding … I mentioned that I thought you and Alasdair would be getting married soon, and Justin disagreed. He was convinced Alasdair isn't the marrying type, whatever the hell that means!"

"I wish you'd told me."

"I assumed Alasdair had said something years ago and Justin had old information. But I kept thinking it was odd that he hadn't proposed yet. I can't really believe he doesn't want to marry you, though. Is it a big wedding he objects to or being married?"

"Both," Leana said sadly.

"I'm going to have to give him a piece of my mind. I'll call him and tell him exactly what I think."

"No you won't." Leana smiled at his indignant tone. "It's none of your business."

"Fine. I'll stay out of it, but I'm going to have such a rant to Justin about it."

"You're allowed to do that."

"You should come and rant with us," Kyle said quickly, the excitement evident in his voice. "Come down to Edinburgh and we'll have a proper catch-up. When are you next off?"

"Monday and Tuesday."

"Perfect. It's so long since we hung out. We can visit all our old haunts and have a big night out. I'll cheer you up."

Leana hesitated for a moment, thinking. "It's actually not a bad idea," she finally said.

~

Elspeth found it slightly off-putting when Isla opened the door on Thursday with a smile. Usually she greeted her by barking, "What do you want?"

"I need something to do," Elspeth said, answering the question that Isla hadn't asked. "Yesterday I went hiking with Lexie. I need to find something to do today so I don't get bored and open the cafe." Actually, she needed to find something to stop her from thinking about Rory and his new girlfriend. *If* he had a new girlfriend. She reminded herself that she still didn't know for sure.

"I'm not going out on the boat today," Isla said, opening the door wider. "I need to get on with a painting. I've been getting a lot of sales at the gift shops around the island, so I need to restock them."

"I thought you'd be annoyed about not selling any here while the cafe's closed."

Isla shrugged. "It's not the end of the world."

"Have you rehearsed that line?"

"Just repeating what Logan said to me," she said with a grin.

"Maybe I could paint with you," Elspeth suggested. By the way Isla was lingering by the door, she suspected her sister would rather be left alone, but she needed something to occupy her.

"Painting is a solitary activity," Isla said.

"I could work alongside you. I won't be in the way."

"My workroom isn't big enough. Sorry."

"We could go outside. Set up in front of the cottage and paint the view of the loch. You used to work out there all the time when you lived in the cottage. Come on, it'll be fun. You can teach me to paint."

Isla didn't look excited by the idea. "It'll just make you more depressed."

"How?" Elspeth chuckled. "I thought painting is supposed to be calming. Art therapy's a thing, isn't it?"

"Yes. But you're a perfectionist. You'll get annoyed at being rubbish at it."

"Who says I'll be rubbish? I might have talents that we never knew about."

"Fine," Isla relented. "But if you turn out to be good I'll hate you forever."

Out in front of the cottage, the warmth of the spring rays felt wonderful on Elspeth's cheeks. As soon as the sun slipped behind clouds, the chill in the air nipped her skin instead.

"I don't understand what's going on," she said to Isla. "I've copied your every stroke but we have completely different pictures. Did you give me a dodgy paintbrush or something?"

"Yes." Isla's voice dripped with sarcasm. "I keep a stash of dodgy paintbrushes for this exact situation."

"What am I doing wrong then? My painting is a load of different shades of blues merged together and yours looks like the loch and the sky and the clouds."

"You're not doing anything wrong. You just can't paint. Some people have natural talent and others don't."

"Hey! You're supposed to be nice to me. Mum's orders!"

"Mum didn't tell me to be—"

"Liar!"

"Okay. Mum said we all have to be extra nice to you."

"I'm fairly sure it was only you who she had to say that to."

"I let you paint with me," Isla said. "Now you're being mean."

"You started it."

"No. I just pointed out that painting isn't something you're any good at. It's a fact. How can facts be mean? I think you should find a different hobby."

"I quite enjoy painting. I might stick with it."

After five more minutes of playing around with the paints, her picture looked no better. If anything, it was getting worse.

Leana's voice drifting from inside the house was a welcome interruption, and Elspeth waved to her through the open kitchen door.

"We're out here," she called.

"What are you doing?" Leana stopped in front of Elspeth's painting and cocked her head to one side. "Is this supposed to be a representation of what's going on in your mind? Because that's quite disturbing."

"No!" Elspeth screeched. "It's the loch!"

"No. That's the loch." Leana pointed at the water in front of them, then at Isla's painting. "And that's the loch. What you have is a waste of paper and paints."

"I've been trying to tell her that," Isla said. "And in comparison I think I was quite polite about it."

"Have you forgotten you're supposed to be extra nice to me?" Elspeth asked Leana.

"Oh, yeah." She patted Elspeth on the shoulder in a condescending way. "What a lovely picture," she said in a sickly sweet voice. "You've done a wonderful job. Isla better watch out … nobody will want to buy her paintings when they see yours."

"I feel like throwing my painting in the loch," Isla said, joining the teasing. "It's embarrassing next to yours. I should call the Louvre and tell them to make space for your masterpiece."

"Shut up!" Elspeth got the giggles and couldn't stop. "I don't understand it. I copied Isla, brushstroke by brushstroke."

"What's this brown smudge?" Leana asked, pointing to the bottom of the picture.

"It's the rocks!"

"Of course. I see it now." She grimaced and shook her head as she exchanged a look with Isla. "Maybe you should stick to baking," she said as the laughter faded.

"Don't worry, I'm only killing time until I can get back to the baking."

"Lexie said you went hiking with her yesterday. That got me

thinking about things you could do in your time off. I came up with two brilliant ideas."

"What?" Elspeth asked warily.

"Don't say no immediately … but I think you should go on some dates."

Elspeth almost laughed at the absurdity of the suggestion. "Considering I struggle with my own company, why would I inflict it on some poor stranger?" She refrained from pointing out that if she couldn't handle a relationship with Rory – the sweetest guy she knew – there was really no hope for her.

"It'd be fun," Leana insisted. "When you split up with Rory, you were saying that he was the only guy you'd ever been with. Why not see who else is out there? We can set up a profile on a dating site and see what happens."

"No way," Elspeth said, trying not to think about the fact that Rory was probably dating again. "I'm not ready for dating."

"What's the other idea?" Isla asked.

"This is a good one." Leana beamed at Elspeth. "Let's go on a trip! You and me – sisters on a road trip."

"You're not inviting me?" Isla asked.

"I didn't think you'd want to come. You could come if you want."

"Where to?" Elspeth asked.

"Edinburgh. Kyle was complaining about not seeing me for ages, so I thought I might drive down for a few days. I've got Monday and Tuesday off, and I don't start until late on Wednesday so it's perfect. Who wants to come?"

"Not me," Isla said. "That's far too much time in a car for my liking."

"I can't," Elspeth said when Leana looked at her. "I have a child, remember?"

"You can leave him for a few days. There are plenty of people to look after him."

"I also have an appointment with a counsellor first thing on Monday morning. Dr Andrews called me about it earlier, and I think she had to pull some strings to set it up so I don't want to miss it."

"Where is it?" Leana asked.

"It's by video so I'll be at home."

"We can go straight after then. Stop making excuses."

Elspeth sank onto one of the patio chairs. If she was honest, she *was* looking for excuses. "It feels a bit weird to go away when I'm supposed to be wallowing in self-pity."

"I'm fairly sure that's not what you're supposed to be doing," Isla said.

"Well, reflecting on my life and what-not." Elspeth rolled her eyes. "Same thing."

"You're supposed to be relaxing and taking some time to collect yourself," Leana said. "Some child-free time in Edinburgh with your favourite sister definitely falls under that."

"Second favourite sister," Isla corrected.

Elspeth barely registered her as she contemplated the idea of a little trip. Maybe a couple of days away would be good for her. "I'd have to talk to Mum. See if she'd look after Arran."

"Of course she will," Leana said. "But Rory could have him anyway."

"Not really. It'd be too difficult for him to be driving between Lannick and Portree during the week. I'll ask Mum."

"So you'll definitely come?" Leana asked excitedly.

"I suppose so," Elspeth replied with a shrug.

CHAPTER TWENTY

"I don't think he's coming," Ava said, leaning close to Jess on Friday evening and breaking her thoughts. "So you can stop watching the door."

"He always comes to the pub." Jess dragged her gaze to Ava. "And he said he was coming. He'll probably be here soon."

"Where are all the hot guys tonight?" Ava asked, scanning the room. "Last time I was here the place was teeming with them."

Jess took a sip of her wine, not really registering Ava's words. "I'm starting to think you might be right and I just need to snog him."

"What?" Ava asked.

"You told me I should kiss Rory."

"Yeah, but from what you've told me since, I'm withdrawing that advice."

"Why?"

Ava winced. "Sorry, but it doesn't seem as though he's over his ex."

"Maybe a fling would help him get over her."

"You can't have a fling with him," Ava said firmly. "You like him too much."

"It could start as something casual and grow from there. We get on so well. I really think that the more time we spend together, the more our relationship will develop."

"You spend plenty of time with him. If he wanted something more than friendship you'd know about it by now. The best thing you can do is stay away from him."

"Play hard to get?" Jess squinted as she mulled the idea over. "It might work. If I back off, he might realise how much he likes having me around."

"No!" Ava almost shouted. "I meant put him out of your head. Move on with your life."

"I can't." She felt fairly pathetic but it was the truth. "Until I know for sure there's no chance of anything happening between us, I can't give up on the idea."

"You're going to get hurt."

"I'm going to invite him over for dinner," Jess said, ignoring the niggle in the pit of her stomach that told her Ava was probably right. "And I'm going to kiss him. Then I'll know once and for all. If he doesn't kiss me back, I'll forget about him and move on." She frowned, sure that would be easier said than done. "I'm going to message him and see where he is."

She didn't get a reply, but spent the next hour alternating between glancing at the door and her phone.

"I think I'm going to go," Ava finally said. "The atmosphere in this place isn't exactly thrilling this evening."

"Sorry," Jess said, realising she was terrible company. "Did you talk any more to Harriet about renting the room from her?"

"I decided to wait a while and see how things go. No sense paying money for rent when I don't really need to. Living with my parents is fine for now."

"That makes sense. I think I'll go home too," she said, when Ava stood and picked up her jacket. There weren't many of their colleagues around, and there was no one that Jess was overly keen to stay and chat to.

In the end she got a reply from Rory the next morning to say he'd fallen asleep on the couch after work. He said he hoped she'd had a good night and would see her on Monday at school. Annoyingly, the message didn't invite conversation, and much as she pondered the idea, she couldn't bring herself to suggest dinner. She needed a reason for them to get together so it seemed more casual.

Sadly, the only excuse she could come up with was the school raffle. She'd decided that approaching businesses in person might yield a more sympathetic response and was tempted to call Rory on Saturday afternoon and ask him to go with her. It was the least he could do, really, since she was doing him a favour in the first place. Except she knew he had Arran at the weekends and that was part of the reason she'd offered to help with the task – he was stretched too thin.

At the reminder that it was all in the name of helping Rory out, she had a surge of motivation and decided to spend the afternoon going round local businesses, seeing if she could drum up some more prizes. Plus, if she could get a load of donations for the raffle, she'd have a good reason to call Rory. She could invite him over the following evening to chat it all through.

After an initial pang of nerves, chatting to local business owners turned out to be really pleasant. People were much more receptive to her in person. She managed to secure a bouquet from the florist, a voucher from one of the gift shops, and a boat trip with one of the tour companies down at the harbour.

Walking up the steep slope from the harbour, the wind whipped at her face, making her cheeks tingle. As the road levelled off at the top of the hill, she turned and looked back the way she'd come.

Boats bobbed on the water and people milled about in front of the row of brightly coloured buildings. It had been a successful morning, and she was proud of the confident way she'd approached the business owners.

She was about to set off for home when she caught sight of one of her pupils walking along the pavement towards her. Paige wasn't the easiest pupil, though from the reports of other teachers, Jess had it pretty easy. As far as she was concerned, Paige was a fairly typical fourteen-year-old; she scowled and exuded a bad attitude, but was never openly disruptive as her other teachers claimed her to be. Jess's first instinct was to look away and pretend she hadn't seen her, but she wasn't quick enough and Paige caught her eye. If she turned away, it would be obvious.

"Hi," Paige said, her usual scowl replaced by a shy smile.

Jess straightened up. "Hi, Paige. How are you?"

"Fine, thanks." A man stood beside her – Jess had barely registered him but suddenly felt his eyes on her and realised it was the guy she'd spoken to in the bar a couple of weeks ago. She wracked her brain for his name. Gary.

"How do you two know each other?" he asked with a frown.

"She's my chemistry teacher." Paige flashed him a puzzled expression. "Do you know Miss Gibson?"

He shifted his weight and Jess was amused by how uncomfortable he looked. "We ... erm ... "

"Oh God!" Paige rolled her eyes dramatically. "Please don't tell me you slept with my teacher?"

"No!" Gary snapped. "We just got chatting in the pub one night."

Jess was amused by the sudden tinge of red at Gary's cheeks. She thought back to him telling her he hadn't noticed her in the pub before and decided she was in the mood for a bit of teasing. "You might be mistaking me for someone else," she said mischievously. "I don't recall seeing you before in my life."

"Ouch!" Paige said, in her cocky teenage way.

"Ha ha," Gary said dryly. "We met in the Merchant Bar a couple of weeks ago."

"And you tried to chat her up?" Paige asked.

"Aye. But she was having none of it."

Paige laughed. "I've told you before to stay away from the brainy ones. You've got no chance."

"Do you have to be so annoying?" he asked, then glanced at Jess. "Paige is my niece. She's kind of a brat."

"Hey!" Paige leaned her head on his arm. "He loves me really."

"I'd love you to get in the car," he said, pressing the key fob in his hand to open the car nearest to them.

"Aw," Paige crooned. "Am I embarrassing you? You've gone a bit red." Reaching up, she squeezed his cheek then cackled with laughter when he swatted her away.

"Please get in the car."

"If you promise not to try and chat up my teacher again …"

He shot her a fierce look that got her moving towards the car. Pausing before she got in, she glanced at Jess. "See you at school."

"Bye," Jess said.

"So, about dinner …" Gary said as soon as the car door closed behind Paige.

"What about dinner?" Jess asked, smirking.

"I invited you for dinner and you didn't reply."

"I'm fairly sure I said no."

The corner of his mouth twitched to the hint of a smile. "You didn't seem too sure. And maybe you've changed your mind now that you've had a chance to think about it?"

"I haven't," she said firmly. "Thanks for checking though."

His gaze lingered on her. Then he took a couple of steps towards the car. "It was nice to see you again," he said with a bashful smile. "I'll probably see you around."

"Maybe." She smiled at him, flattered by the attention. It put her in a good mood for the rest of the day.

Her positivity rolled over to Sunday too. It helped that it was a bright sunny day, and she went out for a walk to make the most of it. She'd really picked a beautiful part of the world to move to, and it reminded her that she should take more time to appreciate it. Over the summer break she planned to go back to visit her family in Aberdeen, but she'd definitely spend some time exploring Skye too.

She managed not to think too much about Rory until Sunday evening when she found herself with nothing to occupy her. Nothing on TV held her interest and she was too restless to read.

Feeling as though she had nothing to lose, she called him.

"How was your weekend?" she asked when he answered.

"It was fine until about half an hour ago." His voice was filled with irritation and he sounded distracted.

"What happened?"

"I dropped Arran at home and Elspeth told me she's going away for a couple of days."

"With Arran?"

"No. She's going away with her sister. Arran's staying with Elspeth's parents."

"Is that a problem?" She wasn't sure what he was so annoyed about.

"The problem is she told me as an afterthought. She didn't ask if *I* could look after Arran, just arranged everything and then told me what was happening."

"It would be difficult for you to have Arran during the week, wouldn't it?" She wanted to take his side, but she was struggling to see what the problem was.

There was a short pause. "Yes. But that's not really the point. It's annoying that I'm only involved in his life at the weekend and on Wednesday evenings. Apparently the rest of the time is nothing to do with me any more."

"That must be hard," she said quietly.

"Sorry. It really annoyed me."

"You sound as though you could do with a drink," she said hopefully.

"I'd love a drink," he said on a sigh. "But I've got a pile of marking to tackle when I get home."

The disappointment made her insides feel heavy. "Are you driving?"

"Yeah. Just pulling up at home now. Anyway, I'm sure you didn't call to listen to me rant. How's everything with you? Have you had a good weekend?"

"Yeah, it was good." She made a conscious effort not to mention her efforts for the fundraiser. Soon, it would sound like her only topic of conversation. She also wanted to keep it for an excuse to call him another time. "I was pretty lazy," she said. "But I managed to get out and enjoy the fresh air today…" She was about to tell him about her walk, exploring the local area, but he swore loudly, interrupting her. "Are you okay?"

"Yeah, sorry. One of Arran's toys is on the back seat of my car."

"And that's a bad thing?"

"It's this big dinosaur toy. It's one of his favourites and he likes to sleep with it." He let out a low growl. "Now I'm going to have to drive all the way back there."

"Doesn't he have a different toy he can sleep with for a couple of nights?"

"He has loads. Unfortunately, it doesn't work like that. I'm going to have to go. I'm sorry."

"It's fine. I'll talk to you at school tomorrow."

He told her to have a good evening and left her feeling a mixture of annoyance and frustration. She'd told Ava that she was sure their relationship would progress if she just spent time with him. But him never having any time was a pretty big hindrance to her plan.

CHAPTER TWENTY-ONE

L eana was assaulted by a flood of memories as soon as they arrived in Edinburgh. Even trying to find a parking space near the Castle Hostel made her feel nostalgic.

"This spot is where I first met Alasdair," she told Elspeth, pausing as they walked along the quiet street. She smiled as she looked around, her mind taking her right back to that night. "He wasn't wearing a shirt or shoes and I thought he was homeless."

"I know," Elspeth said impatiently.

"It was his birthday and his friends had played a joke on him. Which means it's almost exactly three years ago." He'd still be in America for his birthday, and Leana felt a brief pang of disappointment that she wouldn't share it with him.

"Come on," Elspeth said, adjusting the strap of her backpack. "I want to see the hostel."

Leana continued walking alongside Elspeth. "I hate the time difference. I really want to call Alasdair now but he'll be asleep."

"You can call him later," Elspeth said. "We've only got today and tomorrow, so you need to focus on showing me around Edinburgh not moping over Alasdair."

"You've been to Edinburgh before. It's not as though I need to play tour guide."

"I've never been with you," Elspeth said. "I want you to show me all of your favourite places."

"I was trying to. That spot back there where I met the love of my life is a favourite place of mine."

Elspeth laughed. "I don't want the Leana and Alasdair love tour, thanks! You're supposed to be cheering me up. Don't drag me around all the places you went on dates and the place you first kissed."

"I might give you that tour," Leana said, grinning. "But first you get to see the Castle Hostel …" She raised a hand to indicate the wonderful old building as they approached. "I can't wait to see Denis and Ben."

Thankfully, she didn't have to wait long; her old boss and colleague were chatting away in the foyer when they walked in, and she hugged them both tightly.

"It always feels emotional coming back here," she told them, after she introduced Elspeth. "This place feels like home away from home."

"It's always good to see you," Denis said. "It's only a shame you never stay long enough for me to put you to work behind the bar."

"Well, I'll be at the bar this evening," she said cheekily. "Just on the other side of it."

"I presume Kyle will be joining you?" Ben asked.

"Yes. Judging by his messages, he's very excited."

"That lad's always excited." Denis walked to the reception desk and got them their room key. "You're in your old room," he said as he handed it to Leana.

Leana beamed. "Thank you."

"No worries. Some of us have got work to do, so we'll see you in the bar later."

She gave Ben another hug then set off for the stairs, indicating Elspeth should follow with a quick flick of her chin.

"Oh my goodness!" Leana squealed as she walked back into her old room. "It hasn't changed a bit."

"In the last thirty years?" Elspeth asked, looking around the sparse room with a frown.

"I know, it's very basic." Leana tried to look at it without the sheen of nostalgia and had to admit it was fairly drab. Twin beds were separated by a small wooden cabinet, and there was a matching wardrobe and desk at the other side of the room. "It's so full of memories." Her lips twitched to a smile as she remembered the first time Alasdair had stayed over with her. That story was probably a bit intimate to share. "I remember the first time Alasdair took me on a date and I was pacing around this room while I got ready. I was as nervous as anything."

Elspeth groaned and flopped onto the bed nearest the door. "Will you shut up!" she said as she propelled the pillow towards Leana's head.

"Sorry. I'm feeling very nostalgic." Yet again, she had the overwhelming urge to call Alasdair and mentally calculated the time in California. He wouldn't be awake for hours.

"What's the plan then?" Elspeth asked.

"Let's go out and have a walk around. Then we're meeting Kyle and Justin down in the bar later."

"I want to go clothes shopping before we leave," Elspeth said.

"We'll do that tomorrow. Come on. I'm hungry. Let's find food."

After a stroll around the quaint cobbled streets of the Old Town, they found a cafe for dinner then set off back to the hostel to get changed for the evening. The plan was to meet in the hostel bar, but knowing Kyle he'd have them dancing in a club by the end of the night. Even on a Monday night, Kyle would know the best places to party.

"Are you having a shower?" Leana asked Elspeth as she switched the hairdryer off. At the same time, she read a message on her phone from Kyle saying he was down in the bar.

"Yes." Elspeth said, standing from the bed where she'd been scrolling through her phone. "And don't rush me. I hardly ever get a night out. I'd like to take my time getting ready."

"I'm not rushing you. I'll be at the bar with Kyle. Come down when you're ready."

"See you in a bit," Elspeth said as she disappeared into the bathroom.

Leana was happy to have some time to chat to Kyle and Justin without Elspeth around. She could fill them in on the situation with Alasdair and get everything off her chest.

Downstairs she spotted Kyle immediately, chatting to Ben at the bar. He jumped up as soon as he saw her and embraced her tightly.

"Where's Justin?" she asked.

"Got held up at work. He'll join us later. Where's Elspeth?"

"In the shower."

"Perfect." He sat down and pulled the neighbouring stool closer to him, patting it in an invitation for her to sit. "Tell me everything while it's just the two of us. I want to know exactly what's going on with Alasdair and whether we need to start picking teams. Obviously I'm Team Leana."

"I don't think you need to pick teams," she said as she perched on the stool. Ben placed a bottle of beer in front of her and she smiled at him in thanks.

"Really?" Kyle asked. "I've been so worried that you might split up."

"We're not splitting up," she said, giving him a reassuring pat on the leg.

"What are you going to do then? Give up your dream of a big white wedding, or henpeck him until he gives in and agrees to it?"

"Hopefully there are more options than that," she said with a small smile. "I'm definitely not keen on the henpecking. I was just really shocked when he said he didn't want to get married.

I'd always assumed we would, but I'm not about to split up with him over it."

"I'm glad. I was worried it would cause a rift between me and Justin if we had to take sides."

"Really?" She smirked and took a long swig of beer. "That's what you were worried about?"

"That and your happiness. Obviously! I always worry about your happiness first. That's a given, so I didn't think I needed to mention it." He swivelled on his stool and waved excitedly to Elspeth as she walked into the room.

"Alasdair's calling me," Leana said, pulling her phone from her pocket.

"He has the best timing." Kyle pushed her off her stool. "Go somewhere else to speak to him so I can listen to Elspeth's problems while you're gone. I can be everyone's agony aunt. I love the drama," he said with a grin.

Leana told Elspeth she'd be back in a minute, then answered her phone as she moved to find a quiet spot. Instinctively, she walked out of the hostel and wandered down the road a little way.

"I kept wanting to call you all day," she said. "I didn't want to wake you though."

"I'm glad I caught you," Alasdair said. "I take it you arrived safely in Edinburgh?"

"Yes." She smiled as she looked around. "And I'm standing in the place where we first met." Alasdair was quiet and she wondered if they'd lost the connection. "Are you still there?"

"Yes. Sorry. I was thinking about that night." He fell quiet again. "I miss you," he said after a moment.

"I miss you too," she said, wishing he was there with her. "How's California?"

"It's okay. We arrived in San Francisco yesterday afternoon, then played a gig last night. It ended up being a late one so I'm a bit done in today."

"You never could keep up with Ghost Moon when they go out partying, could you?"

"No. I'm remembering why I ditched them for the quiet life."

"Because they're too wild for you? That's the reason?"

"What else?" he asked with mock innocence.

"Maybe it was that big house overlooking the loch?"

He laughed. "It's a nice house. But it was more to do with a gorgeous red-head who lived by the loch."

"She must be very special," Leana said cheekily.

"She is," he said, his tone deadly serious.

Leana's throat felt thick as her emotions swelled in her chest. "I love you."

"I love you too. What have you got planned this evening? Are you going out with Kyle and Justin?"

"Yes. I presume it will be a sedate and civilised evening."

He laughed again. "I highly doubt that. I wish I was there."

"I wish you were too."

"Call me tomorrow," he said. "If you're not too hungover to operate the phone."

"I told you, it's going to be a quiet night."

The sound of his laughter left her feeling all warm and fuzzy when she headed back into the hostel.

Leana woke several times over the course of the following morning. Each time she groaned through a pounding headache and went back to sleep again.

"We should get up," she muttered in Elspeth's direction when she thought they should put an end to the snoozing and do something productive with the day.

"Why?" Elspeth grumbled.

"Because it's midday. We leave tomorrow morning, so we need to make the most of the day."

"I'm not sure I can move, even though this is probably the most uncomfortable bed I've ever slept on."

"The mattresses are terrible," Leana agreed. "You can see why I moved home." She forced herself to sit up, then smiled despite her throbbing head. "I told Alasdair we'd be having a quiet, civilised evening."

"I don't think there was anything civilised about the amount of alcohol we drank. Poor Justin had to be up for work this morning."

"I don't envy him. Do you want to go shopping?"

"No. It sounds like hell." Elspeth pulled the pillow over her head. "Let me sleep a bit longer."

Leana showered, then went out for coffee and bagels to coax Elspeth awake. It did the trick, and they finally set off on foot to the main shopping street. The fresh air didn't help her hangover as much as she'd have liked, and shopping was about the last thing she felt like doing. They wandered in and out of shops on Princes Street, both of them equally unenthusiastic.

Late in the afternoon, with neither of them having made any purchases, they ducked into a pub and ordered cheeseburgers with chips and a large glass of Coke each.

Leana finally felt better and Elspeth perked up too.

"Kyle says he's dying," Leana said as she read a message from him.

"I'm glad it's not just us who can't handle hangovers," Elspeth said.

"He wants us to go and visit him at work."

"I'm not sure I can drink alcohol yet." Elspeth sucked her Coke through the straw. "I'd like to see where he works though."

"It's not far from here," Leana said. "We can walk over there and see him for a while then head back for an early night."

"It's annoying that we have to leave again tomorrow," Elspeth said. "I think I could have done with a longer trip."

"Have you heard from Mum? How's Arran?"

"She messaged and said he's fine. He'll be quite happy

staying with them. They'll no doubt let him watch as much TV as he wants and feed him full of sweets. There's a chance he'll be disappointed when I get back."

"I doubt that. I'm sorry we haven't really done much. It wasn't exactly an exciting getaway for you. We even failed at shopping."

"It's fine," Elspeth said. "It's good to be somewhere different. I might have spent all day thinking about my hangover, but it was a change from thinking about what a mess I've made of my life."

"You haven't made a mess of your life," Leana said gently. "I don't know how you can think that. You have a beautiful child and a successful business."

Elspeth rolled her eyes. "My successful business is currently closed and I'm fairly certain my beautiful child would rather live with his dad. Oh, and I somehow managed to screw up a relationship with a perfect guy. I'm not sure how you can argue my life isn't a mess."

"I can argue it all day," Leana said. "And I can also argue that you're being too hard on yourself."

"Can we not talk about this?" Elspeth said sadly. "I wanted to get away and forget about it all."

Leana drained her drink, trying hard to keep her thoughts to herself before giving up on it. "If you think Rory's the perfect guy, why don't you try and sort things out with him?"

"Because I kicked him out," Elspeth snapped. "I can't suddenly change my mind. And I'm not even sure I want to."

"But you're angry with yourself for messing things up with him and hate the thought of him seeing someone else," Leana pointed out, tilting her head.

"It's not as though I can tell him I might still want to be with him but I'm not quite sure so could he please hang around until I sort my head out."

"Sometimes I think you know exactly what you want but you're scared to admit it."

"It's complicated," Elspeth said, her shoulders sagging. "I hurt Rory. It would be unfair of me to mess him around now. If he's seeing someone else I need to find a way to be happy for him and get on with my life."

"But if you talk to him—"

"I really don't want to discuss it. This is supposed to be a stress-free couple of days away from everything. Let's go and see Kyle." She stood to leave and Leana followed her lead.

The atmosphere was a little tense as they strolled in the direction of the bar where Kyle worked. They hadn't got very far when Leana stopped abruptly.

Elspeth turned to face her. "Judging by your silly grin, I presume you're going to tell me another soppy story about Alasdair. If this is the spot where he first told you he loved you, I might actually vomit."

"It's not," Leana said. "This is where we were standing the first time he kissed me. We'd been at Kyle's bar and we were walking home. It had been raining and I remember it looked so pretty with the glow of the streetlights reflecting off the wet cobblestones ... Elspeth!" she shouted, as her little sister strode away from her.

"I can't listen to you any more," Elspeth called over her shoulder. "All this gushy stuff isn't good for someone who's trying to get over a break-up."

Leana hurried after her and slipped her arm through Elspeth's. "Maybe you should stop trying to get over it and work on fixing things instead."

"You're really annoying," Elspeth muttered. "And you're actually making me think more alcohol is a good idea."

"I'm sorry," Leana said. "I'll stop talking about Rory."

"And Alasdair?"

"Yeah, okay." As though he knew they were talking about him, Alasdair chose that exact moment to call. Leana grimaced as she looked at the phone screen. "Sorry," she whispered to

Elspeth before she answered. "Guess where I am?" she said to Alasdair.

"Edinburgh?"

"Ha-ha! Where exactly?"

"If you say the Black Rose Tavern I'm going to be very jealous."

"We're just walking there. I showed Elspeth the place we first kissed and now she's in a bad mood with me." She grinned at Elspeth as she spoke. "Apparently it's not the tour of Edinburgh she was expecting."

"Sounds like a good tour to me," Alasdair said. "Don't forget to warn her about stalkers in the Black Rose."

"Stalkers?" Leana asked.

"Yes. I once played a gig there and some crazy woman showed up, saying she'd been looking for me in every bar in Edinburgh."

Leana laughed loudly. "Not *every* bar in Edinburgh!"

"I've still not managed to get rid of her," he said lightly.

"Edinburgh must have a real problem with stalkers then. I had a guy follow me back to Skye, and I can't seem to get rid of him either." She turned to see Elspeth put two fingers near her mouth in a vomit gesture. "Elspeth thinks we're sickening," she told Alasdair.

"We are a bit," he agreed, before his tone turned serious. "I hate that you're in Edinburgh without me."

"How's everything there?" she asked.

"It's good. Not as much fun as when you were here."

She swallowed hard, wondering if he really meant it or if he was trying to redeem himself over the whole marriage issue. "We're at the bar," she said. "I better go."

He told her he loved her before ending the call.

"You two really are sickening," Elspeth said. "I definitely need a drink now."

CHAPTER TWENTY-TWO

E lspeth had initially felt uneasy about the trip to Edinburgh. Surprisingly, her chat with the counsellor on Monday morning put her mind at ease. She'd only mentioned it in passing, but it had led to her talking about how guilty she felt when she left Arran with anyone. After chatting it through, she'd felt much better. Everyone needed a break sometimes, and being a good mum meant taking care of herself too.

Almost as soon as they left home, she felt lighter. The time in Edinburgh with her sister was refreshing. It was just a shame they only had such a short amount of time. Waking early on Wednesday morning, it occurred to her that she could stay longer. Leana needed to get back to work, but as long as her parents were happy to look after Arran, there was no reason why Elspeth couldn't stay. A few extra days would further recharge her batteries.

While she showered and called her mum, Leana slept on without stirring. Eventually, Elspeth nudged her awake.

"You have to leave soon," she said as she gave her sister's shoulder a gentle shake. "You won't make it back for work otherwise."

She grunted and swatted Elspeth away. "It's going to be a very long day. Can you drive so I can sleep on the way back?"

"I'm not coming back with you." Elspeth smiled, thinking it sounded a bit dramatic, as though she was running away from her life. Which she was, but only for a few more days.

Leana sat up, squinting at Elspeth. "What do you mean?"

"I don't have a job to get back to, and I spoke to Mum and she's happy to look after Arran, so I'm going to stay here for a few more days. I'll have to check if I can stay in this room or if I need to move to a different one, but Denis was saying the hostel isn't full so it should be fine."

"What are you going to do on your own?"

"I don't know. Probably just relax like everyone keeps telling me to. I'll wander the city and explore. Being on my own for a while is very appealing. I never seem to have any time to myself."

"How long will you stay?"

"Until the weekend." She shrugged. "I'll have to check how I can get back with the train."

"It'll take you forever to get back with public transport. You'll waste a whole day on trains and buses and hanging around at various stations."

"I quite like the sound of it," Elspeth said. "It's probably as close to going travelling as I'll ever get."

"Are you sure you'll be all right on your own?"

"Yes! I'm excited. Now go and have a shower. I'm going to see if I can find coffee, and I'll ask about staying longer."

She found Denis downstairs and he was very accommodating. From the way he tapped on the computer at the reception desk, she was certain he had to rearrange bookings for the rooms, but he insisted it was fine for her to stay in the same room. She thanked him profusely and headed for the coffee machine in the communal lounge.

"I can stay in this room," she told Leana excitedly when she rejoined her upstairs.

"I'm jealous. I'd like to stay here on my own for a few days. Why don't you get in touch with Kyle and meet up with him and Justin again?"

"I quite like the idea of being on my own."

"Don't tell him you're still here then. He might decide you need looking after and get all motherly." She sipped at her coffee, then picked up her backpack. "I should go. Last chance to change your mind and come with me."

"No, thanks." She gave Leana a big hug. "Give Arran a cuddle for me."

"I will."

After Leana left, Elspeth sank onto the bed and smiled to herself. Being alone in a city felt like an adventure, and she was determined not to dwell on her problems or what was going on at home. For once, she was going to focus on herself and enjoy the freedom of being able to do whatever she wanted, whenever she wanted.

For most of Wednesday that meant wandering aimlessly around the stunning city, browsing shops and sitting in cafes to watch the world go by while someone waited on her for a change. The feeling of being anonymous was new and exhilarating and she loved every minute of it.

Late in the afternoon, she remembered it was Rory's night to come over. She sent him a quick message to say she wouldn't be back for another few days and that Arran was with her parents. She figured he could get in touch with them to arrange if he'd go over that evening or wait and have Arran at the weekend.

He sent her a few messages, asking why she'd changed her plans and when she'd be back. The messages put a bit of a dampener on her mood, but she patiently replied until he seemed to be placated.

In the evening she ate dinner in the hostel bar and had just finished eating when her phone rang. It was Rory, and she headed out of the bar when she answered, then continued up to her room.

"Where are you?" she asked, wondering if he'd gone to see Arran or not.

"At the cottage with Arran."

"Are you putting him to bed there? I presumed he'd stay at my parents' place."

"It seems like that was the plan." His tone was frosty. "But nobody bothered to ask me."

She held the key card over the lock, then pushed the handle down when the light turned green. "Was I supposed to check with you that it's okay for Arran to stay with my parents?" she asked, confused by his attitude.

"No. It's not that I have a problem with him staying there. I just don't understand why you didn't ask me to look after him. I'm his dad. It feels as though you only let me know about your plans as an afterthought."

"I assumed it would be easier for him to stay with Mum and Dad during the week. You wouldn't be able to pick him up from nursery and drop him off in the morning with work."

"If I stay at the cottage with him, I can drop him off before I go to work. Then I only need someone to pick him up and watch him until I get back."

"Okay. Whatever you want."

"So you don't mind me staying at the cottage? I'll sleep in the spare room."

"It's fine. But you sound annoyed with me. Are you angry that I didn't come home today?"

"No. But when it comes to Arran you should talk to me first and not the rest of your family. Just because we agreed I'd have him mostly on the weekends doesn't mean I don't want to know what's going on with him the rest of the time. If you're away, I think it's better for me to stay with him. It's less disruptive."

"You're right. I'm sorry. I should have talked to you about it first." She'd honestly thought she was making things easier for Rory, but she supposed she could have checked with him first. "Can you put Arran on the phone?" she asked as she heard him playing in the background. They switched to a video call, but she only caught a glimpse of Rory's profile before he handed the phone to Arran. He didn't speak to Elspeth again and the call ended abruptly once she'd had a chat to Arran and wished him goodnight.

So much for forgetting about everything at home.

The following day Elspeth woke up late and spent a lazy morning at the hostel. In the afternoon, she strolled along Princes Street looking around clothes shops. She treated herself to a couple of pairs of jeans and a few tops and enjoyed picking out some new clothes for Arran too. Usually she was fairly frugal and bought his clothes second-hand or took hand-me-downs from a couple of women in Lannick with older boys. It wasn't often that she bought anything new for herself either.

On a whim, she ducked into a hairdresser and asked if they had time to give her a trim. They asked her to come back in an hour, so she killed some time getting a sandwich and a salad in a cafe nearby.

Walking to the hostel at the end of the day, with her hands full of bags and her hair bouncing just below her shoulders, she felt great. It was amazing what a haircut and new clothes could do.

At the hostel, she slipped into her new skinny jeans and a cute pale-blue shirt. She was about to message Rory to check everything was okay at home, then thought better of it. If there was a problem, he'd have been in touch with her.

Not wanting to put her new look to waste, she ventured down to the hostel bar. It was busier than it had been on previous evenings and she felt a little self-conscious as she walked in. The previous evening there'd been other people sitting alone, but now everyone seemed to be in groups and chatting away.

Denis caught her eye and she slipped onto a stool across the bar from him.

"What can I get you?" he asked.

"A beer, please."

He flipped the top off a bottle and handed it to her. "How was your day?" he asked as she paid for her drink.

"Really good. I went shopping."

"Not my idea of fun," he said. "But I hear some people enjoy it. I thought you might be off doing something touristy."

"No. Maybe tomorrow."

He smiled and moved along the bar to serve someone else. Ben was behind the bar too and waved a greeting at her as he served a group of people a little further along from her.

"That hair!" a voice beside her said loudly, startling her.

Turning, she came face to face with a tall, slightly imposing guy who she guessed to be a few years older than her. His hair fell in dark, tight curls, and when his face broke into a smile it lit up his face.

"Excuse me?" she said with a polite but nervous smile.

"You've got the most beautiful hair I've ever seen." He reached out a hand as if he was about to touch it but just held his palm close to it. "It's so fiery. Like flames."

"Thanks ... I think."

"Yes! It's a compliment. You drew me to you like a beacon."

She took a swig of her beer, wondering whether leaving the comfort of her room was a mistake.

"I'm Kendrick. You can call me Ricky or Ken or Rick. Whatever you want. I'm going to call you beautiful."

She let out a soft laugh. "My name's Elspeth."

"Elspeth! A stunning name for a stunning lady." He lifted her hand to his lips and kissed her knuckles before she had time to pull away. "We're going to be great friends. Can I buy you a drink?"

"I've got one." She gestured to her beer.

"A shot then. Let's drink shots together. Are you on your own?"

She glanced around. "Yes," she said, hoping that wasn't a mistake.

"Not any more." He flicked a curl away from his eye. "I'm going to introduce you to all my friends. Get ready for a brilliant night."

While she struggled for something to say, Kendrick waved frantically to Ben.

"What can I do for you, Kendrick?" he asked with a sigh.

"We'd like shots," he said excitedly. "We'd all like shots. Let's get shots for everyone in here. How much tequila have you got?"

Ben smiled. "Let's not do that again. Go and count your friends. You should just buy shots for them."

"Everyone here is my friend," he said dramatically.

"Then let's say the people whose names you know. And you should ask them if they want a drink first."

"Okay. Back in a sec." He hurried away.

"Is he on drugs?" Elspeth asked Ben.

"The consensus is no. It seems as though that's his personality."

"Really? Is he likely to come back? Should I run away now?"

"He's actually a really nice guy. Once you get used to him."

"How long has he been staying here?"

"About a month. He's great at bringing people together. And he seems to have unlimited funds. He's always throwing his money around." Ben fell silent as Kendrick returned.

"I have eight friends who'd like a shot, please. And me and Elspeth make ten."

"I'm fine with my beer," she said. "Thank you."

"Can you bring the drinks over?" Kendrick asked. "I'm going to introduce beautiful Elspeth to my friends!"

"Oh, I'm actually fine here," she said, but Kendrick had her hand and pulled her from her stool. She looked at Ben in a panic.

"Resistance is futile." He gave her a wink before she was dragged away.

"This is Elspeth!" Kendrick announced when they stopped at a large group of people sitting around a couple of tables which had been pushed together. "Hasn't she got beautiful hair? I'll bet she has fire in her soul to match her fiery hair."

Elspeth touched her hair, glad that it was looking healthy and glossy after her appointment that afternoon.

The group waved collectively and a couple of women at the end motioned to a spare chair next to them. They didn't seem at all perturbed by Elspeth joining them and introduced themselves with handshakes and smiles. Danielle was from Ireland and Molly was Australian. There was some bustle as Ben arrived with a tray of shots.

Danielle grimaced as she knocked hers back, then looked to Elspeth.

"Kendrick likes to round up anyone who's on their own. No one here really knows each other. At least they didn't until recently."

"He gathers people up like lost sheep," Molly added. "I met him a few nights ago and I feel as though I've known him forever. He's introduced me to loads of new people too." She grinned at Danielle.

Elspeth picked up her beer. "I have to say, I was feeling a bit self-conscious sitting on my own at the bar."

"What's your story?" Molly asked. "Are you travelling? You sound local."

"I live on the Isle of Skye," she said. "It's the other end of the country, so I'm not local. Although, I suppose compared to Australia I am. I'm just having a few days away."

They chatted easily for the next half an hour and she was about to leave when Ben appeared behind her and passed her a fresh beer. He waved her away when she tried to pay, which left Danielle and Molly giving her teasing looks when he left.

"I think you've got an admirer," Molly said.

"No. He's an old friend of my sister. I think she told him to look out for me."

"That's sweet," Danielle said. "You're not interested in him then?"

"No. He seems lovely. He's quite old though."

Molly spluttered a laugh. "He's not old. You're just a baby. I'm glad you're not interested. I've got my eye on him for a holiday fling!" She smiled mischievously.

As Elspeth made her way through her beer, she got chatting to the friendly Welsh guy beside her and then an American couple opposite her. The conversations started to blur into each other after Molly brought her another beer.

"I think I'm going to have to go to bed," she finally said.

Molly grabbed at her arm and jokily told her she had to stay. "She's trying to get away!" she called loudly.

Elspeth was laughing when she felt strong hands on her shoulders and looked up to see Kendrick looming over her.

"I'm tired," she said. "I'm going up to bed."

"You have to answer a question correctly first!" someone called in a drunken slur. In response, everyone around the table fell about laughing.

"What are you talking about?" Elspeth asked as she stood up. "I'm going to bed. Goodnight!"

Kendrick stood squarely in front of her, blocking her way. Over his shoulder, she caught Denis and Ben watching the commotion. They both looked amused, and Elspeth had the feeling everyone was in on a joke that she wasn't.

"I have one question for you," Kendrick said loudly. "If you answer it correctly you may go to bed without any protests from me."

"What?" she asked, frowning and feeling as though everyone in the room was looking at her.

"The question, Elspeth with the fiery hair and even more fiery spirit ... the very important question I have for you is ..." His eyes sparkled and he threw his arms out to the sides. "Have you danced today?"

Elspeth's cheeks heated up as everyone around her chuckled. "No," she said quietly.

"What was that?" Kendrick asked.

"No, I haven't danced today."

"Then you can't possibly go to bed. What is the point of a day without dancing?"

"I don't want to dance," she said as he held a hand out to her.

His eyebrows jiggled, and she couldn't help but laugh as he spun her under his arm. With one hand on her back and the other holding hers, he waltzed her around the space beside the tables. Amid excited cheers, others began to dance around them, making Elspeth feel less of a spectacle.

Finally, Elspeth slipped away from Kendrick, leaving him to dance with someone else.

"He's a character, isn't he?" Ben asked, coming to stand beside her at the edge of the dancers.

"He's hilarious." She couldn't stop her smile as she watched her new friends boogie around their makeshift dancefloor.

"Every night ends in dancing when he's around. And he has a knack of encouraging everyone in the room to dance."

"Everyone?" Elspeth asked.

"Well, not everyone. I'm here to work."

"You could take a break, couldn't you?"

"Not to dance, no!"

"Oh, come on." She pulled on his arm.

"Get off! Five minutes ago you were the one protesting about being dragged up to dance."

"And now it's you," she said, taking his hand and pulling him into the throng. "One dance!"

Shaking his head, he slipped an arm around her waist and gave in to the rhythm of the music. Feeling utterly free, she beamed as she danced with Ben, and also strategically manoeuvred him towards Danielle and Molly.

"Have you met Molly?" she asked Ben when the song came to an end. "She's from Australia."

"Nice to meet you," Ben said.

"You should dance together," Elspeth said. "I need to get another drink."

"I need a drink too," Danielle said, giving Elspeth a knowing look.

Ben rolled his eyes. "I'm supposed to be working."

"I'm sure you've got time for another quick dance!" Elspeth replied.

She headed to the bar with Danielle, then looked back to see Molly and Ben dancing together, both of them looking very happy with the situation.

"Molly's going to be your friend for life now," Danielle said.

"I'm having fun," Elspeth said, grinning. "I think I might be drunk and I should probably go to bed, but I kind of want to keep dancing."

"One more drink and one more dance!" Danielle said mischievously.

It was another hour before Elspeth slipped away upstairs. Her face was fixed in a grin and she laughed to herself when she fell into bed.

It had been quite an unexpected day.

CHAPTER TWENTY-THREE

The thudding in Elspeth's head got gradually worse as she woke. Blinking, she sat up quickly, realising the thudding was actually someone knocking repeatedly at the door.

"Who is it?" she asked, her voice croaky as she fought her way out of sleep.

"Molly and Danielle!" a loud voice boomed, making Elspeth wince.

She only vaguely remembered getting changed into her pyjamas and noticed her discarded clothes strewn across the floor as she stumbled across the room to open the door.

"How did you know which room I'm in?" she asked blearily as Danielle put a takeaway coffee in her hand.

"We asked at reception," Molly said.

The two of them filed into the room, and Elspeth moved to put the cup down as the heat seeped through to her hand. Hastily, she picked her clothes off the floor and flung them on the bed.

"It was a great night last night," Danielle said, dropping onto the extra bed. "You've got a nice room. So much better than bunkbeds!"

"My sister used to work here," Elspeth told her, "so we get treated like VIPs. As much as possible in a hostel anyway. She was here with me but I decided to stay longer when she went home."

"I'm glad you stayed," Molly said. "You're a great wingwoman."

"Did anything happen with you and Ben?" Elspeth asked.

A smile spread slowly over Molly's face. "I don't like to kiss and tell."

"So there was kissing?"

"There might have been! Anyway, you need to get dressed. We're going out."

"Where are you going?"

"*We're* going for a walk up to Arthur's Seat. There's a bunch of people going. Kendrick organised it. He's always organising something."

"It's great," Danielle said. "We don't have to plan our days any more. We just follow Kendrick."

"I don't know." Her plan to spend time alone was disintegrating quickly.

"What else are you going to do?" Molly asked.

"I was thinking of spending the day aimlessly wandering around the city," Elspeth replied with a small smile.

"Get dressed," Danielle said, moving to the door. "Everyone's meeting downstairs in half an hour."

Elspeth murmured her agreement and headed for the shower.

When she walked into the reception area half an hour later, Kendrick greeted her exuberantly with a big hug. She recognised a few others in the group from the previous evening, and Kendrick introduced her to a couple of people who she hadn't seen before. As she followed the crowd out of the hostel she counted eleven of them. It felt slightly strange to walk through the city with a bunch of people who she barely knew, but she decided to go with the flow and not overthink it.

They got a bus to Holyrood Park, then ambled towards the hill known as Arthur's Seat. As they walked, she enjoyed chatting to the random people she was with. It was interesting to hear where they were all from and what they were doing. They all seemed to have such exciting lives compared to her. Although they were impressed when she said she ran a cafe on Skye. She neglected to mention Arran, not because she was ashamed of him, but because she was enjoying just being herself and not someone's mother. It also meant she didn't have to deal with the inevitable questions about her teen pregnancy. People always found that fascinating.

In the afternoon Kendrick had booked a tour of The Real Mary King's Close. Elspeth wasn't sure she liked the idea of an underground museum, but she ended up being glad that she went along. The warren of 17th-century streets and alleyways hidden beneath the Royal Mile was incredible. The costumed tour guide regaled them with stories about the people who'd lived and worked in those streets and how the plague had run rampant in the area.

They'd just come back into the daylight when Elspeth noticed she had a couple of missed calls from Rory. She'd call him back from the hostel.

Not having eaten much all day, she happily went along when someone suggested getting dinner. They took over a couple of tables in a spacious pub in the heart of the city. Elspeth's steak pie had just arrived when her phone rang again. Not wanting to talk to Rory in front of everyone, she declined the call and instead sent a quick message asking if everything was okay. When he said everything was fine, she said she'd call him later.

Back at the hostel, their group went to their respective rooms with the plan of meeting in the bar later. Elspeth was glad she'd treated herself to new clothes and was excited about wearing another new outfit that evening. First, she pulled out her phone and called Rory.

"How's Arran?" she asked, hearing him in the background. "I thought he'd be in bed by now."

"He wanted to talk to you first." Rory sounded impatient and gruffly told Arran to stop jumping around.

"Put him on," Elspeth said, then smiled at the sound of Arran's voice. "Are you being a good boy for Daddy?" she asked.

"Yes!" he shouted loudly. "When are you coming home?"

"Soon. In a couple of days. Are you having a nice time with Daddy?"

"Yes! He's sleeping at our house."

"I know. That's exciting, isn't it?"

"We're going to have pancakes for breakfast tomorrow," he told her excitedly.

"You're so lucky. Give the phone back to Daddy for a minute. I think you need to go to bed soon." She told him she loved him and there was some background noise before she heard Rory's voice again.

"How's Edinburgh?" he asked.

"Good, thanks. I'm enjoying it."

"When are you coming home?"

"Saturday or Sunday. I'm not sure yet. I have to check the train times."

"It's Saturday tomorrow," Rory pointed out.

Elspeth's brain whirred; the week had gone quickly, and without a routine she'd lost track of days.

"Probably Sunday then."

"The trains will be a nightmare on Sunday," Rory said. "Do you want us to drive down and pick you up?"

"No." She was surprised by the offer. "I'm fine. Thanks, though."

"My parents would like to see Arran anyway, so we could drive down tomorrow and stay with them for a night and then pick you up on Sunday."

"Don't do that. It's too much trouble. You were with your parents a few weeks ago for the school holidays. I honestly don't mind getting the train home."

"Can you at least tell me exactly when you'll be home? Make a decision, please."

Elspeth sank onto the bed, feeling her shoulders tense. "Does it even matter whether I come home tomorrow or on Sunday? Of course I'll tell you when I know, but there's no need to stress about it."

"You have a child, in case you've forgotten." His tone was full of bitterness. "It would be nice for him to know when you'll be back."

Elspeth hesitated before she replied, trying not to lose her temper. "If you can't cope with looking after Arran for a few extra days this week, you should ask my parents to have him until I get back."

"I can cope with him fine," he snapped.

"Okay, but I'd rather he was with my parents. They wouldn't make me feel guilty for having a holiday. And they definitely wouldn't call me and ask if I've forgotten I have a child."

He was silent for a moment. "Sorry, it came out wrong. But Arran keeps asking when you'll be home, and it would be nice to know what to say to him."

"Tell him I'll be home on Sunday," she said through gritted teeth. "I'll let you know what time. Give him a kiss from me." She ended the call without bothering to say goodbye.

After such a great day, Rory had managed to completely ruin her mood. Especially because he reiterated her own insecurity that it was selfish of her to leave Arran and take some time to herself. Perhaps she ought to go home the following day.

Abandoning the idea of another night at the bar, she got ready for bed and snuggled down under the covers. She'd exchanged numbers with Danielle and Molly, so she sent them a message saying she was worn out after the day of sightseeing and was going to bail on drinks. Curled up in bed, she half expected them to come and bang on the door and insist that she go and party with them, but it was all quiet and she was asleep before she knew it.

CHAPTER TWENTY-FOUR

Considering how early she'd gone to bed, Elspeth was amazed when she woke up to find it was already late morning. The long sleep had been refreshing, and after showering she felt full of energy. Skipping out on the drinks the previous evening had been a good call.

As she checked her options for getting home, she realised she should have got up earlier. With the stops and changes it would be midnight before she got home. She'd also need to rope someone in to picking her up from the bus station at Kyle of Lochalsh, and she was sure they'd all grumble about coming out so late. It would make more sense to get up early the following day and go then. That was how she reasoned it anyway. If she were honest, it was more to do with the fact that she wasn't quite ready to go home yet. The feeling that she'd been summoned by Rory didn't sit well with her either. Having some time to herself didn't make her a bad mother, and it was unfair of him to make her feel that way.

On impulse, she messaged Molly and asked if she and Danielle had plans for the day. The reply came immediately to say that they were meeting downstairs at midday to explore the city some more. Elspeth said she'd see them there even though she hadn't specifically been invited. She loved the hostel and how people grouped together to do things.

As she was strolling around Holyrood Palace that afternoon, Elspeth's phone rang. She tensed as soon as she saw Rory's name on the display. What did he want now? Couldn't he hold the fort for a few days without calling her all the time? She wouldn't mind if there was a reason for the calls, or even if he was cheerful when he called. But every time he phoned he put her in a terrible mood. Tomorrow she'd be home again and he could annoy her all he wanted, but she refused to let him ruin her last day in Edinburgh. Dropping her phone into her bag, she turned her attention to the paintings hanging on the wall of the grand room.

Eddie, an English guy who'd been with them the previous day too, sloped up beside her. "This is all lovely," he said. "But I reckon it must be almost beer o'clock."

She checked her watch and grinned at him. "It's actually five past beer o'clock!"

Reminding herself she was on holiday, she ordered fish and chips in the pub close to the hostel that Kendrick led them to for dinner. A week of eating unhealthily wouldn't hurt. Her phone buzzed yet again and she ignored it, only pulling it out of her bag when they exited the pub. The missed calls from Rory had been accumulating all afternoon and she felt a stab of guilt for ignoring him. She told herself that if there was a problem with Arran he'd have left a message, and she'd have had calls and messages from her whole family. She could wait until she was alone to call him.

The plan was for everyone to go back to the hostel to get changed before another night out. Kendrick had suggested drinks in the hostel bar before moving on to a club. Since she had to be up early, Elspeth would give clubbing a miss but was keen for one last night in the hostel bar.

Up in her room she got ready for the evening, intent on calling Rory right before she went out. She'd probably need a drink after she spoke to him, but she was determined not to let him ruin her evening. She put more effort into getting ready than usual, carefully applying make-up and styling her hair with the blow-dryer on the low setting rather than just blasting it as she usually did.

"I'm coming!" she said, in response to a knock at the door. Molly and Danielle had already warned her that if she tried to bail again, they'd come and drag her out. She was grinning at their tenacity when she reached for the door handle. "I'll meet you down there, I have to make a quick … phone call … Hi."

Rory's brow was creased into a frown as he glared at her. "Hi."

CHAPTER TWENTY-FIVE

The trip to Edinburgh had lifted Leana's spirits for a wee while, but it also made her miss Alasdair more. Another three weeks without him felt like forever.

When she started her shift on Saturday afternoon, she slipped into autopilot, so it took her a while to notice the familiar faces sitting at the table near the window. She felt slightly nervous as she walked over to say hello to Conor and Patrick. If previous experience was anything to go by, she was probably about to embarrass herself somehow.

"The food's so good here that we had to come back," Conor said, smiling up at her.

"Glad you like it," she replied, taking in their empty plates. "How's everything with the music? Did you manage to get it all finished?"

Conor's gaze was fixed on her, his lazy smile giving warmth to his features. "We did. Finally we have tracks recorded."

"What will you do with them?" she asked. "Send them to record companies?"

"No. We'll upload them ourselves. You'll be able to download the EP from your preferred platform soon."

"You'll have to send me a link." She picked up their plates. "Do you want more drinks?"

Patrick shook his head but remained mute.

"I think we're going to finish these and head off," Conor said.

"Give me a shout if you need anything," she said as she left them.

Ten minutes later, she was pouring a pint for Douglas, one of the regulars, when she saw Conor and Patrick walking to the door. She called goodbye to them. Conor said something to Patrick, then wandered to the end of the bar, tipping his chin at her.

"Decide you fancy another drink?" she asked. He shook his head and leaned with his forearms on the bar. "I was wondering if you'd like to go out for a drink with me sometime?"

Leana searched his face, trying to make sense of the question. "You mean like a date?" she asked, moving closer and lowering her voice.

"Yes." His smile widened. "You look surprised …"

"I am. Partly because every time I've seen you I've managed to embarrass myself, so I'm surprised you'd want to go on a date with me. But also because I have a boyfriend … who you know."

"I wasn't sure what the situation was with Alasdair. In his messages he was vague about when he'd be back from America. I didn't know if he was staying long-term. And when I overheard you on the phone with him, you didn't sound particularly friendly so …"

"So you thought you'd try your luck?"

"Yeah. But you guys are together?"

"Yes. He'll be back in a few weeks."

"Okay. My turn to be embarrassed then. Sorry if I made you uncomfortable."

"No, not at all." She actually felt quite flattered that he'd asked her out. "It's a nice change to me embarrassing myself."

"Can't blame a guy for trying," he said as he straightened up. He tapped a finger on the bar and seemed to be contemplating saying more. "Patrick and I are often out in Portree on the weekends. If you ever fancy joining us for a drink, give me a shout. I think we owe you a drink or two to say thanks for letting us use the studio."

She smiled and nodded.

"You've got my number," he said before he left.

Leana was staring at the door when Douglas's voice interrupted her thoughts.

"I hope Alasdair's coming home soon. The vultures are circling."

"He's just a friend," Leana said.

"A friend who asked you out on a date?"

Leana chuckled. "Good to know there's nothing wrong with your hearing." She glanced at the plate in front of him on the bar. "What have I told you about eating your veg?"

He let out a quick groan before picking up a piece of broccoli and putting it in his mouth. "You'll make someone a good wife anyway. You've got the nagging perfected."

She muttered that it wouldn't be Alasdair as she moved to serve a couple who'd just walked in.

By the time her shift ended, her feet were aching and she was glad to slip her shoes off at home. She was walking through to the living room, intent on calling Alasdair, when her phone rang. As she sank onto the couch she answered the video call to be met with the sight of Alasdair sitting up in bed with no top on. The desire to snuggle up next to him was overwhelming.

"Isn't it the afternoon there?" she asked. "Are you having a nap?"

"No, I just woke up. We were out last night."

"You look terrible," she said, taking in the dark circles under his eyes.

"Thanks a lot." He shuffled down the bed and dragged a hand through his hair.

"I reckon you could do with a few early nights."

"Probably," he said. "How was work?"

"All right." She relaxed into the couch cushions. "Conor and Patrick came in for a meal."

"They weren't pestering you to let them use the studio again were they?"

"No. They got everything done the other weekend. Conor's a bit of a flirt, isn't he?"

"Not with me," Alasdair said, then frowned at the phone screen. "Was he flirting with you?"

"I think there was a bit of a misunderstanding. He thought we'd split up and you'd moved to America."

"Why, what was he saying?"

"He asked me out for a drink."

"Seriously?"

"Yes." She laughed. "A guy *seriously* asked me out on a date. Don't sound so shocked!"

"I'm shocked because he's been out drinking with me and I let him use my studio, and now he's trying to move in on my girlfriend."

She was taken aback by the genuine annoyance in his tone. "I told you it was a misunderstanding. And I put him straight."

"Good." He rubbed the back of his hand across his forehead. "I can't believe I told you not to feel threatened having them in the house, when it should have been me who was worried."

"Don't be daft. Of course you don't have to worry. Why are you in such a bad mood?"

"Because some guy's hitting on my girlfriend while I'm stuck at the other side of the world."

"Oh, yes. Poor you … stuck in California!" She rolled her eyes and made him laugh. "You are having a good time, aren't you?" she asked seriously.

"Yes." He looked weary. "I just wish you were here."

"I had to work," she said. When he didn't reply, she could

feel his irritation radiating through the screen. "Are you annoyed with me for coming home?"

"No." He paused. "Maybe. Work was an excuse. You could definitely have taken more time off, you just didn't want to."

Leana felt her body tense. Conversations about her job always rankled her. "Can we not have another conversation about how it doesn't matter whether I turn up for work or not?"

"I didn't say that. But realistically you could have taken some more time and it wouldn't have been an issue. I don't know why this has turned into an argument. All I said was I wish you were here with me. It was supposed to be a nice thing."

"Sorry," she said. "I'm tired. I think I might go to bed."

"Shall we try and talk again the same time tomorrow?"

"I'm working in the day so I'll be finished earlier."

"Okay. I'll get up earlier. Just call me when you get home from work."

She promised she would and ended the call.

As usual, Alasdair's comments about her job left her feeling unsettled. Instead of going to bed she reached for her laptop. The thought of studying nursing had niggled at her for long enough. Maybe doing some research into courses might help her make a decision one way or another.

CHAPTER TWENTY-SIX

Having Rory in front of her left Elspeth so shocked that it took her a moment to get her brain in gear so she could formulate words.

"Is Arran okay?" Guilt at ignoring his calls hit her hard.

"He's fine. Are *you* okay? I've been trying to call you all day."

"I'm fine." She gestured for him to come in. "I was busy."

"What if something had been wrong with Arran? You can't just ignore my calls. We've been through this before."

"I was about to call you back. I knew there was nothing urgent or you'd have left a message. Why are you here?"

"I decided to drive down to my parents' place today so you could come home with us tomorrow."

Elspeth tried to stay calm as she registered what he was saying. "Where's Arran?"

"With my parents. When you didn't answer your phone I was worried, so I thought I'd come and check on you."

She tilted her head. "Do you realise I'm an adult?"

"What?"

"I don't need you deciding when I should come home. And I don't have to answer the phone to you if I don't feel like it."

"I wasn't deciding when you should come home. You said you were coming on Sunday. I thought I'd save you the trouble of getting the train. And why on earth couldn't you just answer the phone?"

"Because every time I've spoken to you this week you've been in a bad mood with me. I was sick of you trying to ruin my holiday."

"I wasn't trying to ruin your holiday. You said you were going away with Leana for a couple of nights and then you didn't come home. Which would be perfectly fine if you didn't have a child who was missing his mum."

Elspeth sat on the corner of the bed. "Can you please stop with the guilt trip?"

Moving to look out of the window, Rory kept quiet for a moment. "I'm sorry," he said when he turned back to her. "I spent all day worrying about you, and I'm probably not in the best frame of mind."

"Well, I'm sorry you drove all the way over here, but as you can see I'm fine."

His gaze travelled over her. "You look really good."

"Thanks. I went shopping and got a haircut."

"Since I'm here, can we talk?" He leaned against the desk. "I feel as though we never get to talk without Arran around."

"What do you want to talk about?" she asked.

He looked thoughtful, as though he was choosing his words carefully. "We agreed when we split up that we'd be honest and open with each other. For Arran's sake. But I haven't always been honest with you …"

Elspeth averted her gaze. As though calling her in a bad mood wasn't enough to sabotage her holiday, now he was about to confess that he had a new girlfriend. While she'd been away it had been lovely to put that thought out of her mind.

Given how grumpy Rory had been with her recently, the thought of him seeing someone else should be easier to bear. But even when he was driving her crazy, her feelings for him were still there, and she wasn't sure she'd ever be in a position to hear him talk about another woman without it physically hurting.

"Do you want to get a drink?" she blurted out. "There's a bar downstairs. We could get a drink and have a chat." With other people around, the conversation might not feel so intense, and there was a chance she might be able to get through it without turning into a blubbering wreck and begging him to take her back.

The reprieve in the conversation was welcome as they walked downstairs together. It was still early in the evening so the bar was relatively quiet. Elspeth recognised a lot of people sitting at the tables along the far wall and waved a quick greeting to Danielle and Molly, who gave her questioning looks, presumably wondering who Rory was. She shrugged and went to get drinks.

"I've got a bone to pick with you," Ben said across the bar. "Your sister told me to keep an eye out for you but she neglected to mention you're as bad as she is when it comes to partying!"

"I heard *you* had a good night," she said cheekily.

His eyebrows twitched. "What did Molly say?"

"Nothing! I'm winding you up. Can we get a couple of beers, please?"

He flicked the tops off two bottles.

"This is Rory, by the way," Elspeth said as she paid for the drinks. "Arran's dad."

"Nice to meet you." Ben shook his hand. "Leana was always talking about your little fella when she was working here. Always showing us photos. I bet you're looking forward to getting back to him," he said to Elspeth.

"I can't wait," she said.

"When do you leave?"

"Tomorrow."

"Enjoy your last evening," he said before wandering away.

"Shall we grab a table?" Elspeth suggested, leading Rory away from the bustle so they'd be able to talk easily.

"It seems as though you've been having fun," he remarked as they sat down. "You know a lot of people."

"I'm no expert on holidays," she said testily, "but I thought having fun was the whole point."

"It is. I wasn't having a go at you. I'm glad you've enjoyed your trip."

She took a long swig of beer. "What did you want to talk about?" They may as well get the conversation out of the way, then he'd leave and she could drown her sorrows at the bar.

"I wanted to talk to you about Arran splitting time between your place and mine. I should have brought it up ages ago."

Elspeth's heart felt as though it had dropped down her chest. That hadn't been what she was expecting. Suddenly him announcing that he was seeing someone didn't seem quite so bad. It was probably better than him telling her it wasn't fair that she had Arran six nights a week while he got one. Especially because she didn't have much of an argument; it wasn't fair, but logistically that was the way it worked with Rory's work and the half-hour drive between Lannick and Portree. She supposed it didn't make much difference to her if he picked him up on Friday evenings instead, though she was happy with the current setup.

"It's not practical for us to have equal time with him," she said slowly. "What were you thinking?"

He stared at her, looking slightly confused. "I wasn't thinking I should have him more. I wondered if you thought it would be better for him not to stay over at my place?"

Through her confusion, Elspeth thought she must have either misheard or misunderstood. "What do you mean?"

"Would it be better if he has one bedroom? At your place?"

"I ... erm ..." Fleetingly, it crossed her mind that he was trying to get Arran out of the way while he enjoyed the pleasures of a new relationship, but she dismissed the thought immediately. Rory would always put Arran first. "Why?" she asked.

"I think maybe it's confusing when he stays with me. Unsettling for him."

"I don't think so. Why would you think that?"

He shifted his beer bottle as condensation slid onto the table. "Because I don't think he likes staying at my house. I hate the thought of forcing him to spend time at my place when he wants to be at home."

"But he loves being at your place."

Rory shook his head. "He spends the whole time asking for you. He cries every time I put him to bed at my house."

"I always thought he prefers you. I'm always jealous that he loves you more. Which is pathetic," she said, blinking back tears.

"That's definitely not true."

"Why didn't you tell me about him crying at bedtime?" As ridiculous as it was, she felt an odd sense of relief at the thought of Arran asking for her when she wasn't there.

"I was scared you'd say he shouldn't stay over. And I thought he'd probably stop after a while, but I feel terrible every time I tuck him into bed."

Elspeth smiled sadly. "When he's with me he's always asking for you. Every time he goes to bed at home, he cries because he wants you. That's why I wanted to talk to the doctor. I thought our break-up had traumatised him."

"But she said it was fine?"

"She said it's probably a phase. That kids are like adults and get more emotional the more tired they are, so him getting upset at bedtime doesn't sound like anything to worry about."

Rory visibly relaxed and took a long drink of his beer. "That's a relief. I was starting to take it personally."

"It's definitely not you," Elspeth said. "You're a great dad and Arran thinks you're a superhero."

"Thanks." He held her gaze in a way that made her stomach quiver with butterflies. At the sound of someone calling her name, she turned and caught sight of Kendrick approaching their table.

"Beautiful Elspeth!" he crooned. "Come and sit with us. Bring your friend!" He introduced himself to Rory before lifting Elspeth's hand and pressing it to his lips. "Come and join us," he said again.

"I'll come over in a bit," she said.

"Drinks?" he asked as he backed away.

"We're fine, thanks."

"He seems like a character," Rory remarked once Kendrick was out of earshot.

"He's very entertaining." She picked at her beer label, trying to think of a way to steer the conversation to Rory's relationship status. The fact that he still gave her butterflies bothered her. Her emotions were a jumble, but she couldn't kid herself that she didn't have feelings for him. If he'd moved on, she was better off knowing. "Was there anything else you wanted to talk about?" she asked eventually.

Rory's gaze had been roaming the room, but his attention came back to her at the question. "No. I don't think so."

"Okay." She fiddled with a section of her hair. "I was wondering if you're seeing someone."

His eyebrows shot up. "If I'm seeing someone?" he repeated.

"Yes. Do you have a girlfriend? It's fine if you do. Obviously, we're both free to see other people. It would just be good to know … in case Arran says something …"

He stared at her before speaking. "I don't have a girlfriend. Are *you* seeing someone?"

"No." She scrunched her nose up at the ridiculous question. "It's just that Arran talks about someone called Jess so I wondered …"

"Jess is a friend from work. I bumped into her one day when Arran was with me, that's all."

"You're not together?"

"No. She's just a friend."

"Good." She swallowed hard. "I mean, it's fine either way, but it's good to know."

Her stomach fluttered again at the smile he flashed her, but the atmosphere was broken by Ben putting more drinks in front of them. Two beers and two shots of bright green liquid.

"Courtesy of the madman!" he said with a quirky grin. "I mean Kendrick."

When she looked across the room, Kendrick had a shot glass held aloft. She raised hers in reply, then knocked it back, grimacing as it burned the back of her mouth.

"I'm driving," Rory said.

Ben chuckled. "Elspeth gets extra drinks then. This could be an interesting night."

"I need to slow down." She was already feeling a little woozy. There was a chance it was the alcohol that was stirring up her feelings for Rory too.

As Ben left them, Molly and Danielle appeared and pulled up chairs.

"It seems as though you made a new friend and ditched us," Molly said jokily.

"This is Rory," Elspeth said. "He's my ... erm ... he's ..."

"Ooh the suspense," Danielle said, her eyes sparkling with amusement.

Elspeth looked to Rory, who appeared as amused as the girls and clearly had no intention of helping her out. "He's the father of my child," she finally said.

"You crack me up," Molly said as they all fell about laughing. "Shall we get more shots?"

"No." Elspeth eyed the collection of drinks on the table. "Rory's not drinking, take his."

"Don't you drink shots?" Molly asked him as she took it.

"I've got to drive back to my parents' place in a bit," he replied.

"No." Molly looked at him sternly. "Come out clubbing with us. It's going to be a brilliant night."

Danielle looked across the room to where Kendrick was encouraging people to dance. "Let's go and boogie," she said, standing.

"I'll be over in a minute," Elspeth said, then watched the two of them join the lively group at the other side of the room. "You could stay," she said, the words coming out quickly and casually as she looked at Rory. "It might be a laugh."

He looked thoughtful. "You do have two beds in your room."

"I've always been impressed by your observational skills," she said, shifting her leg so it knocked against Rory's under the table.

CHAPTER TWENTY-SEVEN

While Rory went outside to call his parents and check it was okay for them to look after Arran for the night, Elspeth went into a panic about the fact that she'd asked him to stay over. She was fairly sure they shouldn't be sharing a bedroom. Especially given the fact that her mind kept taking her to a scenario where they didn't make use of both beds. She was on dangerous ground, but she was also excited about spending time with Rory.

She didn't have long to dwell on it. Kendrick spotted her sitting on her own and made a beeline for her. He sashayed his shoulders when he got close. "Have you danced today, fiery Elspeth?"

"No, I haven't."

"Well, what are you waiting for?" He took her hand and pulled her up.

"I have to dance," she called to Rory who'd just arrived back and was watching her in amusement.

After Kendrick spun her around the dancefloor for a while, she moved to Danielle and Molly.

"So who is he really?" Molly asked.

Elspeth followed her gaze to Rory. He'd moved to sit at the

bar and was chatting to Ben. When she caught his eye, he smiled back at her. "He's *really* the father of my child," she said with a rush of pride.

"No, way," Danielle said. "Seriously?"

"Seriously." Elspeth paused from dancing to get her phone out. She found a recent photo of Arran and held it up. "That's Arran. Our son."

Molly snatched the phone from her. "He's adorable," she said. "Look at his hair. He definitely got that from you."

"He's so cute." Danielle gave a pointed look in Rory's direction. "I can see where he gets that trait from too." The three of them cracked up laughing.

"So is he your husband or your boyfriend?" Molly asked.

"He's actually my ex-boyfriend. But we're on good terms."

"What's wrong with him?" Molly asked. "He's hot and he seems lovely."

"There's nothing wrong with him." Elspeth felt the familiar pang of regret. There was nothing wrong with *him*, but probably something wrong with her to have given him up.

"Did he cheat on you?" Danielle asked.

"No," Elspeth replied.

She frowned. "Did you cheat on him?"

"No."

"I'm confused then," Danielle said with a small shake of the head.

"It's complicated." But when Elspeth glanced across the room to see Rory beaming back at her, nothing felt complicated at all. Everything seemed crystal clear. "I'll be back in a minute." She kept her eyes on Rory as she went to him. "What are you grinning at?" she asked, her lips pulling to a smile as she stood so close to him that her hip rested against his leg.

"You," he replied, passing her beer. "It's good to see you so relaxed."

"I should get away from Lannick more often," she said, then gulped at the beer.

"Not too often." He froze, as though he'd said the wrong thing. "Arran would miss you," he muttered.

"Just Arran?" she said, resting her hand on his knee.

His gaze locked with hers for a moment, then he looked away. "I think everyone misses you."

Removing her hand from his leg, she took a step back. What was she doing? After all she'd put him through, he'd probably never trust her with his heart again. And even if he'd consider giving their relationship another go, she wasn't sure she trusted herself not to hurt him again.

"Do you want to dance?" she asked, knowing he'd say no. She needed to move away from him before the urge to kiss him completely overwhelmed her.

"No!" he said, laughing. "You know I only dance when I'm drunk."

"Keep drinking then," she said, backing away. "I'll be back in a bit."

As she danced, she couldn't stop her mind from churning over the possibility that there might still be hope for her and Rory. She didn't think she'd ever stopped loving him, but her feelings for him had dulled so much that she hadn't been sure what she wanted. That wasn't only true of her feelings for Rory; she'd felt the same about just about every aspect of her life. It had gone on for so long that she'd thought it was her new permanent state, but recently she felt more like her old self again.

Over the next hour she alternated between dancing and chatting to random people and going back to talk to Rory. He seemed content to sit at the bar, and Elspeth swung between the desire to be close to him and feeling completely confused and overwhelmed by her emotions. Surely it was wrong to give him up and then want him back again.

When Kendrick asked her if she wanted to go to a club, she shook her head and went to the bar, leaving him to cajole the rest of his gang to move elsewhere.

"Do you want to dance with me yet?" she asked Rory,

squeezing into the tight gap beside him at the bar. Saturday night was in full swing and the place was rammed.

"No."

"Come on," she said, taking his hand.

"I don't want to dance," he said firmly, but didn't release her hand, instead gently running his thumb over her fingers in a way that sent goosebumps running up her arm. Automatically, she stepped closer to him, slotting into the space between his legs.

"I'm glad you came," she said. "I was annoyed with you earlier. You turning up without asking me felt as though you were interfering, but it's actually nice that you were concerned. And it was really sweet of you to drive all the way down here to give me a lift home." Her eyes locked with his and she was sure he was going to kiss her. She really wanted him to.

"It's great to see you having a good time," he said, his thumb continuing to stroke her hand.

"I liked having you here." She smiled. "Even though you just sat at the bar all evening and watched me. It's like having a bodyguard or something."

"You know I hate dancing," he said with a pout.

"I know." She glanced around the room. "Everyone's going to a club, but I'd rather not. I might go to bed."

"That sounds sensible." He moved off the stool and his body pressed against hers as he slid past her. He kept hold of her hand as he guided her through the throng. They were walking across the reception area when Molly called out to her.

"Aren't you coming to the club?" Danielle asked.

"No." Elspeth walked over and hugged them both at once. "I'm drunk, I'm going to bed."

"Don't blame you!" Molly whispered in her ear, then shot her a mischievous grin.

"I'm leaving tomorrow," Elspeth told them. "But I've got your numbers so we can keep in touch."

"We might venture north and track down your cafe one day," Danielle said.

"You should." Elspeth hugged them again and told them to say goodbye to Kendrick for her. When she turned, Rory was waiting for her and she automatically took his hand to walk upstairs.

"It's great here," she said at the room, tapping the key card repeatedly against the reader to no avail. "I can see why Leana loved it. It must have been different working here though. It's a bit busier than the Old Inn!"

"Just a bit." Rory took the key from her and managed to open the door immediately.

Elspeth laughed as she stumbled inside. "I had a brilliant night. Did you have fun?"

"It was good," he said.

"It would have been better if you'd have danced with me." She took his hand and raised it above her head as she twirled under his arm.

"You're so drunk," he said, smiling down at her.

"I'm not *that* drunk."

"I beg to differ."

"Dance with me," she said, looping her arms around his neck as she stood close to him.

"You should go to bed," he whispered.

Softly, she trailed her fingers along the back of his neck. "I really want to kiss you."

"I'm not sure that's a good idea."

"Please." She pressed onto her toes and leaned closer until her lips met his. Pushing her hands into his hair, she pulled his head towards her but was met with resistance. Rory stepped back so abruptly that she almost lost her balance.

"What's wrong?" she asked.

He let out a long sigh. "You're drunk. And we're not together any more. That's what's wrong."

CHAPTER TWENTY-EIGHT

"I didn't know you were down to work tonight," Leana said when Lexie wandered in towards the end of her shift on Sunday. There were quite a few people having meals, but as soon as it quietened down she'd be able to leave.

"I'm not." Lexie glanced at Nick, who was hanging up their coats in the entranceway. "We came for a drink."

"Speaking of drinks," Douglas called from the table beside the fire, "can I get another, love?"

Leana shook her head. "No. You can't." She nodded towards his plate. "I told you to eat your veg. Do as you're told and I might think about getting you another drink."

"I always end up with more veg when I order from you," he grumbled. "Do you tell the chef to give me extra?"

"Aye. I do. With the amount you drink, you need to get something healthy into your body."

"I don't like veg."

"I'm sick of hearing about it," Leana said. "Eat up and I'll get you another drink. Otherwise, you can go thirsty."

"What kind of place is this?" He shook his head but pulled his plate closer to him and continued eating.

"I can see you're in a good mood," Lexie said as she and Nick settled themselves at the bar.

"Well, it's ridiculous the amount he drinks. He needs to at least eat well."

Lexie smiled. "Do you remember his wife?"

"Doris? Aye. She was sweet, wasn't she?"

"Yes." Lexie beamed. "You sound just like her!"

"Be quiet and tell me what you want to drink," Leana said, shaking her head.

"What's put you in such a cheerful mood?" Nick asked sarcastically when she moved to get their drinks.

"Alasdair, of course!" She concentrated on pouring drinks for a moment, then set them in front of her friends. "Also, I've been thinking about making some changes in my life. I was up until the early hours looking into nursing courses."

"You're still thinking about that?" Lexie asked.

"Yes. I think maybe it's my calling."

Nick grinned and glanced around at Douglas, who was muttering to himself as he ate his greens. "You're certainly suited to a caring role."

"That's what I think," Leana said. "I'm sure I'd be more fulfilled if I had a job that involved helping people."

"Leana!" Douglas called. "I've finished."

"Well done," she replied. "I'll bring you a drink in a minute." She glanced down the bar. Another regular customer was looking at her expectantly. "Do you need help with your lottery numbers, George?" she asked. When he nodded, she wandered along to him. His eyes weren't good enough to fill out the form, so she often had to do it for him. "What are you two smiling about?" she asked Nick and Lexie when she went back to the beer tap to pour Douglas's beer.

"You're always helping," Lexie said. "I don't think you need to be a nurse to look after people."

"You'd make a terrible nurse anyway," Nick said.

"Remember the time I broke a glass and cut my finger? You almost passed out at the sight of the blood."

"I'm sure I'd get over that," Leana said, frowning.

"You're scared of needles too," Lexie pointed out.

"No, I'm not! I just didn't think it was necessary for me to get a flu shot because I have such a strong constitution. I never get ill."

"Aye, right." Lexie looked at her sceptically.

To be honest, she really didn't like the idea of sticking needles in people, but surely they'd teach her to get over that. After taking Douglas his pint, she wandered over to the next table, where a local couple were eating a meal. The woman had their baby in her arms, rocking her gently as she ate with her free hand.

"Do you want me to hold her so you can eat in peace?" Leana asked.

"If you don't mind," the woman said, passing the baby to her.

Leana swayed with her in her arms. "How old is she now?"

"Four months. As long as someone's holding her she's as good as gold. Whenever we put her down she screams. We're hoping it's a phase!"

"She's very cute." Leana set off for a walk around the pub with the little bundle, leaving the tired parents to eat in peace. She ignored the way Lexie and Nick were watching her and smiled down at the baby instead. When she'd returned the baby and went back behind the bar, Nick and Lexie had their heads close together, talking quietly.

"You know you're quite annoying when you sit there giggling and whispering?" Leana said to them.

Lexie beamed at her. "We were just saying we should make a list of all the ways you help people during one of your bar shifts. Then you'd see that you've already followed your calling to help people."

"I'm just not sure I want to spend the rest of my working life pulling pints," Leana said sadly.

Nick shook his head. "You don't just pull pints. As you've demonstrated over the past ten minutes. You make people's lives a little bit better."

"Douglas would probably disagree!" Leana quipped.

"No, he wouldn't," Lexie said. "He purposely doesn't eat his veg so you'll tell him off. He just likes to feel that someone cares. If you're not here, he just eats everything."

Leana sighed. She did actually love her job. Especially interacting with the regulars.

"I, for one, would be very upset if you weren't behind the bar any more," Nick said.

Mary stopped chatting to the customers at the other end of the bar and approached Leana. "You're not thinking of leaving, are you?" she asked quietly.

"I'm exploring my options."

"Oh my goodness." Mary's shoulders sagged. "Aren't you happy here?"

"I am, but—"

"What's going on?" Angus asked, walking out from the kitchen.

"Leana's thinking of leaving us," Mary said, an air of panic to her voice.

Angus shook his head. "We can't have that. Do you know how difficult it is to find good bar staff? What do you want? A pay rise? That's probably due ..." He looked questioningly at his wife.

"Of course you can have a pay rise." Mary patted Leana's arm. "We could make you a manager too if you're not challenged enough. Give you some more responsibilities."

Angus nodded. "You could take over ordering stock, that would be a help."

"What about some office duties too?" Mary said. "I could teach you about the bookkeeping?"

Leana's jaw worked like crazy as she opened and closed her mouth repeatedly. Even if she could think of anything to say, she couldn't get a word in as Mary and Angus discussed which roles she could take over for them.

"I don't have a problem with the job," she said. "I was only wondering whether I might want a different career at some point."

"You've got a job here for life," Angus said. "Don't go looking for anything else." He wandered away as the bell in the kitchen rang.

"Do you need more time off?" Mary asked. "If you need a break, you could take a sabbatical and come back again. We could always organise that."

"I don't think that's necessary," Leana said in a daze.

"Things are quietening down now," Mary said. "Get off home and put your feet up."

After getting her coat, Leana went over to Lexie and Nick. "What just happened?"

"I think you got a pay rise," Nick said with a smirk.

"And I don't need to worry about you leaving any more," Lexie said. "There's no way Mum and Dad would let you go!"

CHAPTER TWENTY-NINE

S adly, Elspeth hadn't drunk enough alcohol that she was numb to the pain of rejection. When she'd got into bed she'd felt hurt and humiliated. On top of that she was angry with herself for thinking Rory might still feel the same way about her. That was partly his fault for giving her mixed signals. He'd driven all the way from Skye because he was concerned about her. But maybe that was more to do with Arran – maybe his concern was because she was the mother of his child and nothing more.

She woke to daylight flooding the room. The noise of Rory gently tapping on his phone was the only sound. He was fully dressed and sitting upright against the wooden headboard on the second bed, which was neatly made and looked as though it hadn't been slept in.

"Morning," she said without moving her head from the pillow.

He gave her a half-hearted smile. "How did you sleep?"

"Fine." As she sat up, her mind tortured her with an image of Rory pushing her away when she'd tried to kiss him. Shaking the memory away, she mumbled about showering and slipped into the bathroom. The warm water soothed her but didn't come close to washing away her humiliation.

"Mum's been messaging me," Rory said when she ventured back into the room feeling a little more human. "They want to take Arran to the zoo this morning. I said that's fine. Now she wants to know if we want to go too or if we'll meet them afterwards. What do you want to do?"

Elspeth sank onto the bed, rubbing her hair with the towel. The thought of going to the zoo with his parents didn't appeal to her. Irritation swept through her, making her whole body feel tense.

"Why don't you just tell me what we're doing," she said, her voice tinged with anger. "That's probably easier considering you seem to think I'm incapable of making decisions."

He snapped his head to look at her. "What's that supposed to mean?"

"It means my plan for the day was to get the train home. But you trampled all over that idea so I guess I'll do what you want."

"You're annoyed with me for coming to drive you home?" He raised his eyebrows. "Do you have any idea what a horrendous journey it is to get from here to Skye on public transport?"

"No," she said, worried she was about to lose control of her emotions and start crying. "I don't have any clue what the journey's like. Because I've never done it. I've never been on a train on my own. I'm not sure I've even been on a bus alone."

"It's much easier in the car. I'm doing you a favour."

"Are you?" She looked directly at him. "Is that why you came here? To do me a favour?"

He squinted in confusion. "I came to check you were okay and drive you home."

"But I told you on the phone that I wanted to get the train home. I also told you I was fine. There was no need for you to turn up here. It's like you wanted to be heroic and swoop in and save me … but I didn't need saving. I was having a great time. And now I feel as though I'm supposed to be grateful to you.

But I'm annoyed that you interfered in my plans as though you know what's best for me." She shifted her gaze when tears filled her eyes. The worst of it was that she knew she wouldn't be annoyed with him for turning up if he hadn't rejected her when she'd tried to kiss him.

"What do you want me to do?" he asked.

She caught a tear at the corner of her eye. "What I *wanted* you to do was look after Arran for the week so I could have some time to myself. Now I guess we'll go and meet your parents at the zoo."

"It doesn't seem as though you want to do that," he said meekly.

"I haven't seen them since we broke up," she said tearfully. "They probably hate me, so spending the morning with them doesn't sound like a lot of fun."

"They don't hate you," he said. "But if you don't want to meet up with them, we don't have to."

"I want to see Arran." She also couldn't stand the thought of spending time alone with Rory. Even being around his parents who hated her would be better than being alone with him. Plus, she knew them well enough to know they'd be polite even if they were annoyed with her. "I'll pack my things. Then we'll go to the zoo."

As expected, Rory's parents made no mention of her breaking up with Rory. They treated her graciously, as they always had done. Arran hugged her tightly when he saw her, then barely let go of her hand as they walked around the zoo. His excitement at the animals eased the tension between her and Rory. After a late lunch in the jungle-themed cafe, they made their way back to the exit, aware of the time and the long journey home.

Spending five hours in the car with Rory didn't exactly fill Elspeth with joy. As she said goodbye to his parents, she was already wishing the journey away and looking forward to the moment when she was back in the cottage and Rory had left again. She needed space to get her thoughts in order. When she was around Rory, everything felt like a jumbled mess.

"Do you want me to sit in the back with you?" she asked Arran as she helped him with his seatbelt. Sitting in the back would make it easier to ignore Rory on the drive.

"No," he said, surprising Elspeth. Usually he begged her to sit in the back with him.

"That's strange," she said to Rory as she walked around the car. He shrugged and got into the driver's seat.

"Can I have your phone, Daddy?" Arran asked as Elspeth clicked her seatbelt into place.

"What do you want Daddy's phone for?"

"To play games," Arran replied.

"Just for a little while," Rory said, unlocking the screen and passing his phone back.

"You let him play games on your phone?" Elspeth asked with a smirk.

"Yes. He was bored on the drive down yesterday so I gave him my phone." He caught Elspeth's eye. "Why is that so funny?"

"It's not." She quashed her grin and affected a low tone of voice. "I think we should have a chat about limiting Arran's screen time. New research is coming to light every day about the adverse effects of screens on children's health. The long-term effects won't be fully known for decades, but all the evidence points to it being bad for mental health." She took a breath and the smile took over her face again.

Rory gave her a puzzled look. "Did you just do an impression of my dad?"

"No!" She howled with laughter. "It was an impression of you!"

His eyes widened and she caught the flash of panic in them. "Oh my God! Are you serious? Is that how I sound?"

"Yes!" She couldn't stop laughing. "I do a really great

impression. Didn't I sound like Daddy?" she asked Arran. He only laughed along with her.

Rory slumped forwards, resting his forehead on the steering wheel.

"I'm sorry," she said, putting a hand on his back. "I couldn't help myself. You can be a bit obsessive about screen time."

He sat up straight. "Because all the studies show that ..." He slumped forwards again. "Just kill me now, please. I've turned into my dad."

"You're not quite that bad," Elspeth said, amused.

As Rory turned the engine on, he glanced in the rear-view mirror. "You can have the phone the whole way home," he said to Arran. "And when we get home, you should probably watch some TV. And maybe tomorrow before nursery you should watch more TV."

"Stop it." Elspeth gave his leg a friendly tap. "He doesn't understand sarcasm."

"I can't believe you're only teasing me about this now. Why didn't you film me and show me what a prat I sounded?"

"You were always so serious about it." Her attention switched out of the window, but she was hit with a memory and couldn't keep from giggling.

"What's so funny now?" Rory asked, pulling out of the car park and onto the road.

She slipped back into a comically deep voice. "I've printed out an article that I found about the dangers of screen time for the developing brain ..."

"Shut up!" Rory said. "You're being mean."

"I think I still have that article," she said. "I might frame it and give it to you for your birthday."

"Is it nearly my birthday?" Arran piped up.

"Still a wee while to go," Rory told him. "Which is good because I'm saving to buy you your own tablet. And maybe a PlayStation or Xbox. Probably both. And I think you should have a TV in your bedroom."

"Ignore Daddy," Elspeth said, grinning as she turned to Arran. "He's being silly."

Rory rubbed at the stubble at his jaw. "All this time I was wondering why you split up with me and it's just become very clear."

Elspeth's smile faded instantly. Even though he was joking, she wanted to tell him that the reason she'd split up with him had absolutely nothing to do with him. She also wanted him to know that she wasn't anywhere close to being able to joke about it. From the look on his face, he realised that himself.

"I'm worried you're going to be really relaxed about screen time from now on," she said, in a bid to get the conversation back to the lighter tone. "Which means I'll need to be the strict one." She shook her head. "I don't want to be the strict one."

"I think it's only fair that you take your turn at being the parent who sounds like a pompous old man."

"Would I have to use the deep voice too?" she asked, smiling again.

"Definitely!"

She pushed her head into the headrest. "I love that you care about that stuff."

"I don't care about that stuff," he said indignantly. As he slowed to a stop at traffic lights, he gave her a sidelong glance. "I always thought I was a cool dad."

"You are," she said, resisting the urge to reach out and give his hand a reassuring squeeze.

By the time they arrived home, Elspeth had lost all thoughts of wanting to be on her own. When she stood outside the cottage with Rory, she hated the fact that he was leaving to go to his home. She wanted him to stay, and it was an effort not to invite him inside.

"Thank you for driving me home," she said awkwardly.

He dug his toe into the gravel on the path. "I was about to apologise for disrupting the end of your holiday."

"It's fine." She felt her cheeks heating up. "I was a bit hungover this morning. I shouldn't have snapped at you."

"Last night was fun," he said, shifting his weight and glancing at the car.

"Yes, it was." At least until the end of the night, but thankfully they seemed to be pretending that hadn't happened.

He looked around her, into the house. "I'm going," he called to Arran.

"Bye," came the curt reply.

"We'll see you on Wednesday?" Elspeth asked.

"Yeah."

He took a step back at the exact moment she stepped forward. She'd intended to hug him, but maybe he thought she was going to try to kiss him again.

"Sorry." He smiled and came forward to hug her. It was something they'd stopped doing, and as soon as she was in his arms, Elspeth realised avoiding physical contact had been a sensible idea. Now she really didn't want to let him go.

"See you soon," he said as he walked away.

CHAPTER THIRTY

On Monday morning Elspeth had another session with the counsellor. After her initial apprehension at the idea of talking to a stranger, she was surprised by how cathartic it felt. It also left her feeling emotionally raw and eager to do something to distract herself from her racing thoughts. She noticed that her desire to reopen the cafe had faded and decided that was a good thing.

Sitting in the quiet cottage, sipping a coffee at the kitchen table, she sent Lexie a message asking how she was. The phone rang moments later.

"Hi," Lexie said. "I started to message you back but decided it was easier to call. How was your trip?"

"Really good, thanks."

"Great. I want to hear all about it. Are you free tonight? I thought Nick and I could come over for dinner. We can bring food."

"I'll cook," Elspeth said, happy to have something to do.

She ended the call feeling much more positive about the day. Shopping and cooking would keep her occupied, and it would be nice to catch up with Lexie and Nick.

Arran was excited to hear they were coming over for dinner

too. From the moment she picked him up from nursery and told him they were coming, he constantly asked how long until they'd get there.

He always enjoyed spending time with Nick. After dinner, the two of them built a fort using the couch and a chair and a couple of blankets. It was hard to tell who was having more fun, Nick or Arran. Once Elspeth had finally coaxed Arran into getting ready for bed, he insisted on Nick reading his bedtime story.

Elspeth and Lexie returned the living room to its usual state and made cups of tea. As they settled themselves in the living room, Elspeth filled Lexie in on her trip to Edinburgh and how she'd ended up hanging out with a bunch of random people in the hostel.

"It was good of Rory to drive down and pick you up," Lexie said, pulling her feet under her on the couch.

Elspeth sipped her tea, which was now only lukewarm. "I kissed him," she said without much thought.

"Kissed who?" Nick asked, wandering in and sitting beside Lexie on the couch.

"Rory," Elspeth said.

"Are you two getting back together?" Lexie asked, smiling hesitantly.

"No. It doesn't seem like it."

"What happened?" Nick asked.

"I kissed him and he pushed me away." Briefly, she covered her face with her hands, wishing she could block out the memory.

Lexie arched her brows sympathetically. "What did he say?"

"I believe his exact words were 'you're drunk'."

"Were you?" Lexie asked.

"Yes. We'd been in the bar all evening. I thought he was flirting with me. Clearly, I read the situation wrong."

Nick looked thoughtful. "Maybe he thought the only reason

you were kissing him was because you were drunk, and he didn't want things to be awkward the next day."

"That makes sense," Lexie agreed. "I mean, he drove all the way to Edinburgh to see you. That definitely seems like he wants to get back together with you. And agreeing to stay the night isn't a normal thing to do if you're genuinely only friends. He's definitely sending you mixed signals."

"I shouldn't have drunk so much," Elspeth said. "It blurred things."

"Did he say anything else?" Nick asked. "Or did he literally just say you were drunk."

"I kissed him," Elspeth said, trying to recall the exact events of that evening. "He pulled away and when I asked him what was wrong he said that I was drunk and we're not together any more … something like that … I think."

Nick leaned back into the couch. "It sounds as though it was the circumstances of the kiss rather than the kiss itself. Didn't you talk about it the next morning?"

"No, we haven't mentioned it."

"You need to talk to him," Lexie said. "Tell him exactly how you feel. You want to get back together with him, right?"

"I think so. But I couldn't blame him if he never wanted me back. I was pretty awful to him."

Lexie shook her head. "I don't think you were. The situation was awful, but you were always honest with him. It's not as though you cheated on him. The relationship wasn't working and you were open with him about that. And you tried to work things out."

"I think it's great how you're so honest with each other," Nick said. "Everything was so amicable because you communicate so well. I think you should continue in that vein and tell him how you feel now."

"I miss him," she said sadly. "But I'm terrified of giving things another go and hurting him again."

"Then tell him that," Nick said.

She slumped back in the chair. "I'll see him on Wednesday. Maybe I'll talk to him then."

Lexie shook her head. "Arran will be here and you won't get a chance to talk to him properly. Besides, you'll drive yourself crazy thinking about it between now and Wednesday. Just go now."

"What?"

"She's right," Nick said. "Go and talk to him. We'll stay with Arran. Just don't be all night."

Lexie gave him a playful nudge and grinned at Elspeth. "Ignore him. You can be all night! We'll take care of everything here."

Elspeth decided not to think about it too much. It would be better to know where she stood one way or another. "I guess it can't hurt to talk to him," she said, standing. "It's not as though I have anything to lose. Except hope, I guess."

"Go!" Lexie said. "I'm ninety-nine per cent sure he'll be happy for you to kiss him when you've not been drinking all evening."

"I'll find out. Thanks," she called behind her as she hurried to the door on a rush of adrenalin.

Jess ignored the pile of marking she had to do on Monday evening and instead went to the supermarket after work, then arrived at Rory's door with a bag of shopping and an over-whelming feeling of determination. He hadn't been in the pub again on Friday night and had sent her a message to say he was away for the weekend but hadn't said where.

When she'd seen him at work earlier in the day he'd looked exhausted. He hadn't hung around in the staffroom, so she hadn't found a time to talk to him. She'd resorted to turning up on his doorstep.

"You look like hell," she said cheerfully when he opened the door in a pair of tracksuit bottoms and a T-shirt.

"I feel like it," he said, dragging his hands through his hair.

She held the shopping bag up. "I brought dinner."

"I was going to finish my lesson plans and go to bed," he said with a weak smile.

"You need to eat." She sounded way more confident than she felt. "How does stir fry sound?"

He paused and Jess's heart pounded. If he sent her away the rejection would crush her.

"It sounds great," he finally said, opening the door wider.

She patted his shoulder as she stepped inside. "You carry on with your work while I cook."

"Thank you." He followed her to the kitchen, where his laptop was open on the table.

Jess got straight to work on dinner while Rory tapped away on his computer. He snapped the laptop shut just before she'd finished cooking.

"That smells amazing." He swivelled in his seat to face her. "I'm starving."

"Almost ready." She pushed the meat and veg around the wok. "Is everything okay with you? You seem stressed."

He rested his elbow on the table and propped his chin on his hand. "Elspeth was away last week so I ended up staying in Lannick with Arran. Then I stupidly decided to drive down to Edinburgh for the weekend."

"To visit your parents?" she asked.

He nodded in reply. "And Elspeth didn't have her car so I drove her home too."

"Elspeth was in Edinburgh?"

He nodded again. "She needed to get away for a while." His eyes glazed over as though he was lost in thought. "I think it did her good."

Jess was slightly confused and focused on the food in a bid

to gather her thoughts. "You went all the way to Edinburgh to give Elspeth a lift home?"

"She didn't have a car," he said again, as though that was a good explanation.

"Right." The stir fry was finished, but she continued shuffling the food around with the spatula.

"What's that look for?" he asked.

She let out a breath and shook her head. "Do you ever think she might be taking advantage of your generous nature?"

"She didn't ask me to pick her up. I thought it would be a nightmare for her to get the train back. But with hindsight, I should have let her make her own way. She wasn't very happy about me turning up."

"Wow," Jess said automatically. "How ungrateful can you get?"

Rory started to defend her then stopped. "Do you mind if we don't talk about Elspeth?"

"I don't mind at all." She lifted the wok from the heat and divided the food between two plates. "How about we compare prizes?" she said, taking the plates to the table and sitting opposite him.

He raised his eyebrows and seemed to be trying to decipher her meaning.

"For the raffle," she said. "How many have you got?"

He slapped a hand to his forehead, then held it there. "I completely forgot. I haven't done anything about it."

"I'm winning then. I have seven prizes lined up."

"I can do it this week," he said. "The list of prizes needs to be included in the newsletter at the end of the week. I still have time."

She shook her head. "Do you want me to do your half of the list too?"

"No." He grinned and picked up his fork. "I'd hate to be accused of taking advantage of your generous nature. Besides, it's just a few phone calls."

"I actually found it's easier to approach businesses in person."

"Has anyone ever told you you're an over-achiever?"

"Lucky for you that I am or you'd have no prizes for the raffle."

He chuckled and loaded up his fork. "What prizes have you got? Anything good?"

She launched into telling him about which businesses she'd approached and what they'd each pledged. It was good to chat about something that wasn't Elspeth or Arran, and she enjoyed the light-hearted banter as he teased her about how much effort she'd gone to while she gently chastised him for his lack of effort.

They sipped wine as they ate, and she topped up their glasses when they'd finished the food.

"Let's drink these on the couch," she said, lifting her glass. He followed her to the living room and thanked her for dinner as he sat beside her.

"You're welcome. I was worried you weren't looking after yourself. You're always so busy running around after other people."

"I definitely feel as though I spend most of my time running around," he agreed wearily. Placing his glass on the coffee table, he sank back into the couch.

Jess did the same. "I think you need a holiday," she said turning her head to face him. They were sitting close enough that her leg rested against his. She wouldn't have to move far to kiss him. Her heart pounded at the thought.

"The end of term can't come fast enough," he said. "Seven weeks of hanging out with Arran will be bliss."

"I don't know what I'm going to do with myself. I'm keen to explore the island more. I haven't really seen much outside of Portree."

"There are loads of amazing places. I used to spend a lot of time exploring with Arran."

"Maybe we could do some day trips together?" she suggested.

He nodded, and his small smile made her insides flutter. With a burst of courage she leaned closer, inching her face towards his. She caught the flash of surprise in his features, but there was no going back.

Her whole body tingled as her lips brushed against his. She felt of flutter of anxiety when he didn't respond. But he didn't pull away, so she took that as a good sign and pressed her lips against his.

"Sorry," she murmured, pulling back when he still failed to respond.

He sat up straighter, blinking a few times in quick succession. "No, I'm sorry. You took me by surprise. I didn't … I mean … I …" He trailed off and took a deep breath.

Jess forced herself not to bolt. If he wasn't interested in her at least she'd know for certain. Glancing at her glass of wine, she debated whether she could blame the kiss on alcohol, but she really hadn't had very much to drink.

"Now I feel awkward." She smiled, hoping to lighten the atmosphere.

"Don't," he said. "I just wasn't expecting that, and my head is all over the place at the moment."

"I didn't mean to complicate things further," she said quietly.

"You didn't. You've been such a good friend. I'm not sure how you put up with me." He reached out and touched her hand, sending shock waves up her arm.

"You're quite easy to put up with," she said, shifting her fingers to entwine them with his. He closed his eyes briefly, his features pained as though he was fighting some internal battle. Feeling as though she had nothing to lose, she kissed him again. She sensed his momentary hesitation, then he moved his hand, slipping it around her back and pulling her closer. He kissed her deeply and their bodies pressed against each other, making her stomach turn cartwheels. She pushed her fingers into his hair, holding tightly as their kisses became frantic.

~

Elspeth was a jumble of nerves when she arrived at Rory's house. Maybe there was a tiny spark of excitement too. As she walked past the front window she caught movement inside. The view was hindered by the tree in the small front garden but he was definitely at home. And there was a chance he'd seen her so it was too late to change her mind and run away.

After ringing the doorbell, she stood taller and pulled her shoulders back. It seemed to take forever for him to answer.

"Hi." The surprise was evident in his features. His hair was dishevelled and he looked slightly flustered. And possibly out of breath. "Everything okay?" he asked, not opening the door any further than necessary. It made her suspicious and she automatically looked behind him.

"Is this a bad time?"

"Yeah. Kind of. I was just in the middle of some stuff."

"Sorry. I wanted to talk to you. It won't take long. Can I come in?"

He glanced behind him. "Could it wait until tomorrow? I'm snowed under with work."

"It will only take five minutes."

"I kind of wanted to speak to you as well, so maybe I could come over to your place tomorrow? Can it wait until then?"

She nodded, thinking about Nick's remark that they were always so open and honest with each other. She was certain he wasn't being honest with her now. If he was working, he could put it aside for five minutes to talk to her.

"I'll talk to you tomorrow," she said, turning and walking briskly away. The sound of the door closing made her turn back. For him to be so abrupt led her to one easy conclusion. It wasn't just today that he'd lied to her. Him saying he wasn't seeing anyone was obviously a lie too. As she walked past the front of the house, she slowed to peer around the tree and into the living room.

Her chest felt as though it was being crushed.

He definitely wasn't working.

CHAPTER THIRTY-ONE

When Elspeth arrived at home, Lexie was stretched out on the couch with her head resting in Nick's lap. He idly stroked her hair while they watched TV. Their casual affection hit Elspeth like a blow to the chest. She'd had that and she'd discarded it as though it was nothing.

"How did it go?" Lexie sat up and muted the TV. "You've not been long."

"Did you chicken out?" Nick asked.

"No." She flopped into the chair. "He lied to me."

"What do you mean?" Lexie asked.

"When we were in Edinburgh, I asked him if he was seeing someone and he said no. But it was a lie."

Nick looked puzzled. "You think he's seeing someone?"

"I know he is. He wouldn't let me in the door to talk. He said he had a lot of work to do and he'd speak to me tomorrow when he had more time. It was another lie. He wasn't working at all. The reason he wouldn't let me in is because his girlfriend was there."

"I feel as though you might be jumping to conclusions," Nick said. "Maybe he really does have a lot of work to do."

Elspeth rested her elbow on the arm of the chair and propped her chin on her hand. "I looked in the window and saw her."

"Oh." Lexie grimaced. "Maybe she's a colleague and they're working together but he didn't want to say that because he thought you'd jump to conclusions."

"They were kissing," Elspeth said on a sigh.

Lexie swore and tipped her head to one side. "Sorry. Are you okay?"

"Not really, no. I'm furious with him for lying to me." For now, it felt easier to focus on her anger and ignore the fact that her heart felt as though it had split in two. "We always said we'd be honest and he lied to my face."

"To be fair, you've been having a rough time," Nick said. "If he lied, it was probably with good intentions."

"Great. He thinks I'm not emotionally stable enough to hear that he's moved on."

Lexie smiled sadly. "I can't imagine Rory lying to you without good reason."

"I can't believe he's seeing someone else. It didn't take him long to get over me."

"You could still tell him how you feel," Lexie suggested. "Maybe he's only moving on because he thinks he has no chance with you."

"How can I tell him I want to be with him? It's not long since I broke up with him, asked him to move out and completely disrupted his life. It'd be cruel to change my mind now when he's rebuilding his life. Besides, who's to say I won't change my mind again next month? Apparently, I'm quite fickle."

"You're being really hard on yourself," Nick said. "It was never a normal situation with you and Rory. You had a fling with him and got pregnant at sixteen. Then you didn't see him for years until he turned up out of the blue, and suddenly you were a ready-made family of three and he moved straight in with you. That sounds like a pretty stressful situation to me."

"That's not really how it was. He didn't move in straightaway. He was living in Edinburgh for a year before he moved here."

"Nick's right," Lexie said. "Having a long-distance relationship is intense, and then he moved in and you had to deal with a new relationship as well as Arran having another parent. It was a lot of change really fast. On top of all that you were running yourself ragged with the cafe. Something was bound to give."

As her throat tightened with emotions, Elspeth shook her head. "I still can't tell him how I feel. I love him and I miss him, but most of all I want him to be happy. I want all three of us to be happy. Rory's started a relationship with someone else and it would be terrible of me to sabotage it. I need to let him move on."

"What if *I* talk to him?" Nick suggested. "I could drop some hints that I think you want to get back with him. Then it's up to him what he does with that information."

"It'll only confuse things even more. I need to figure out how to be happy without him. I can do that." She forced a smile. "Sorry for messing up the evening. But thanks for staying with Arran."

"Don't thank us," Nick said. "I'm wishing we never suggested you go and speak to Rory."

"At least I know where I stand. I'll be okay."

"I'm not working tomorrow," Lexie said as they stood to leave. "Do you want to do something? We could grab a couple of kayaks and bob around the loch."

Elspeth almost declined the offer before realising that keeping herself occupied was probably a good idea. "What time will you be up?"

Lexie shrugged as they moved into the hallway. "I'm up when Nick goes to work. Come straight after you drop Arran at nursery if you want."

She agreed that she would and said goodbye to them at the door. Having a plan for the following day would be a good distraction. Much as the thought of Rory being with someone else crushed her, she was finally feeling herself again, and she refused to ruin her progress by sitting around dwelling on the fact that he was moving on. He was perfectly entitled to.

Elspeth needed to figure out how to do the same.

~

"I kissed him," Jess said excitedly, perching on the far edge of Ava's desk. She'd been happy to find her there when she arrived at work. The staffroom wasn't an ideal place to chat. And she felt as though she was going to explode if she didn't talk to someone.

Ava stopped tapping on her keyboard. "Rory?" she asked.

"Of course Rory!" She glanced around; the door to the hallway was open but all was quiet.

"When?"

"Last night. I cooked him dinner and we drank wine. Then I kissed him, just like you told me to!"

"And he kissed you back?" Ava asked, pushing her hair behind her ear.

"Yes. He was a little hesitant at first." She beamed thinking about it. "I think I took him by surprise. But then he kissed me back and it was incredible."

Ava leaned onto the desk. "Did you sleep with him?"

"No."

"So you kissed him, then said goodnight and went home? You've got more willpower than I have."

"We were interrupted," she said, thinking back on the evening. "Elspeth turned up at the door wanting to talk to him."

Ava put her hands to her cheeks in a slightly dramatic gesture. "His ex arrived while you were kissing him?"

"Yes. But he told her it was a bad time."

"I feel as though this story doesn't end well, but you're smiling so I'm confused."

"It was fine," she said. "Obviously it's slightly strange for

246

him that his ex showed up, but it was okay."

"So he got rid of the ex and resumed kissing you?"

"She kind of ruined the moment. I kissed him again but he was distracted. Then he got all stressed about how busy his week was and how much work he had to do …"

Ava covered her eyes with her hands. "That's bad," she said, peeking out at Jess.

"No. He kissed me back, so he obviously feels something. And when I was leaving he said he'd see me soon."

"Of course he'll see you soon! You work together." Her features softened as she removed her hands from her face. "Do you really not see what's going on here?"

"I think he likes me. The timing isn't perfect, but I'm sure he likes me."

"If he really liked you, he wouldn't have gone cold after seeing his ex-girlfriend. Clearly he still has feelings for her."

"It's slightly irrelevant if she doesn't want to be with him."

"Not if she decides she wants him back. Do you really want to be with someone who'd rather be with someone else?"

"I think eventually he'll realise we're perfect for each other."

Ava grimaced. "Do you remember when you told me that you'd friend-zoned yourself? You were right. He sees you as a friend and that's all. If he'd ever contemplated anything more, he wouldn't have been surprised when you kissed him."

"But he kissed me back," Jess said adamantly. "And it felt as though he liked me."

"I'm sorry," Ava said. "I hope you're right, but from what you tell me I feel very nervous for you."

"I think it's all going to work out. And I'm feeling brave, so as soon as I see him I'm going to ask him out on a date." She glanced at the clock on the wall. "I need to get to my classroom, but I'll see you at lunch?"

Ava nodded while maintaining a look of pity. Not that Jess cared; she knew what she'd felt when she and Rory had kissed, and she wasn't about to let anyone dampen her spirits.

CHAPTER THIRTY-TWO

The morning kayaking on the loch with Lexie was perfectly relaxing. Elspeth wasn't keen to rehash the situation with Rory, so they stuck to neutral topics as they paddled around for a couple of hours. By the time they were walking home again, Elspeth's arms were aching and she massaged her upper arms.

"Do you want to come for lunch?" Lexie asked when they neared her house.

"I'm okay, thanks. I might go and lie in the bath for a while and soothe my aching arms."

"Pathetic!" Lexie said, flexing her bicep. "Enjoy chilling out though. I've got my usual Wednesday morning hiking group tomorrow if you feel like joining again?"

"Won't they mind?"

"No. They loved it when you came last time. Although, I'll warn you that the more they get to know you, the more they'll start to tease you. It's all affectionate … I think!"

"I'd like to come. If you're sure." Again, having a plan for the day seemed wise. "I guess you've already ordered lunches, but I might bake something extra for a treat."

"Perfect. See you tomorrow!"

Elspeth continued along the path alone. When she reached

home she didn't stop but kept going until she reached Leana's house.

The sun came out as she walked through the trees into the back garden. Shafts of sunlight broke through the branches, highlighting the bright greens of the new leaves.

"Hello!" she called out to Leana, who appeared to be having a fight with a bush at the side of the house.

"Hi!" she replied, then stumbled backwards when the roots gave way and the plant came ripping out of the ground.

"What are you doing?"

"Gardening. What does it look like?"

"It looks like the bush did something to upset you."

"Not the bush, Alasdair, but since he's not here I'm taking my anger out on the plants instead."

"What did he do now?"

"Never mind." She pulled off a gardening glove and wiped her forehead with the back of her hand. "Was it you and Lexie I saw out on the loch earlier?"

"Yes. We were kayaking for ages. My arms are killing me."

"Is that your subtle way of saying you're not going to help me with the gardening?"

"If it helps alleviate anger, count me in."

Leana led the way to the patio table and they sat down together. "What's going on?"

"Rory's seeing someone."

She frowned. "Sorry."

"I brought it on myself." Elspeth shrugged, trying not to let herself venture too far along the path of self-pity. "I've been thinking about what you said about me dating. Maybe it wouldn't hurt."

"Really?"

"Yes. I thought you could help me to set up a dating profile."

Leana smiled widely. "No need. I know the perfect guy."

"Who?" Elspeth asked, feeling panicky.

"Remember I told you about the two guys using the recording studio? One of them is really cute. Totally your type."

"Do I have a type?" Unless he was a clone of Rory, Elspeth wasn't sure why Leana would think anyone was her type.

"You'll like him," she said confidently.

"I've changed my mind," Elspeth said. "I don't want to date anyone. I thought we'd have a laugh looking through profiles on dating sites. I'm not really ready to go on dates."

"We could make it really casual. I'll come too. They invited me out for a drink to thank me for letting them use the studio. I only need to message and take them up on it. That way you can meet him and see what you think. If you like him, you can arrange a proper date. Otherwise we'll have one drink and leave."

"I actually hate the thought of dating." Elspeth dropped her head to the table, feeling pathetic. The only person she wanted to date was Rory. But that wasn't an option, she reminded herself. And if she wanted to move on she needed to be proactive. While she'd been in Edinburgh, meeting new people had been great. Maybe it would be the same – she'd meet some new people and have fun. It didn't need to be a big deal.

"Okay," she agreed. "Set it up."

Leana beamed. "I'm excited."

"I'm glad one of us is." Stretching her neck, she lifted her chin, enjoying the sun on her cheeks. "Have you spoken to Lexie recently?" she asked, changing the subject.

"Mostly just at work. Why?"

Elspeth pursed her lips. "She's quiet. I get the feeling there's something going on with her. But I also have the feeling that I'm not the person anyone wants to discuss their problems with at the moment." She gave Leana a pointed look.

"What's that supposed to mean?"

"It means that no one wants to bother me with their problems. Like before when I asked you what Alasdair had done to make you want to kill plants."

"That bush was already dead." Leana looked thoughtful. "At least I think it was. And it's not that I don't want to bother you with my problems. I just don't particularly want to talk about it."

"Whatever you say. But if you get a chance, check Lexie's okay. She's more likely to talk to you."

"Is she off today?"

"Yeah."

"I might call in before work. She always seems fine when I see her though."

"Maybe I'm imagining it." Elspeth stood up. "I'll leave you to murder plants. I need to go shopping."

By the time she'd finished at the supermarket it was already time to collect Arran, and all thoughts of soothing her aching muscles in the bath had been forgotten.

"We're going to Granny and Grandad's house," she told Arran as she lugged shopping bags from the car.

"Why?"

"To cook dinner." Her dad's comment about them never eating at their place any more had been niggling at her since he'd said it. She thought it might be good for her and Arran to have more bustle around some of their mealtimes.

Arran was happy to be given jobs in the kitchen and enjoyed the time as much as Elspeth did. They made pizzas from scratch and baked a sticky chocolate cake too. Usually when she was baking she didn't have the patience to let Arran help her and would shoo him away, telling him she was working. To be fair, it *was* always work. Having time to bake for her family felt like going back to basics. It reminded her of all the times she used to bake after school.

The kitchen was a complete mess when her parents arrived home.

"Hello!" Christine said, surprised but clearly pleased to see them. "What's going on?"

"We've been cooking and baking," Elspeth said.

Arran leaned affectionately against his grandad's leg. "We made a cake."

"Trying to butter us up, are you?" Keith asked Elspeth.

"No. Why would I be trying to butter you up?"

"I thought you might have come to beg us to let you open the cafe again."

"No. Just dinner," she said, putting the first pizza in the oven. "No ulterior motives I promise."

"Good." Keith lifted Arran into his arms. "Another couple of weeks off will be good for you. Actually it's only a week and a half now really."

Elspeth straightened up, her brain whirring. Had she really been off work for two and a half weeks? "The time's flying by," she said. "I don't know if I'll even want to go back so soon. I might make it six weeks off."

"Oh bloody hell." Keith took a seat at the table. "This is going to backfire, isn't it? We tell you to take a month off and then six months later I'll be begging you to go back to work!"

"No." Elspeth smiled. "But I'm starting to see the benefit of the time off. When I do open up again, I'm going to cut back on the hours. I don't want to work six days a week and never take any holidays."

"You definitely need to find some balance," Christine agreed, peering into the oven. "Logan's coming for dinner too, by the way."

"I assumed so. Hopefully I've made enough."

Christine helped her start tidying up while Keith played with Arran. The oven timer had just started to beep when Logan walked in, dressed in his usual work attire and covered in paint splatters.

"Something smells good." He walked over to the cake on the counter and ran a finger through the soft chocolate icing before sticking it in his mouth. "Did I forget someone's birthday?"

Elspeth slid the large pizza onto the waiting plate and put the second one in the oven. "I just felt like baking a cake," she said, blowing the hair away from her face.

Logan slung an arm around her shoulders. "That's a funny coincidence because I feel like eating cake."

"Is there ever a time you don't feel like eating cake?" she asked.

"No." He grinned then took his usual seat at the table, rubbing his hands together when Elspeth set the pizza in the middle of them.

It didn't really feel long since she and Arran were living with her parents. Back then, Elspeth had regularly cooked for the family. She'd forgotten how much she enjoyed it. When it was just her and Arran it wasn't the same. She made whatever was easy and stuck to foods that he'd eat without too much complaint.

She'd missed the bustle of the dinner table too and smiled away as they all went around chatting about their respective days at work.

"Why do you look so happy?" Logan asked when Elspeth got a sudden fit of the giggles that she struggled to contain.

She didn't even know what she was laughing about and could only shake her head as she calmed herself down so she could eat. "No reason," she said, taking a bite of pizza. "I'm just happy." It wasn't something she'd expected she'd be able to say for a while. After seeing Rory entangled with another woman, she'd been convinced she'd struggle to be happy about anything for a long time, but she seemed to be able to compartmentalise that information quite nicely.

"Your holiday seems to have done you good," Keith said. "I thought you'd hate being in a big city on your own."

"I loved it. And I wasn't on my own. I made loads of friends." She told them all about Kendrick, and Molly and Danielle and all the other interesting people she'd met, and about the sightseeing she'd done. Arran loved hearing about the underground museum. She promised she'd take him sometime when he was older.

With so much chatter and with cake to eat, dinnertime stretched on. Finally, Elspeth noticed it going dark outside and took Arran home to get ready for bed.

"I like eating at Granny and Grandad's house," he said when she tucked him in.

"Me too." She kissed his forehead and switched the light off. "We'll do it more often."

CHAPTER THIRTY-THREE

L exie had enjoyed the early morning kayaking trip with Elspeth. It felt good to be able to relax out on the water without the responsibility of looking after a group. In the afternoon she was busy planning a hike when Leana arrived unexpectedly.

"When will Alasdair be home?" she asked, once they were settled at the kitchen table, steam rising from the cups of tea in front of them.

Leana looked weary. "A couple of weeks."

"You don't seem too thrilled about his return."

"I'll be happy when he's home. Another two weeks just feels like a long time. We ended up arguing on the phone yesterday. It was his birthday and he was in a terrible mood. He's still annoyed with me for not staying over there with him. And I'm annoyed with him for staying. Plus, the whole wedding issue is hanging over us. I'd like to resolve that somehow."

"How are you going to do that?" Lexie blew on her tea before taking a sip and wincing as it scalded her tongue.

"I don't know. I'd like to talk to him more about it."

"But you still love him? The worst-case scenario is you don't get the wedding you want?"

"You're making me sound petty," Leana said, a small smile tugging at her lips.

"I don't mean to. It's not petty. And I completely understand; I was upset when I thought I wouldn't get the wedding I wanted."

"That was different. There was never any question of Nick not wanting to get married. And he was determined to make sure you got the wedding you wanted."

"True." Lexie nodded. "But it's not worth losing Alasdair over. That's my point."

Leana stared sadly into her drink. "It's not only the fact that I won't get a big wedding that bothers me. It's that Alasdair's okay with me missing out on something that I've been dreaming about. When you were getting married, Nick was on a mission for everything to be perfect because he wanted to make you happy. Apparently, Alasdair isn't as concerned with my happiness."

"You've been happy up until now, haven't you?"

Leana tapped the side of her mug. "Whose side are you on exactly?"

"Yours. Always. But that doesn't mean I'm going to nod my head and agree with every word you say." She could absolutely see Leana's point, but she also thought she and Alasdair were perfect for each other, regardless of their different views on marriage. "I want you to be happy. And it always seemed as though you were happy with Alasdair. Besides, I'm fairly sure he'll cave and go along with getting married to keep the peace."

"I don't want to marry him if his heart's not in it. It would be a nightmare to plan a wedding without him caring about it."

Lexie grinned. "You could probably ask Logan what that's like. Isla definitely wasn't interested in planning their wedding."

"She wanted to marry him, though, it was only the big wedding that she objected to. I don't understand why Alasdair objects to marriage so much."

"Lots of people do," Lexie said. "It doesn't make him a terrible person."

"It makes him very annoying," Leana huffed.

"No one's perfect. And no relationship is perfect. But I think you have it pretty good." She kept thinking of Elspeth and how much she missed Rory. She didn't want to see Leana go through that.

"You're annoyingly level-headed these days. There was a time when you'd have told me not to stand for not getting everything I wanted and insist that I find someone who'd treat me like a princess."

"Well you're not a princess." Lexie rolled her eyes. "And getting *everything* you want is just greedy. As long as you're generally happy you can let a few things slide. If you think you'll be miserable for the rest of your life because you missed out on a wedding then you shouldn't stay with Alasdair. Personally, I think you'll end up being happy with Alasdair even if you don't get married. But what do I know?"

"It looks as though you're in a good position to be giving out relationship advice actually. You seem to have ended up with everything you want."

"Yeah." Her smile slipped and she brought her mug to her lips in an attempt to hide it.

"What's going on?" Leana asked, arching her brows. "Elspeth was worried you had something on your mind. She's right, isn't she?"

"It's nothing," she said, shaking her head.

"Tell me then."

Slowly, she set her tea down again. "We want to have a baby."

Leana smiled. "That's amazing."

"Yes. We decided after we got married that we wanted to start trying to get pregnant. But so far it hasn't happened."

"Oh." Leana's smile fell away. "Sorry."

"It's probably not a problem. We haven't been trying for that long, but I was starting to get stressed about it so I had a good talk with Nick about it."

"I guess it can just take a while," Leana said.

"That's what Nick said." She paused and shifted her gaze out of the window for a moment as a small brown bird hopped along the front wall. She was fairly sure it was a warbler. Nick would have been able to tell her for certain. She looked back at Leana. "After I talked to Nick I felt better, but now he seems really down. He pretends to be cheerful, but I think he's really worried."

"I suppose he would be," Leana mused. "*If* there's a problem, it's likely with him, isn't it?"

Lexie squinted, confused. "Why would you say that?"

"You got pregnant before without any problem," Leana said, as though it was obvious.

"Oh, no," Lexie whispered, covering her face with her hands. "Of course that's what's bothering him. I'm such an idiot. I even mentioned the abortion, but I never even thought about it like that."

"I'm sure everything will be fine. Like you say, you haven't been trying for very long. And even if there's a problem, there are lots of other options. IVF and stuff. But I bet it won't come to that."

"I hope not," Lexie said.

Leana finished her tea. "I'm sorry. I have to get to work. Or do you want me to hang around? I can call Mary and tell her I'll be late."

"No, thanks. I'm fine." She was actually happy to be alone. It would give her time to gather her thoughts before Nick got home.

When Nick walked in an hour later, Lexie was still sitting in the kitchen, lost in thought. She checked the time as he jolted her from her trance.

"Today's gone fast," she remarked as he bent to kiss her.

"How was Elspeth this morning?"

"She actually seemed okay."

"That's good. I feel bad for encouraging her to go and see Rory last night. Remind me not to interfere in other people's relationships."

"We weren't interfering." Standing, she slung her arms around Nick's neck. "We were giving advice and support. Today I did the same for Leana and she thinks I'm in a good position to give relationship advice since I'm clearly an expert on healthy, happy relationships."

His brow creased. "I don't know if this is a good time to point out that I've just got home from work and there's no dinner on the table." He tightened his arms around her waist and gently kissed her. "So you're definitely not in the running for wife of the year, but I agree that our relationship is pretty solid."

She gave him another peck, then took his hand and led him to the living room. "I need to talk to you."

"Oh, no. Did I leave the toilet seat up again?"

She squeezed his hand then took a seat on the couch. "I want to talk about the baby situation."

The atmosphere changed in an instant.

"I told you it'll be fine," Nick said. "It just takes some time."

"I know, and you made me feel better about it. But now you seem stressed."

He shrugged. "I'm fine."

"I was talking to Leana about it," she said slowly. "And she pointed out that since I was pregnant before, maybe you're worried that there's a problem with you ..."

"You spoke to Leana about it?" He crashed back onto the couch, closing his eyes briefly. "Is everyone in Lannick going to be talking about me being infertile?"

"No!" she said in a rush. "Leana would never say anything to anyone. But is that what you think? That you're infertile?"

He eyed her sadly. "I think if there's a problem, the logical assumption is that I'm the problem. Surely you think so too?"

"It honestly hadn't occurred to me until today. I kept thinking it's my fault that I'm not pregnant."

"Why would you think that?"

Lexie paused, not even sure she wanted to voice her thoughts. They weren't logical and she knew Nick would tell her so. "I keep thinking about the abortion," she said eventually. "And thinking that the universe is punishing me for it."

He entwined his fingers with hers and looked at her intently. "The universe wouldn't punish you, because you didn't do anything wrong."

She bit her lip as her chin quivered. "I know that really, but that's where my mind goes."

He pulled her close and she nestled against his chest while he rubbed her back. "Don't torture yourself over a decision that was the right choice for you at the time."

"I'm trying not to," she murmured. "But you need to stop worrying too."

"Yeah, I know. Stress affects fertility. Which basically just adds an extra layer of stress to my stress."

Sitting up, she looked at him quizzically.

"Now I'm stressed about being stressed," he said.

"I don't want to do this," she said on a sigh.

"What?"

"I don't want to spend our first year of marriage worrying about something that we don't have control over."

He frowned. "Do you want to put off the baby plans?"

"No. I just don't want us to get consumed by thinking about it. Six months ago we got married and I was so unbelievably happy. Nothing has changed since then." She put a hand on his leg. "I love you even more now than I did six months ago, and I love our life. We should be perfectly happy and enjoying married life."

His lips twitched upwards. "Leana's right – you do give good relationship advice."

"So you'll stop worrying?"

He grimaced. "I'll try."

"There's no point obsessing over this," she said. "Either it happens or it doesn't. And if it doesn't, we'll figure it out together. Okay?"

"Yes." He put a hand on her cheek and kissed her deeply.

"Good." She gave him a teasing smile. "That means we can go back to just having sex when we feel like it, not because we feel we have to."

His eyebrows shot up. "Has that been happening? You have sex with me when you'd rather not?"

She laughed at his expression. "There were just a couple of times when I'd probably have rather gone to sleep. Don't pretend there haven't been times when you've just gone along with it too."

"Well there was that one time I was waiting up to see the Northern Lights and you insisted you were at your most fertile and dragged me inside."

"You weren't going to see the Northern Lights," she said, amused. "I've lived here all my life and I've never seen them."

"Well you probably would have done if you'd have sat outside with me that night instead of dragging me up to bed."

"I'll stop dragging you up to bed in future," she teased.

"I don't think that's necessary." He scrunched his nose up. "The Northern Lights are probably overrated."

CHAPTER THIRTY-FOUR

After dinner on Tuesday evening, Jess sat staring at her phone. She'd hoped for an opportunity to talk to Rory at work, but when she'd seen him in the staffroom he'd been embroiled in conversations. They'd exchanged a smile, but finding time to speak to him privately in work hours would always be difficult. Now, her thumb hovered over the screen of her phone while her brain flitted between calling him or messaging, and what she'd say in either case. A message felt easier, but then she'd have the inevitable wait for him to reply, and she wasn't sure she could take it.

The melodic chime of the doorbell disrupted her thoughts and she moved automatically to the door.

Her lips stretched to a wide smile at the sight of Rory on the doorstep. "I was just about to call you." She held up her phone as though offering proof.

"Perfect timing then." He looked at her expectantly until she stepped aside and held out her arm in a welcoming gesture.

"I already ate," she said, as he wiped his shoes on the mat. "Otherwise we could've had dinner together. I might have some beers if you want one?"

"No, thanks. I can't stay for long, but I wanted to speak to you about last night."

She had a sinking feeling but managed to keep smiling as she led the way into the living room.

"I feel really awkward," he said as he followed her. "I thought it was best to come and talk to you about it so we both know where we stand."

"Yes," she murmured, as they sat on opposite ends of the couch.

"I think I may have given you the wrong impression." His brow creased in a frown as he held her gaze. "You've been such a good friend, but my life is a mess at the moment. I'm not ready to be in a relationship with someone new."

The heaviness in Jess's chest was crushing and she wasn't sure she could speak. "I really like you," she said quietly. "And when I kissed you, you kissed me back."

He swallowed hard. "I like you too. You've been a really great friend. When you kissed me, I got caught up in the moment. I wasn't thinking. But with the way things are at the moment, with Elspeth and Arran, it just won't work. I'd end up hurting you and I don't want that."

Too late, she thought sadly. It felt as though he was stabbing her in the heart. With a great effort, she forced herself to smile. "Bad timing?"

"Yes." He rubbed at the back of his neck. "I really want us to be friends. We can still be friends, can't we?"

Swallowing the lump in her throat, she returned his smile. "Of course."

"Thank goodness." He sighed. "I was worried things were going to be awkward."

"No," she said, lying. She would definitely find it awkward being around him, although that wouldn't be anything new. At least before she hadn't known what she was missing. Now, she knew what it was like to kiss him, so not being able to would be even worse.

"I managed to rustle up a couple of raffle prizes in my lunch break today," he said, changing the subject.

"What did you get?"

He hesitated, looking slightly sheepish. "A two-hour kayaking tour at the activity centre in Lannick and a painting by a local artist."

Jess glared at him. "Is the artist Isla?"

"They're good prizes," he said through a laugh.

"I take it you know someone at the activity centre too? You're such a cheat!"

"Taking easy options isn't cheating. I'll try and get a few more prizes too. Can you email me your list and I'll make sure it's ready for the newsletter on Friday?"

"Yeah, sure."

He stood and his eyes sparkled with amusement. "And don't worry, I'm not going to take the credit. You put so much effort into it. I'll make sure Imogen knows that."

"Don't you dare!" Jess shrieked. "Next time she'll ask me."

"Hopefully." He dodged out of the way as she swiped at his arm.

"You're mean."

His features turned serious. "I do appreciate you helping me with it."

"I know."

"You're a great friend," he said, taking a step towards her and wrapping her in a hug.

The scent of him was overwhelming, and she wanted to stay cocooned in his warm embrace. Unfortunately, he released her almost immediately and headed for the door.

"I heard Imogen looking for someone to cover your last lesson tomorrow," Jess said at the front door, remembering a conversation she'd overheard with the headteacher earlier that day.

"I've got an appointment," he said. "I need to leave an hour early. Imogen was really good about it."

"Everything okay?" Jess asked, her mind whirring as to what kind of appointment it could be.

"Yes." He set off down the path, clearly not wanting to divulge any more information. "I'll see you tomorrow."

After closing the door behind him, Jess let out a long breath. She felt like screaming. Why couldn't things work out as she wanted them to? She consoled herself that it was a matter of bad timing and not that he didn't like her.

She'd just have to be patient.

Elspeth was layering a lasagne when Rory arrived on Wednesday afternoon. He hadn't come over the previous evening as he'd said but had messaged to say he'd come over on Wednesday as usual and speak to her then. It didn't make any difference to Elspeth. After seeing him with his girlfriend, she no longer had anything to discuss with him.

He called hello as he wandered down the hallway, and once again it irked Elspeth that he casually wandered into her house. More so now, since he wouldn't even let her across the threshold at his place. Maybe now would be a good time to ask him to knock instead of letting himself in. A bit of formality between them might make the fact he had a new girlfriend easier to bear. It would also be easier if he'd tell her about his new relationship status instead of treating her like a child who he needed to protect.

"Elspeth?"

"Hi," she said.

"You're spilling." He indicated the spoon in her hand.

"Oops." A dollop of meat sauce splattered to the floor before she had a chance to move it back to the pan.

"You were miles away," Rory remarked.

"Yes." She glanced at the clock on the wall. "You're early."

Surprise flashed in his eyes, then vanished. "I had a meeting this afternoon, so someone was covering my class. The meeting finished early so I came straight here."

"What was your meeting about?"

He shrugged. "The usual school stuff."

It struck Elspeth as odd that they'd arrange a meeting during school hours. "Didn't your meetings always used to be in the evenings?"

"Yeah. It was just an extra thing." He looked pointedly around the kitchen. "Where's Arran?"

"Over with Logan. You can go and fetch him. Or he'll probably be back as soon as he notices your car."

"Sorry about the other night," he said quickly. "At my place. I didn't mean to be rude."

"It's fine." She arranged lasagne sheets in the dish, then began adding another layer of sauce.

"What did you want to talk about?"

"Oh … erm …" She almost laughed at the idea of telling him why she'd gone to visit him on Monday evening. That would be a little awkward now.

"Was it about what happened in Edinburgh?" he asked. "Because I wanted to talk to you about it too. I know you were drunk, but—"

"But that's no excuse for kissing you? I know, and I agree. It was completely inappropriate. I was drunk and I got carried away. It's a good job you're sensible and put a stop to it. I honestly didn't mean to complicate things."

"Right." He took a seat at the table. "That's what I thought, but I wanted to check."

"It won't happen again, I promise."

The buzz of his phone came as a nice distraction, and Elspeth turned back to the food, proud that she'd made it through the conversation calmly.

"Sorry," Rory said. "I just need to take this call."

She turned in time to see him stride towards the front door,

269

putting the phone to his ear and answering with a somewhat formal tone before he stepped outside.

"Something important?" she asked when he came back five minutes later.

"Sort of." His mouth twitched to a smile. "It was work stuff."

Elspeth stared at him, wondering why he looked so amused by a work phone call. She decided it was probably Jess calling him.

"What were we talking about before?" he asked.

"Drunken kisses," she said.

"Oh, yeah."

"It's good that we talk about this kind of stuff so we both know where we stand." She took a breath. "So I should probably tell you I have a date."

"A what?"

"A date. With a guy." She turned her back to him and continued with the cooking. "It's probably not even worth mentioning, but Leana wanted to set me up with this guy, and I thought it might be fun so I agreed I'd meet him."

"Right," Rory said weakly.

"I thought dating other people is the sort of thing we should talk to each other about, so I wanted to mention it." When he didn't reply, she turned and caught him staring at her before snapping his gaze away quickly.

"Thanks for letting me know."

"I didn't want you to hear about it from anyone else."

"Yeah."

"So if there's ever anything you want to talk to me about, feel free."

He walked to the table and tapped the edge of it. "I should probably go and track down Arran. See what he's up to. I might take him for a walk before dinner. Work up an appetite."

"Good idea," Elspeth agreed. "It'll be half an hour at least." She turned to find he'd already gone. It was an hour before he reappeared with Arran. He was quiet as they ate and left imme-diately after he'd put Arran to bed, saying he had work to do.

Elspeth forced herself to believe that he really did have work to do and not that work was his code word for a petite brunette called Jess.

CHAPTER THIRTY-FIVE

While Elspeth drove, Leana pulled the visor down to look in the mirror. After pressing her lips together, she dragged her brush through her hair.

"You're making me nervous," Elspeth said. "Why do you care how you look? Do you fancy one of these guys?"

"No. I like to look nice for myself. No one else. And why are you nervous? It's just a drink."

"Why did you pick Friday night? Rory always goes out in Portree on Fridays. What if we bump into him?"

"Which pub does he go in?"

"I don't know. They rotate around the pubs each week. Or at least they used to."

"You told him you were going to start dating anyway, so it's not a big deal. If we see him, you can politely ignore each other."

Elspeth wasn't sure she was capable of politely ignoring Rory if she saw him. Going on a date felt weird enough as it was. If she bumped into Rory, she'd probably need to make a quick exit.

When they walked into the Isles Inn she did a scan of the

place, but it was quiet and there was definitely no sign of Rory. Leana smiled at the two guys standing at the end of the bar and hugged them both before introducing Elspeth.

They settled themselves at a table, Elspeth opting for a soft drink, despite Leana's suggestion that she should leave the car in Portree and let her hair down. She managed to smile along with the conversation as Leana chatted to the guys about their music, but her heart wasn't in it. It definitely didn't feel like a date. She wasn't even sure which one of them Leana wanted to set her up with. Based on looks, she guessed Conor. Patrick was nice too, if a little reserved. He made an effort to chat to her when Leana and Conor were engrossed in a conversation about how he'd got into music.

After an hour, Elspeth would have quite liked to go home, but Leana seemed to be having a good time. She was chatting away and getting through drinks rapidly.

"Shall we go somewhere else?" Patrick asked when they finished the latest round of drinks. "It's pretty quiet in here."

"I'm up for that," Conor said, then looked questioningly at Leana, who nodded her agreement.

Outside, Elspeth took Leana's arm and slowed their pace as they walked a little way behind. "I want to go home," she whispered to her sister.

"No," Leana complained. "Not yet. Why don't you have some drinks? We can get a taxi home."

"I'm not in the mood for a night out. I'd rather be at home drinking tea."

"Elspeth! Will you act your age for once? Didn't the doctor tell you to have fun?"

"No. She didn't." Elspeth's mood nosedived even further at the reminder of her visit to the doctor.

"Well I think you should have some fun," Leana said. "Stay for a bit longer at least."

Elspeth agreed to another half hour, but was determined that she was leaving after that.

The Merchant Bar was busy and the noise and bustle came as a bit of a shock. There were no tables free, and the music was at a level where you had to speak loudly to be heard. Once they had drinks, Elspeth smiled at Patrick, then glanced at Leana, who was laughing away with Conor. It didn't look as though she'd be keen to leave anytime soon.

Elspeth had just run out of small talk with Patrick when a voice called out to her and she looked along the bar to see a familiar face walking towards her.

"Ruth!" She greeted her warmly, happy at the distraction. Ruth was good friends with Lexie, but Elspeth knew her pretty well from nights out in Portree. "How are you? I haven't seen you in ages."

"I'm good, thanks." She looked at Patrick. "Sorry. Am I interrupting?"

"Not at all." Elspeth introduced the two of them.

"Do you mind if I hang around here with you for a wee while?" Ruth asked, glancing over her shoulder.

"Of course not," Elspeth said, trying to figure out why Ruth seemed so on edge.

"I'm on a date," she explained, grimacing slightly.

Patrick chuckled. "I take it it's not going well?"

"He's awful. I was going to leave, but then I spotted you, so I told him I was just going to say hello to a friend. I'll finish my drink, then discreetly slip away."

"Which one is he?" Elspeth asked.

"End of the bar. Tall with a green checked shirt."

Elspeth peered through the people standing along the bar. She gasped, then stifled a laugh. "Henry? You're on a date with Henry?"

"Do you know him?" Ruth asked.

"I went on a date with him once," Elspeth said, thoroughly amused. "Has he been showing you photos of his hamster?"

"Yes!" Ruth shrieked. "He's the most boring guy ever. And

I'm a vet's nurse. I love animals. But he showed me a two-minute video of a hamster running on a wheel."

"Are you serious?" Patrick asked.

"Unfortunately, yes." Ruth laughed loudly. "I can't believe you went on a date with him too."

"I lasted about five minutes. Then I faked a headache and left."

Patrick grinned. "Poor guy."

"No!" Elspeth and Ruth said at once, then laughed.

"At some point you'd think he'd realise that his hamster photos are scaring women away," Ruth said.

Elspeth shook her head. "Obviously not."

"I'll be right back," Patrick said, then set off towards the bathroom.

"I'm really sorry," Ruth said to Elspeth. "Are you two on a date?"

"Sort of. Don't worry about it, though. I was glad of the interruption."

"How come you chose the Merchant Bar? Are you trying to rub Rory's nose in it?"

"What do you mean?"

"Rory's always in here with work on Fridays. It seems odd to have a date in the same place your ex is."

Elspeth looked frantically around the room. "Rory's here?"

"Yes. Didn't you know?"

"I had no idea."

"He's with his colleagues, over by the window."

Elspeth still couldn't see him. Then a guy moved aside and she was staring straight at him. He was sitting at a small table with two women but looking directly at Elspeth. He flashed her a brief smile before snapping his gaze away.

"This is awful," Elspeth murmured. Her heart was pummelling against her rib cage and her chest felt tight.

"You could always move to another pub," Ruth suggested.

"It's not even a proper date. Leana was trying to set me up with him."

"What's going on with Leana?" Ruth asked, her gaze drifting along to Conor and Leana, who were deep in an animated conversation. From the way Leana was leaning into him, she seemed pretty drunk.

"Alasdair's in America and Leana's in a bad mood with him. But I think everything will be fine." Elspeth was tempted to go over and tell her to stop flirting with Conor, but she suspected the advice wouldn't be well received.

Patrick arrived back and asked them if they wanted another drink. Elspeth declined and contemplated going home. She looked across to Rory and felt sick when she saw the woman beside him had a hand resting on his shoulder. There was no way she could stay around and watch them fawning over each other.

"I'm going to go," she said. "I've got to be up early in the morning."

Patrick was ordering drinks and hadn't heard her.

"Sorry." Ruth leaned towards her and lowered her voice. "I feel as though I sabotaged your date."

"You're doing me a favour. I don't feel so bad leaving now." She glanced in Patrick's direction, then smiled at Ruth. "He's sweet. You should stay and hang out with him."

Ruth grinned. "So I abandon my date and steal yours instead?"

"I don't see why not. Someone may as well have some fun." She gave Ruth a hug, then tapped Patrick on the shoulder and said goodbye to him, before making her way over to Leana.

She was standing very close to Conor, chatting away with a huge smile on her face.

"I'm going home," Elspeth said, tugging on her arm to get her attention. "Do you want to come?"

"Don't go home yet. Stay out longer."

Elspeth shook her head. "If you want a lift home, I'm going now."

"I'll get a taxi," Leana said, immediately switching her attention back to Conor.

"Bye, then!" Elspeth wandered away. Pausing with a hand on the door, she looked over at Rory. He was chatting with the two women and didn't notice her.

It occurred to her that she'd never been on a date without wishing she was with Rory.

CHAPTER THIRTY-SIX

"You can stop looking for her," Jess said, when she got sick of Rory's attention drifting around the room. "She's already left."

He gave her a quizzical look. "What?"

"Elspeth. I saw her leave a while ago. I presume that's who you're looking for."

His gaze drifted yet again. "Leana's still here."

"As are we!" Ava said pointedly.

"Sorry." He turned to sit squarely at the table again and took a sip of his drink.

"How long were you with her for?" Ava asked.

"Not that long. About eighteen months. I think maybe we moved in together too soon, but it's a strange situation when there's a child involved."

Ava's features scrunched up. "I thought he was like four."

"He is. Five in October."

"Isn't he yours then? Biologically, I mean."

"Yeah, he is." Rory shook his head as though tuning into the conversation properly. Jess already knew the story but was quite intrigued to see Ava's reaction when she heard it. "I didn't know he existed until he was two and a half."

Ava rested her elbows on the table, leaning closer to Rory. "You didn't know she was pregnant?"

"No." Rory smiled, seeming amused by Ava's shock. "I was on Skye for a holiday. Elspeth and I had a fling and I left again before I knew she was pregnant. I only found out when I came for another holiday a few years later."

"No!" Ava's eyes looked as though they might pop out of their sockets. "You've got to be kidding me? Are you winding me up?"

"I'm serious," he said.

"Why didn't she tell you?"

He shrugged. "We'd only known each other for a couple of weeks. She just decided to raise Arran alone."

"Hang on," Jess said, thinking she must have mis-heard. "You told me she didn't have your number or any way of contacting you."

He scratched at his jaw. "I might be drunk."

"So drunk that you've forgotten the reason why the mother of your child didn't mention you had a kid?" Ava asked.

His shoulders shook as he chuckled. "No. I mean drunk enough to tell the real story. Usually, I tell a different version. The truth makes Elspeth sounds like a horrible person."

"So she knew how to get in touch with you?" Jess asked, shocked.

"Yes. But we barely knew each other. And she was really young."

"So you arrived back here to find a toddler running around who looks like you?" Ava asked.

"Pretty much." His brow was wrinkled, but a hint of a smile played at his lips.

"Weren't you furious?" Jess wasn't sure how he could ever have forgiven her, never mind get into a relationship with her.

"I was a bit annoyed at first," he said. "But I sort of understood. And things probably turned out for the best. At least I like to think so. I don't know what would have happened if I'd found out I had a kid while I was at uni."

"That's insane." Ava took a sip of her drink, then turned as someone called her name. "I'll be back in a bit," she said and wandered over to the next table.

"Elspeth really has left," Jess said, when Rory looked over his shoulder yet again.

"I wasn't looking for Elspeth. I'm wondering who the guy is that Leana's with. She's got a boyfriend."

"She's your ex-girlfriend's sister. I don't see why it's any of your business who she's with."

"Elspeth was on a date with the other guy," Rory said, apparently not hearing the irritation in Jess's tone. "I guess it didn't go well. That's one positive to the evening."

"You're kind of pathetic, you know?" she murmured.

"What?"

She hadn't really intended for him to hear, but she also didn't particularly care. Reaching for her glass, she was surprised to find it empty. She could've sworn she'd only just got a fresh one.

"Did you just call me pathetic?"

She sighed. "It's obvious that she's not interested, but you still follow her around looking for scraps of attention. Although she probably enjoys that."

"What are you talking about?"

"Surely even you can see how badly she treats you. I mean, she was pregnant and didn't bother to tell you. And she has you running around, chasing down to Edinburgh after you, and then she was rude to you when you got there."

"Because she didn't ask me to go there. She didn't want me there."

"Exactly. She doesn't want you! But you chase after her anyway. Tonight she brought a date into the pub that you go in every week. If that doesn't convince you that she doesn't want to get back with you, I don't know what will."

"I don't think she did it on purpose." His brows twitched

together. "You don't understand how it is. We have a child – it's not as though I can walk away and have nothing to do with her."

"That's true." Jess stared at him, then put a hand over her mouth as a manic burst of laughter bubbled out of her.

"What's funny?"

"I just realised how pathetic I am! How can I sit here and judge you for pining over someone who isn't interested?" The laughter fell away and she stood up. "I'm not doing this any more."

"Doing what?"

"You." She waggled a finger between the two of them. "Us. This. I'm done." She began to walk out.

Rory stepped in front of her. "What are you talking about?"

"I can't be friends with you." Her eyes locked with his and a wave of sadness swept through her.

"I don't understand. The other day you said—"

"I said whatever I needed to say to keep you close. But I don't want to be just friends. It's torture and I refuse to do it." She bit on her lip as everything suddenly felt very clear. "You're not even a good friend. You don't care about me."

"Of course I do," he said frantically.

"You never ask about me. All we ever talk about is you and your problems. You never ask how I am."

"I do," he insisted.

"I'm not doing it any more," she said, as much to herself as to Rory. "I'll be polite to you at work but that's it. I don't want anything to do with you outside of work."

"Don't say that." His eyes looked so pitiful that she almost wanted to take it back and wrap her arms around him. She wouldn't, though. He'd said it was bad timing, but that wasn't the problem. No matter how long she hung around, he was never going to fall in love with her. She'd only get her heart broken repeatedly.

She looked at him sadly. "Bye," she whispered before stepping around him and striding away. Halfway across the room her chin wobbled and tears welled in her eyes. Stepping out into the fresh air, she paused and wiped at her cheeks.

"Hello!"

The cheerful voice startled her, and she squinted to see who it was and if they were speaking to her.

"Now you really do look like you've never seen me before in your life." He shifted his weight. "I'm Gary. We met at the pub and then the other day with my niece ..."

"I know who you are," she said, averting her gaze.

"Are you okay?" His voice turned warm and full of concern.

"Yes," she lied. "I'm fine."

"Do you smoke?"

"No." She gave a bemused shake of the head. "Do you?"

"No."

"Sort of a weird question then."

His face broke into a smile. "I thought maybe you'd come out for a smoke."

"No. I'm heading home."

"Didn't you bring a jacket?"

Her shoulders drooped and she let out a sigh that was part growl. "I left it inside."

"I suppose you could always go back for it," he said, a hint of mocking in his tone.

She took a step and glanced in the window. Rory was nowhere to be seen, but she was still tempted to abandon her jacket rather than face going back inside.

"I had a bit of an argument with someone," she told Gary.

"I see. You stormed out? Having to go back to collect your belongings is always a let-down after you've made a dramatic exit."

"Exactly," she said, managing a small smile.

He moved closer to her, peering over her head and into the pub. "Can you see it?"

"It's on the hook on the wall there." She pointed to near where her colleagues were sitting and chatting away.

"What colour is it?"

"Grey."

"Okay. I'll get it, but if someone starts accusing me of theft you need to come in and put them straight."

Jess didn't have time to comment. When she turned, he was already walking into the pub. Lingering beside the window, she ducked out of the way when any of her colleagues turned in her direction. After a moment, she saw Gary pawing through the coats. He looked quite suspicious and she stifled a laugh, then nodded vigorously when he held up her coat.

"Thank you so much," she said when he arrived back outside.

"No problem." He held the jacket out.

As she pushed her arms into it and pulled her hair out from the collar, she looked at Gary and felt slightly awkward. "I should get home."

"Is it far? I can walk with you if you want."

"That's okay. I think you've been quite gentlemanly enough for one evening." She took a few steps away. "Thanks again for getting my jacket."

He gave a one-shouldered shrug and flashed a quick smile.

"Jess!" he called out before she'd got very far down the road. She paused and he hurried to catch up to her. "I know you've already turned me down twice, so I might seem a bit desperate now, but they say the third time's the charm… so I wondered if you might go out for dinner with me sometime." He shoved his hands into his pockets. "If you say no, I promise not to ask again. I realise it might be getting creepy."

Jess grimaced. His timing couldn't really be worse. But he seemed sweet enough, and there was a chance that a date was exactly what she needed to take her mind off of Rory. "I don't know," she said when the silence drew on too long. "I thought you weren't even supposed to be dating at the moment." She recalled the conversation when she'd first met him in the pub.

"Dating's fine," he said, with a boyish smile. "I have to be respectable about it. Which is why I asked you for dinner and not just a drink."

"I see," she mused, mock-seriously.

"I also think Isla would approve of you."

Jess let out a delicate cough, thinking that Isla probably wouldn't approve of her – at least not if she knew she'd been chasing Rory. "I doubt that," she murmured.

"She would," Gary said confidently. "And Paige says you're her favourite teacher, which is a massive compliment. Usually, she hates all teachers on principle. But she really likes you. Your classes are her favourite, apparently."

"That's a lie! She looks bored stiff in all my lessons."

"Oh, that's just her face," Gary said, jokily. "She can't help that, bless her. But the scowl appeared when she became a teenager, so I'm confident she'll grow out of it at some point. She's not a bad kid really."

Jess couldn't help but smile at Gary's description of her.

"She said you almost blew up the classroom once," he went on. "Almost killed the whole class in her version of events. Oddly enough, I think that's why you're her favourite teacher."

"I didn't almost blow up the classroom," Jess insisted, chuckling. "It was a small, controlled explosion – designed to get the attention of the class who weren't in my control at the time. They listen to me much better since then."

"Nothing like making kids fear for their lives to get them to listen!"

"Well, it worked!"

As they both fell silent, the atmosphere felt strained.

"So are you going to break my heart for the third and final time or what?" he asked.

Jess wavered, unsure whether or not agreeing to go out with him was a good idea. Finally, she threw caution to the wind. "Okay. I'll have dinner with you."

He blinked rapidly.

"Sorry, was that the wrong answer?" she asked, amused.

"I just got used to being rejected by you. Definitely the right answer, though." He took her phone when she held it out to him, and he called himself before handing it back. "Should I call you tomorrow to arrange something?" he asked, looking slightly flustered. "Or do I wait a couple of days? What's respectable?"

"You can call me tomorrow."

"Okay, great." He beamed at her and took a step back before he hesitated. "Are you sure I shouldn't walk you home?"

"I'm fine, thanks. I'll talk to you soon."

He smiled again before setting off back towards the pub.

Jess felt a small glow of satisfaction as she continued along the road. It definitely hadn't been the best night out she'd ever had, but it hadn't turned out too badly either. At least she was finally ready to put an end to her infatuation with Rory. And who knew what might happen with Gary? If nothing else, he'd be a distraction.

At the end of the road, she paused and turned back. Gary was standing outside the pub, watching her. He raised a hand to wave and she did the same. Then he disappeared inside the pub and Jess went on her way.

It felt much better to be the one who was chased rather than the one doing the chasing.

CHAPTER THIRTY-SEVEN

Leana had been drinking too fast, but she was having fun and hadn't been at all tempted to leave with Elspeth. Alcohol had washed her inhibitions away and she automatically swayed to the music. When the volume was turned up a notch, she reached for Conor's hand to get him to dance with her. He was laid-back and easy-going, which was a good combination when Leana felt like letting her hair down.

"I must be drunk," he said, leaning close to her. "I don't usually dance."

"I love this song," she replied. "I can't not dance." It didn't occur to her to protest when he put a hand on her hip and danced closer to her. There was no harm in dancing. She smiled at him, then felt momentarily confused by the pressure on her arm. He was squeezing too hard. Except when she looked down, it wasn't him at all.

Rory pulled her roughly by her elbow. "What the hell are you doing?"

"Dancing," she said, squirming out of his grip.

Conor took a step towards Rory. "Have you got a problem?"

"I have actually," Rory snarled in reply.

Leana stepped between them, placing a hand on Rory's chest to stop him getting any closer to Conor.

"She's got a boyfriend," he said. "Stay away from her."

"We were only dancing," Conor said, shaking his head.

Rory glared at Leana. "Where's Alasdair?"

"In America," she said, sure he knew that.

"I've seen you flirting and dancing with this numpty all night." Rory slurred his words slightly. "What are you doing rubbing up against some guy in the middle of the pub?"

"We were only dancing," Leana said weakly, but Rory's words sobered her and she felt a stirring of guilt.

"What happened to Elspeth?" Rory asked.

"She went home ages ago."

"Because of me? She can't even stand to be in the same room as me?"

"You're drunk." Leana took his arm. "You need to go home."

"I'm not leaving you with that guy."

"I'm going home too," Leana said, then turned back to Conor. "Sorry. I have to go."

"Who's he?" he asked. "Are you okay going with him?"

"I'm fine. He's family. I'll see you around." As she walked to the door, it occurred to her that she'd actually go out of her way to make sure she *didn't* see him around. Rory's words had hit her hard and she felt terrible for her behaviour. She might tell herself that it was all harmless flirting and dancing, but if Alasdair carried on like that with another woman she'd be furious. Not that he would, she thought sadly.

"Do you want to stay in my spare room?" Rory asked when they stood on the street outside the pub. The air was cold, and Leana wrapped her arms around herself, then shot a hand out to steady Rory when he stumbled off the pavement.

"I just want to go home," she said.

"I'll walk you to the taxi rank."

"Are you sure you don't need me to help you get home?"

"No. I'm fine." He swayed as he walked beside her. "Apart

from the fact that Jess hates me and Elspeth wouldn't have anything to do with me if we didn't have a child. Otherwise I'm fine."

Leana gave him a sidelong glance. The self-pity was unattractive, but she felt sorry for him. "You're just drunk," she said as they approached the square where two taxis were waiting.

"Where's Alasdair?" Rory asked again.

"America," she said on a sigh.

"I know! I mean *why*. Why isn't he here with you?"

"That's what I keep wondering." She couldn't help but smile at his drunkenness.

"He should be here with you," Rory said opening the taxi door for her. "He's such a prat."

"Maybe." Leana squeezed Rory's arm and got into the car. Then she shuffled across and gestured for him to get in too. "We can drop you off on the way. I'm not sure you'll make it home otherwise."

"I'm fine," he said, but followed her into the car.

"You're going to have the hangover from hell."

"You too!" he said, laughing.

"Probably." She flopped back in the seat. "I miss Alasdair."

"I don't understand why he's in America," Rory said loudly. "Not when he could be here with you. I'm going to call him and tell him what an idiot he is!"

"Thanks," she said, appreciating his concern. "Maybe you should just go to bed though."

They arrived outside his house a couple of minutes later. "Sorry," he said, looking back at her when he'd got out of the car.

"What for?"

Lines appeared beside his eyes as he squinted in concentration. Then his features softened and he laughed. "I've no idea!"

"Just go to bed," she said, then called goodnight as he banged the door closed behind him.

· · ·

Leana spent most of the journey home fighting her eyelids in an effort to stay awake. She messaged Alasdair asking if he was up but didn't get a response until she was putting her key in the lock at home.

"What's going on?" he asked abruptly when she answered the call.

"I don't know," she said, confused by his tone. "I'm just getting home. What do you mean?"

"Rory called me to tell me you spent all night flirting and dancing with some guy."

Leana let out a long breath as she wandered through to the kitchen. "I was out with Elspeth. We met up with Conor and Patrick, that's all. Rory was in the pub and he came over completely drunk at the end of the night."

"Rory reckoned it was just you out with Conor and Patrick."

She got a glass out of the cupboard, then moved to the sink. "Elspeth left early. I was having a good time so I stayed out. It's not a big deal."

"So you weren't flirting with Conor?" he asked angrily.

"I was talking to him."

"And *dancing* with him?"

"It was only a bit of a laugh," she said.

"Really? Because Rory thinks I should be getting on the next plane back. He's rambling about how I'm about to lose you."

"Rory's drunk," she said, irritated.

"So are you by the sound of it."

"And that's a crime, is it? Excuse me for having fun while you're off on an extended holiday! What do you expect me to do, sit around pining for you?"

"I didn't expect you to go on dates with other guys. Is this because I said I don't want to get married? Are you trying to make some kind of point?"

"No." She wandered back along the hall, taking her glass of water with her. "And I really don't want to have this conversation now. Not when you seem intent on arguing."

"Can you blame me, after I've had Rory on the phone, telling me Conor's had his hands all over you in the middle of the pub?"

Leana paused at the foot of the stairs. "I told you, we were just dancing."

"Where are you?" he asked quickly.

"At home. I already told you that."

"Are you on your own?"

She leaned heavily on the bannister and took a steady breath before answering. "What exactly are you implying?"

"I'm just wondering if Conor felt the need to escort you home?"

As her blood pumped furiously, Leana made her way up the stairs. "I'm going to pretend you didn't ask that. I'll talk to you tomorrow. I'm hanging up now."

She heard him call her name before she pressed the button to end the call. He called back almost immediately, but she silenced the phone and switched it off.

CHAPTER THIRTY-EIGHT

Caffeine did little to make Leana feel any more human on Saturday morning. For once, she was glad she and Alasdair were in different time zones – it gave her breathing space so she could get her thoughts in order before she spoke to him. His words had shaken her, and she'd had a restless night, constantly drifting in and out of sleep. While she could admit that dancing with Conor bordered on being inappropriate, the idea of her going home with another guy left her speechless. She couldn't believe Alasdair had even considered it.

As she was making her second cup of coffee, she was drawn to movement through the patio doors and spotted Elspeth and Arran wandering up the garden. Automatically, Leana poured a coffee for her sister too.

"Morning," she said as she slid the door open.

"You look rough," Elspeth remarked while Arran continued to wander around the garden.

"I feel it." She handed over the mug of coffee and retreated into the warmth of the kitchen.

"How was the rest of your night?" Elspeth asked, following her inside.

"Not great. I should have left with you."

"Hindsight's wonderful, isn't it? What happened?"

"I'm surprised you don't already know. Where *is* Rory? Isn't he supposed to have Arran today?"

"He overslept so he's running late."

"He better not come anywhere near me. I feel like killing him."

"Why? What happened?" Elspeth looked suddenly pale. "Actually, I'm not sure I want to know. Does it involve his new girlfriend? Was he all over her in the pub?"

"No." Leana looked at Elspeth in concern. "Is that why you left early?"

"I wasn't having a good time," she replied, avoiding the question.

"Sorry. I thought you'd get on with Conor."

"Oh, it was Conor you were trying to set me up with? That was a bit of a non-starter since he only had eyes for you. I presumed Patrick was for me." She smiled. "Ruth had a good time with him anyway. She messaged me this morning in a panic, checking she wasn't stealing him from me."

"At least someone had a good night," Leana said, perching on a stool.

"What happened?"

"I was dancing with Conor, and Rory came and told me what he thought of that."

Elspeth's eyes widened. "Seriously?"

"Yeah. Then he called Alasdair and told him all about it."

"Rory really did that?"

"Yes. He was very drunk. I had to take him home – I was worried he wouldn't make it otherwise."

"So he didn't go home with his girlfriend?"

"No. And I got the impression he's not seeing anyone."

Elspeth chewed her bottom lip and stared into her coffee. "So how was Alasdair after Rory called him?"

"We had a big argument and I hung up on him. Can you believe he thinks I'd cheat on him?"

She shook her head. "I also can't get my head around the fact that Rory would tell him that. What was he thinking?"

Leana ran a hand over her face. "It's all such a mess."

In the silence, Elspeth pulled her phone from her pocket and read a message. "Rory's on his way. I better get Arran back home to meet him."

"Please do. I don't want him coming around here."

"I don't think Rory would have called Alasdair maliciously. He must have been really drunk."

"I know, but I can't face him at the moment."

Unfortunately, she didn't have a choice in the matter. An hour after Elspeth left to take Arran home, Rory turned up on the doorstep.

"I don't want to speak to you," she said, all set to close the door on him.

"Listen to me for a minute, please." His hair was a mess and he looked so pathetic that Leana couldn't bring herself to slam the door in his face.

Instead she propped her hands on her hips as she waited for an explanation.

"I'm sorry," he said, looking straight at her with bloodshot eyes. "I should never have called Alasdair."

"No, you shouldn't. I was only dancing. Why would you tell Alasdair I'm cheating on him?"

Rory winced. "That wasn't my intention. Everything came out wrong."

"How exactly was it supposed to come out?" she snapped.

"I was annoyed with *him*." He paused and glanced at the car, where Arran sat in the back, staring at his lap, presumably at a toy.

"You were annoyed with Alasdair?" Leana asked, not quite connecting the dots.

"Aye. He's in America when you'd clearly rather he was here with you. He has everything and he takes it for granted." He ran a hand through his hair, then scratched the back of his head. "I honestly wasn't trying to cause problems between you."

Leana dropped her hands to her sides as she relaxed.

"Can you please not hate me?" Rory asked sheepishly. "I feel as though Arran is the only person who wants anything to do with me at the moment."

When he looked so pitiful it would be almost impossible for Leana to stay angry with him. She also suspected his heart was in the right place when he'd called Alasdair. Stepping forwards, she put her arms around him and he sagged into her embrace.

"I'm really sorry," he said again.

"It's all right." Leana pulled away. "It would've been nice if Alasdair hadn't been so quick to believe I'd cheat on him."

"You'll sort things out, though, won't you?"

"Aye." She walked to the car with him and peered in at Arran, who was concentrating on a game on Rory's phone. "I'm sure everything will be fine." As Rory went to get in the car she stopped him with a hand on his arm. "Are you still in love with Elspeth?"

He sighed heavily. "Yes."

"I don't think she knows that."

"It doesn't make any difference if she knows it or not. To be honest, it's probably better if she doesn't know."

"She misses you," Leana said quietly. "You should talk to her. Tell her how you feel."

His brow creased. "She seems happy."

Leana wasn't sure *happy* was the right word, but when she thought about it, Elspeth had her old calmness back. For a while she'd been manic and would get upset at the smallest thing. She definitely seemed more stable.

"Maybe it's a good time to speak to her then," she said.

He shook his head. "She's happy and it's nothing to do with me. I don't want to complicate things for her."

"Are you okay?" she asked as he opened the car door.

"I'll survive," he replied wearily. "I'll call Alasdair later and explain."

She shrugged and told him not to worry about it.

He managed a small smile before he left.

It was early afternoon when Leana's phone rang, and she tried to calculate the time in California as she answered. She hadn't expected to hear from Alasdair yet.

"You're up early," she said, her tone automatically turning frosty.

"I've hardly slept. I'm really sorry about last night."

She didn't reply.

"I'm at the airport."

"Where are you off to now?"

"Home," he said, as though it should be obvious. "I'm coming home."

Leana sat bolt upright on the couch. "You don't need to come home early. I'm not cheating on you. Rory was just drunk and rambling."

"I know that. But I want to come home. I have to transfer a couple of times, but Josh's assistant arranged it all for me and drove me down to LAX."

Her chest swelled at the thought of seeing him. "When will you arrive?"

"Monday morning."

"Good," she said as it hit her just how much she'd been missing him. The thought of seeing him soon felt like a huge relief.

"I should have come home when you did."

"It's fine," she said. "Just come home and everything will be okay."

There was an announcement in the background. "I have to get on the flight. I'll message you later and let you know what time I'll get back. If I get the train to Kyle of Lochalsh, can you pick me up from there?"

"I can come to the airport. The train will be annoying after all that traveling."

"I think the flight lands pretty early. I don't mind getting the train."

"Just send me the details."

When they ended the call, Leana felt a flutter of excitement in her stomach. She tried hard not to dwell on the fact that he was jumping on a plane because he thought she was cheating on her and focused on the fact that she'd have him home soon.

CHAPTER THIRTY-NINE

When she thought it through, Leana realised that driving the two hours to pick Alasdair up from Inverness airport on Monday would mean leaving the house around six o'clock in the morning. A two-hour drive at that time wasn't appealing, especially because she was working the evening before so wouldn't get to bed until late.

As it turned out, she was awake before sunrise anyway and wished she'd arranged to meet him at the airport. Restless, she made a coffee and stood by the window, cradling the mug to her chest as she watched sunlight gradually seeping onto the horizon, making the still water of the loch sparkle. On her phone, she checked the status of Alasdair's flight from London. It had been delayed by twenty minutes but was due to take off any time. Her phone vibrated and showed a new message from Alasdair. He said he was waiting to take off from Gatwick and would see her later.

Quickly, she checked the time. If the flight hadn't taken off yet she still had time to meet him at the airport. Maybe. He'd have to wait for his bags, so she should be able to make it. But only if she stopped thinking about it and left immediately. After one last slug of coffee she made a quick dash around, pulling on a hoodie and grabbing her purse and the car key. She was in the car in a matter of minutes and set off up the drive, playing with the heat controls as she shivered.

The journey felt unbelievably slow, and she alternated between watching the road and checking the time. Several times she picked her phone up to message Alasdair and let him know the change of plans, but she stopped herself, keen to surprise him. The only flaw to the plan was if she didn't make it on time and he left before she found him. She decided to wait. If it looked as though she'd be late, she'd message him, but she thought she should make it just in time.

When she finally parked the car at the airport, she was a bundle of nerves and excitement. Rushing through the airport, she lingered for a few minutes at the arrivals gate before dashing to the information desk. The arrivals screen indicated the flight had landed, but she wanted to know if he'd have got his bag and come through yet. The woman told her the baggage had come through but couldn't say much more than that.

In a panic, Leana took her phone out. Alasdair's phone went straight to voicemail, ,and she paced around the arrivals hall, pondering her options. If he was going to take the train he'd have to get a taxi to the station. After a moment she set off towards the exit, scanning all around as she jogged towards the taxi rank. There was no sign of him anywhere. Feeling defeated, she sank onto a bench and tried calling him again.

She felt a rush of relief when he answered. "Where are you?" she asked.

"On my way home," he said, then laughed gently.

"What's so funny?"

"Nothing. I have to go. I'll talk to you later."

"Wait!" she screeched at the phone as the line went dead. "Where are you?" she demanded, immediately trying to call him back.

"Here," a voice said, so close she could feel the breath on her cheek.

Startled, she whipped around to find Alasdair standing behind the bench, beaming at her.

"I wanted to surprise you," she said, standing and rushing around to him. "But I thought I'd missed you."

"Perfect timing," he said, folding his arms around her. "It's so good to see you."

"You too," she said, feeling emotional as she buried her face in his shoulder. "I'm so glad you're back."

Pulling back, he took her face in his hands. "I'm sorry I stayed away so long."

"It's fine," she said, fighting off tears.

He kissed her lightly, then sighed as he gazed into her eyes. "You look amazing."

She took a step back to look down at herself. "I look a mess."

"I was looking at your face, not your clothes." He frowned. "Are they your pyjamas?"

"No!"

"I swear I've seen you wear them for bed."

"It's loungewear," Leana said, running a hand over the soft cotton trousers. "You can wear them for bed or around the house … or to the airport."

He chuckled. "Did you wear them for bed last night?"

"Maybe," she said, stifling a smile. "Stop teasing me. I was in a rush to get here in time. I didn't stop to think about things like getting dressed."

"I still think you look amazing." He pulled her close again and kissed her properly.

"How was the journey?" she asked when they broke apart.

"Horrible. I've hardly slept in days."

"Want to go home?" she asked, trailing her fingers over the back of his neck.

"I'm dying to get home." He took the handle of his case, then held her hand as they walked back through the airport.

He spent the first part of the journey telling her all about his travels with Ghost Moon. Most of it she'd already heard as they'd spoken on the phone so often, but it was good to hear it all in person.

"It sounds incredible," she said when his stories wound down.

"It was." He turned his head on the headrest and gazed at her intensely. "But I spent most of the time wishing you were with me."

Leana's attention flicked back to the road and she stared straight ahead. "You still think I should have stayed out there with you?"

"It's a bit irrelevant now," he said through a yawn.

"Yeah." She drummed her fingers on the steering wheel. "I really like my job, you know?"

He paused and she could feel his gaze on her. "I know."

"I was looking at university courses. I thought about becoming a nurse, but it would mean moving away."

He shifted in his seat. "Are you serious?"

"I seriously thought about it," she said. "But I don't really want to."

"I'm confused."

She cast him a sideways glance and caught the look of intensity in his features. "When I started working at the pub, I never expected to stay there long-term. But I enjoyed it, so there didn't seem to be any reason to do anything else."

His brow was wrinkled. "But now you want to do something different?"

"I thought maybe I should. You have such an amazing career, and sometimes I get the feeling you think I should do more with my life."

"Where did you get that idea from?" he asked, sounding genuinely perplexed.

"You always make it sound as though my job isn't very important. As though it doesn't matter whether I turn up to work or not. Like when we were away and you thought I could just stay away because it's only a bar job."

"That's not what I meant."

"That's how it sounded."

He reached for her hand. "The reason I thought you could take time off is because I can see how much Angus and Mary value you. I don't think they would care about you taking extra time off as long as you came back eventually."

Leana's lips twitched to a smile. "You might be right about that. They overheard a conversation about me leaving and immediately offered me a pay rise and a promotion."

"See!" He laughed. "That's great." Gently he stroked his thumb over the back of her hand. "I would never think that working in a bar isn't good enough for you. If it weren't for you working in a bar, I wouldn't currently have a job in the music industry."

"How did you figure that one out?" she asked dubiously.

"Because until I met you, I was convinced I had to follow a certain career path. I probably would have worked in an office forever." He smiled lightly. "I remember the first time you met my parents and my dad was being all condescending about the fact that you worked in a bar, and you didn't care. All you cared about was the fact that you enjoyed what you did and it paid the bills. You didn't care what anyone else thought."

"I care what *you* think," she said.

"I think it's great how much you enjoy your job."

She squeezed his hand, then pulled it from him to change gear.

"So you're not going to make me move across the country while you get a degree?" he asked.

She looked at him in surprise. "Would you?"

"If it was what you wanted."

"That's good to know." She grinned at him. "I'd like to stay in Lannick for now. Especially since I just got a promotion."

She told him all about the conversation with Angus and

Mary and the extra responsibilities she'd have in the pub, then they fell silent for the rest of the drive. Alasdair dozed for the last half hour but perked up when they drove through Lannick.

"Finally home," he said when they walked through the front door.

"I can make some lunch," Leana said. "I bet you're starving."

"I just want to go to bed."

"You need to stay awake for the day to get your body clock back in the right time zone."

"Really?" he asked, slipping his arms around her waist and pulling her close.

"Yes. If you go to sleep at the normal time you'll get over the jet lag much quicker."

There was a twinkle in his eyes as he kissed her. "I said I want to go to bed. I didn't say anything about sleeping."

"I should probably come up with you," she said between kisses. "Just to make sure you don't fall asleep."

"That sounds like a great idea." He deepened his kisses, making her stomach flutter with anticipation.

CHAPTER FORTY

"You're supposed to be keeping me awake," Alasdair said when Leana blinked her eyes open on the couch in the middle of the afternoon. They'd been watching a film, but she'd obviously nodded off.

"Sorry." Her neck was at an uncomfortable angle and she groaned slightly as she lifted her head from the cushion. "Why are you sitting on the floor?" she asked in a daze. "You insisted on spending a fortune on the couch, the least you could do is sit on it."

"I'm not sitting," he said. "I'm kneeling."

"Same difference. You're still on the floor. Did I nudge you off the couch in my sleep?"

"No."

Sitting upright, Leana stretched her neck, then looked down at Alasdair. "What are you doing?"

He rested his hand on her knee then uncurled his fist to reveal a blue velvet ring box.

"Oh, you've got to be kidding me?" Leana blurted out.

"What?"

"You better not be proposing."

"That was the plan," he said slowly.

"Sorry." She shook her head and sighed. "Go on then."

"You've put me off my game now? I had a speech prepared …"

"You already told me you don't want to marry me," Leana said, unable to hide her irritation. "I'm not sure what you could say to convince me otherwise."

"I thought *you* wanted to get married?"

"I did. But I don't want to marry someone who doesn't want to marry me."

"I want to be with you forever," he said, raising his eyebrows as panic flashed in his eyes.

"I know. But you don't want to get married. You're only asking because Rory told you I was flirting with someone, so you got jealous and jumped on a plane home. The fact that you think I'd cheat on you tells me we absolutely shouldn't get married."

"I didn't think that." He got up from the floor and sat beside her. "And I bought the ring weeks ago, so that's definitely not the reason I'm proposing."

"But it's why you came home early?"

"I came home because I missed you. I'd been wanting to fly back since the moment you left without me."

"So why didn't you?"

"Because it was a really great opportunity … and I felt a bit pathetic that I couldn't manage a few weeks apart from you."

"Okay. But it still seems as though you thought you might lose me, so you decided you'd better get back and put a ring on my finger quick."

"That's not how it was." His features tensed and he looked thoughtful for a moment. "I'll admit I was jealous. I hate the thought of you dancing with some other guy. But hearing Rory so upset about Elspeth put things into perspective. I have everything I want right here, and I will do anything to make you happy."

"Even marry me?" she said, leaning back into the couch.

"Yes. I love you and I want to be with you forever."

"We can do that without getting married."

"If you want to get married, I'm quite happy to."

"Which is not the same as you wanting to. I don't want to organise a wedding knowing you don't care either way."

"So you won't marry me now no matter what I say?"

"I don't think so." She reached for the ring box and opened it up. "Oh, that's pretty."

He looked at her in earnest. "Please will you marry me?"

Hesitantly, she took the ring and slipped it onto her finger. It hit her knuckle and wouldn't budge any further. "That's not a good omen."

"I didn't know what size, so the woman in the shop said she'd give me an average size and you can get it adjusted."

"Great. I have fatter than average fingers?"

He let out a low groan and flopped back on the couch. "Can you please just say yes and put me out of my misery?"

That would probably be the easiest thing to do, but Leana couldn't quite rouse herself to be enthusiastic about it any more.

"I missed you so much when you were away," she said, turning to face him. "I hated it. Since we met, I've always hated any time we've spent apart. I can't imagine you not being in my life. And the more I think about it, the more I realise that it doesn't matter if we're married or not."

"I want you to be happy. If you want a wedding, I want you to have one."

"I don't need a wedding." She gazed at the ring as her mind whirred. "I would like to be married to you at some point. I always imagined that when we had kids we'd be married."

"Okay," he said.

"How would you feel about a shotgun wedding?" she asked in amusement.

He chewed on his lip. "What?"

"A shotgun wedding … you know when people get married quickly because they're pregnant…"

"I know what a shotgun wedding is. I'm just not quite sure what you're trying to tell me ..."

She spluttered as she laughed. "I'm not pregnant! I meant we should get married *when* I'm pregnant. Just nip off to the registry office without telling anyone. Sometime in the future! Not now."

"I don't think people generally plan a shotgun wedding. We could sneak off to the registry office at any time."

"Let's do that then," she said, shuffling closer to Alasdair.

"We're not going to get around to it until we have kids, are we?"

"Probably not. Did you really think I was pregnant?"

"Yeah."

"Did you freak out? You seemed pretty calm."

"I freaked out a little bit," he confessed. "My heart's beating as though I've been running."

She lay a hand on his chest and felt his heart pounding. "Does the thought of it scare you that much?"

"No." He put a hand over hers and looked her in the eyes. "My heart rate goes crazy when I'm excited too."

Leana couldn't help but laugh. "That was a smooth recovery!"

"I meant it!" he said adamantly before breaking into a grin.

CHAPTER FORTY-ONE

On Wednesday afternoon, Arran declared he was bored about five minutes after he got home from nursery. Then he took to repeatedly asking Elspeth how long it would be until Rory got there. When she got fed up with the question, she sent him to look out of the window for him arriving. The poor boy had a long wait but it kept him quiet. At least until he saw Keith arriving home from work; then he dashed to put his shoes on and ran out of the door shouting that he was going to play with Grandad.

An hour later the front door opened again. "Did you have fun?" Elspeth shouted. "Dinner's almost ready and Daddy should be here soon."

"It's me," Rory said as he appeared in the kitchen doorway.

"I thought you were Arran. He's at my parents' place." She put a tray of chips in the oven before she turned to him. "Do you think you could knock instead of letting yourself in?"

He stared at her as though she'd said something crazy. "You want me to knock at the door and wait to be let in?"

"Yes. I think that would be better. If you don't mind?"

"I do mind, actually. Why do I suddenly need to knock on the door?"

"Because it's not your house anymore." She'd expected he might be a little grumpy about the suggestion but hadn't thought he'd be so openly annoyed by it. "I would never just walk into your house without knocking."

"I wouldn't care if you did." Clearly he was in the mood for an argument and Elspeth half wished she hadn't raised the subject.

"The other day you wouldn't even let me in the door. Now you're claiming I shouldn't even bother knocking?"

"I was in the middle of something," he said.

"Some*thing* or some*one*?" Elspeth muttered under her breath.

"What?"

She shook her head. "Never mind. Do you want to go and fetch Arran?"

"I actually wanted to talk to you. I've got some news. I was going to wait until Arran was in bed, but I may as well get it out of the way."

"That sounds ominous."

He stretched his neck and she noticed how tired he looked. "Can we go and sit down?" he asked, then set off to the living room without waiting for a reply.

"You're worrying me," Elspeth said. "I take it from your mood that it's not good news?"

"I thought it was." He sat on the chair, hunched forwards with his hands clasped together. "But I don't think you'll like it. I've been putting off telling you, and now I've stressed myself out worrying about how you'll react."

Elspeth took a seat on the couch. "If it's about your girl-friend, I already know."

"What?" he asked, staring at her.

"I asked you if you had a girlfriend and you lied to my face."

"No, I didn't."

"Oh, come on! I saw you kissing her. If she's not your girlfriend, she's at least someone you're dating, or a friend with benefits. You don't have to hide it from me."

"You saw me kissing Jess?"

"Yes. I could see you through the window."

Rory dropped his head to his hands.

"It's fine," Elspeth said. "I just wish you'd felt you could tell me about her."

"I didn't tell you about her because there's nothing to tell."

"So you're saying that I didn't see you kissing her?"

"No. I kissed her." He leaned back in the chair but refused to look at Elspeth. "She is just a friend, though. At least she was. I messed everything up."

"How do you mean?"

He caught her eye and seemed to debate how much he should say. "I didn't realise how she felt. I think I might have inadvertently led her to believe that we might be more than friends."

"Kissing a woman could definitely give her that impression," Elspeth said.

"I didn't kiss her." He gave a discreet shake of the head. "Not really. She kissed me and I might have kissed her back. It was only that one time."

"You don't have to explain yourself to me. We're not together any more."

"Yeah I know, and you don't care if I'm seeing someone else. That's great!"

"What's your problem?" she snapped, trying to figure out why he was so annoyed with her.

"You!" he growled. "You're my problem. You want to date other people and you want me to date other people. And you want me to knock on the bloody door." He sighed, and his eyes shone with tears when he looked at her. "I don't want any of those things."

Elspeth's heart rate quickened. "What?"

"I'm not seeing anyone else. I can't stand the thought of

being with someone else. And every time I come here I feel like a visitor in my own home. It's bad enough as it is. I don't want to knock at the door." He buried his face in his hands.

"I'm confused," she murmured.

"I'm not saying I *won't* knock on the door. I will, but you wanted us to be honest, so I'm telling you I hate the idea."

Elspeth's thoughts were jumbled and she fought to get everything straight in her head. "Why did you come to Edinburgh?" she asked.

He turned to look at her. "What?"

"Why did you come to Edinburgh when I was there?" She shook her head, realising it sounded an odd question. "I thought that maybe you still had feelings for me, but then you pushed me away when I tried to kiss you."

"Of course I still have feelings for you. But when we got back to the room and you were drunk, the situation felt completely manipulative."

"What do you mean?"

"I mean that it was just like you said: I turned up expecting you to be grateful. I wanted to be all heroic and sweep in to save you. Except you were clearly having a great time. I stopped you from kissing me because I thought you were only doing it because you were drunk. And because you were grateful that I came all the way to Edinburgh to check you were okay."

"It was pretty sweet," she said.

He tilted his head. "I don't want you to be with me because you're grateful to me. Or because you're drunk."

"But you still want us to be together? After everything?"

He looked at her for a moment, his jaw tense. Then he nodded slowly. "I know you want to date other people, and I'll have to find a way to be okay with that. But I hate it." His voice broke on the words and he dropped his gaze to the floor.

"I don't want to date other people either," she said slowly. "I only did it because I thought you were seeing someone."

His features were serious when he looked at her. "What are you saying?"

"I'm saying that I didn't try and kiss you because I was drunk or because I was grateful to you. I just wanted to kiss you."

"Are you serious?"

Nodding, she got up and moved over to him. He sat up straighter and she sank onto his knee.

"I miss you so much." Tears filled her eyes. "I'm so sorry for everything."

"You don't have to apologise," he whispered, running a hand over her hair. "I miss you too. All the time."

"Can I kiss you now?"

He smiled. "You can kiss me anytime you want."

Trailing her fingers through his hair, she moved slowly closer until her lips touched his. He closed his eyes and slipped his arms around her, holding her tightly. Then he parted her lips with his and kissed her deeply.

Kissing him made butterflies dance in her stomach and every inch of her skin tingle. When he drew back, he looked at her in confusion.

"This is not at all how I expected the afternoon to go. I honestly thought you'd moved on and wanted to see other people."

"No," she said, stroking his hair. "I've never wanted to date anyone other than you."

"So you just went on a date with that guy because you were annoyed that you thought I was seeing someone else?"

"No. I wasn't annoyed with you. Well, a little bit, but after how much I'd hurt you, I didn't want you to feel bad about seeing someone or think that you couldn't move on with your life. I hate how much I hurt you."

He swallowed hard. "You said you didn't love me any more."

"I'm sorry. It's hard to explain. It wasn't that I didn't love you. More like I lost interest. That sounds horrible, but it wasn't just you. It was like I didn't have the energy to care about anything."

"And now you feel better?"

She nodded. "It's like everything went black and white for a while and now the colour has come back on."

"I'm glad." He ran his fingers over her hair and pulled her face to his again, kissing her softly.

After a moment, she pulled away. "What was your news?"

"I quit my job," he said with a smile.

"You did *what*?"

"I handed in my notice yesterday. I'll leave at the end of the school year. Then I'll start my new job in August."

"What new job?" she asked, with an inkling of what he was going to say and hoping she'd guessed right.

"I had a job interview at Lannick High School last week."

"And you got it?" she asked as her eyes blurred with tears.

"Yes. It was all a bit of a whirlwind. Mary overheard the headteacher talking about the job vacancy in the pub and she thought I might be interested, so she called me and let me know. I sent over my CV before they even advertised the position. The headteacher invited me in for an interview and offered it to me immediately. That was only last week."

"That's amazing," Elspeth said. "Congratulations."

"Thank you. I was pretty happy about it for about ten seconds."

"Why ten seconds?"

"I'd been at the interview last week. He called and offered me the job when I was here. But then you started telling me how you were going on a date with some guy. That sort of ruined my mood. And then I was panicking that you might not want me so close."

"I definitely want you close. And Arran's going to love it. You'll be able to see him more during the week."

"Yeah." He gave her an odd smile, and it occurred to her that if they were back together and he was working in Lannick, he'd probably want to move back in with them. That would be logical.

Her heart was beating erratically when he drew her close again, embracing her tightly.

"I missed you so much," he whispered against her cheek.

"I missed you too," she said at the same time that she heard the front door burst open and Arran shouting for Rory. Elspeth removed herself from Rory's lap just before Arran ran into the living room. He jumped over the arm of the chair, diving onto Rory.

"Hi!" Rory tickled him and gave him a big hug.

The oven timer began to beep and Elspeth went back to the kitchen to finish getting the dinner ready. Her mind whirred constantly, trying to figure out what was going on. Was she really getting back together with Rory? After convincing herself it wasn't a possibility, it was hard to let herself believe it.

When she caught Rory standing in the doorway watching her, she walked over to him and took his hand.

"Do you really want to be with me?" she asked in a rush. "After how awful I've been."

"I don't think you were awful. You can't help how you feel." He rested his hands on her hips. "Honestly, I want to be with you more than anything. But I'm also terrified of it not working out."

"Me too." Her eyes filled with tears. "I'm scared I'll hurt you again."

He put a hand to her cheek and wiped a tear away with his thumb. "I'll risk it," he said. "Maybe we should take things slowly."

She nodded, then kissed him. Arran walked in so she pulled away quick, feeling as though they were doing something they shouldn't.

"I'm hungry," Arran said, sitting up at the table.

"Dinner's ready now," she said, moving to put it on the table.

While they ate, Elspeth's thoughts were all over the place,

and she struggled to concentrate on the conversation between Rory and Arran. She kept catching Rory looking at her and forced herself to smile. Everything felt complicated, and she was filled with worry when she should be ecstatic.

"Are you okay?" Rory asked when he came down from putting Arran to bed. Elspeth had been sitting at the kitchen table, staring into space.

"Yes." She stood and went to him. "I'm just not sure where we go from here." It would be so easy to fall back to the way things had been before they split up, but she didn't think that was a good idea.

"I was thinking we could do something on Friday night," he said. "We could go out for dinner or I could cook for you at my place."

"That sounds like a date," she said, her lips twitching upwards.

"I'd like to take you on some dates." With his hands at her waist, he pulled her close to him. "I think we skipped the dating phase in our relationship."

"We did," she agreed. "I think dating is a good plan."

He gave her a soft, lingering kiss, then left her smiling to herself at the thought of going on a date with him.

CHAPTER FORTY-TWO

"I thought we were coming to your place," Isla said when Elspeth ushered Arran into their house on Friday afternoon. Jasper padded out from the kitchen and went straight to Arran, who stroked his back.

"I decided it might be easier for you to look after him here," Elspeth said, dropping Arran's backpack by the shoe rack inside the door.

"Has that got his pyjamas and toothbrush in it?" Isla asked.

Elspeth tried to smile but felt tense and was certain it was more of a grimace. "Yes. You don't mind him staying over, do you?"

"No. Does that mean you're intending to stay at Rory's place?"

"I don't know." Elspeth followed Isla to the kitchen, while Arran wandered towards the living room with Jasper trailing after him. "I thought it might be good to have the option. But he also suggested we take things slow... I don't know what that means. I was really excited and now I'm nervous, and I'm not sure why." She paused and looked down at the new jeans and top that she'd bought in Edinburgh. "How do I look?"

"Same as you always look. Why?"

"Because I'm going on a date," she said loudly. "I want to look nice. I put a dress on but that felt weird, so I got changed. Should I have gone for a dress?"

"It's Rory," Isla said. "I don't think he cares what you wear."

"*I* care. I want to look good."

"Have you shaved your legs?"

"Yes."

Isla's lips twitched to a smile. "You're definitely planning on staying over then."

Rolling her eyes, Elspeth leaned against the sideboard. "It all feels strange. Why am I nervous? It's Rory. It makes no sense."

"No, I get it," Isla mused. "It's like going on a first date but already knowing the person is the love of your life. That definitely warrants a few nerves."

"You're not helping," Elspeth said.

"Sorry. I'm teasing, but clearly you're not in the mood for jokes."

"You're right," Elspeth whined. "It feels like a first date. Except usually the stakes are pretty low on a first date. If it doesn't work out, you've not lost anything. But I love Rory. I need this to work out."

"He loves you too," Isla pointed out. "So the odds are in your favour."

"It didn't stop me from ruining everything before, did it?"

"Don't be dramatic," Isla said. "Everything will be fine. Can you please stop fidgeting?"

"No! I'm too nervous."

"What time are you leaving?"

Elspeth checked her watch. "About now. Do you think it was a bad idea to go to his place? I thought it would be more relaxed than going out for dinner, but now I'm not so sure. Being around other people might be easier."

"It's a bit late to change your mind now. Rory's cooking, isn't he?"

"Yes. I'm not changing my mind. I'm just panicking."

"Once you get there you'll relax. It's only Rory, for goodness' sake."

Elspeth wandered into the hallway. "What do you think he meant when he said we should take things slow?"

"I've no idea. Maybe you should ask him."

The front door opened and Logan walked in, greeting them both and slinging his arm around Isla's shoulder. She half-heartedly shrugged him off, telling him he needed a shower, but it only encouraged him to embrace her more fully.

"It's the big date night, isn't it?" he said to Elspeth. "You look nice."

"Thank you."

"She's stressed," Isla remarked.

"Have you shaved your legs?" Logan asked, causing Isla to aim a playful elbow at his ribs.

"Oh, my god!" Elspeth screeched. "You two had a conversation about that. You're bloody weird, you know!"

"I already asked her," Isla told Logan.

He chuckled. "Apparently it's a sign of how committed you are to the date."

"Well, obviously I'm committed. It's Rory." Elspeth ignored their smirks and shouted for Arran. "I'm going," she said when he ran into the hallway. "Be a good boy. I'll see you tomorrow." Crouching, she gave him a hug and a kiss, then thanked Logan and Isla for looking after him before stepping outside.

Her heart felt as though it was in an unnatural rhythm the whole way over to Portree. On Rory's doorstep, she took a deep breath to try to calm herself down. As she reached for the doorbell, she remembered the conversation about letting themselves into each other's houses. After contemplating it for a moment, she pushed at the door handle and shouted hello as she stepped inside.

"I'll be one minute," Rory called from upstairs. "Make yourself at home."

She slung her jacket over the bannister, then made her way to the kitchen and stood looking out over the garden. The small patch of grass was bordered by a hedge on two sides and a panel fence at the other.

"Sorry it's such a mess," Rory said, getting straight to work on loading a pile of dishes into the dishwasher. "I intended to tidy up but I got held up at work. I managed to shower," he said, flashing her a quick smile. "I'll have to nip to the shop, but at least it means you can choose what you want to eat."

"Sorry," Elspeth said as he collected a couple of dirty mugs from the table. He put them into the dishwasher, then closed it before stopping to look at her.

"What for?"

"You look exhausted. I should be cooking for you."

"I offered."

"You also suggested we could go out to eat. Shall we go out instead?"

"Whatever you want. I don't mind cooking, though."

"You've been working all week," Elspeth said. "I don't want you running around after me."

He sighed and moved towards her, pausing before slipping his arms around her waist. "I'm quite happy to run around after you," he said, resting his forehead against hers.

"How about we order pizza?" she suggested.

His shoulders sagged. "I had great plans for a romantic evening."

"I just want to spend time with you. I don't care what we eat or how romantic the setting is." Lightly, she kissed his lips and her stomach fluttered wildly.

"I have wine at least," he said as he hooked a stray strand of hair behind her ear. "I'll open that and order pizza. And hope that the living room is in a better state than the kitchen."

Elspeth felt much more at ease as they settled onto the couch. She pulled her legs under her and looked at Rory intently.

"What's going on with you?" she asked, taking a sip of wine.

"How do you mean?"

"I mean you look worn out, and I don't know what's going on with you any more. I miss knowing all the little things about your life. Before, if you'd had a bad week, I'd know all about it. Now I don't know what's happening with you."

"Work's been hectic recently," he said thoughtfully. "And …" He trailed off, shaking his head.

"What?"

"Nothing. It'll sound as though I'm complaining. I don't want to spend the evening complaining."

"Just tell me what you were going to say."

He looked thoughtful. "I was going to say that when I have Arran with me, I try to focus on him. Which is good because it means I don't do much work at the weekends any more. But …"

"You cram all your work into the times when you don't have Arran?" Elspeth asked. She knew he wasn't trying to make her feel bad, but she felt guilty nonetheless. "And you spend a lot of time driving over to Lannick to pick Arran up or drop him off." She looked at him sadly. "I should've offered to drive him to you sometimes."

He reached for her hand. "I would have asked if I'd wanted you to. I never minded driving him around."

"I'm sorry."

"Don't be. I shouldn't have said anything. It's not your fault."

Elspeth let out a humourless laugh. "Of course it's my fault."

"It doesn't matter anyway. In a few weeks it'll be the school holidays and I can relax. And then I'll be working in Lannick, which will make everything easier."

Not if he was still living in Portree it wouldn't. Elspeth wondered if he was planning on moving back in with them. It would be logical. And practical, with him working in Lannick. She was surprised he hadn't mentioned it. Though she wasn't sure what she'd say if he raised the subject. She should be excited by the thought of it, but mostly she felt a vague feeling of unease.

The doorbell saved her from bringing it up and they were distracted by the arrival of the pizza.

"Do you know when you'll open the cafe again?" Rory asked as they ate in the living room.

"I'm nervous about it," she admitted. "I feel really good now, but I'm scared of working too much and ending up back where I was before."

"Can you cut down on the hours?"

"Yes. That's what I'm planning on doing, but it's hard over the summer when we're busy. It seems wrong to miss out on the business."

"You need to be strict with yourself. Make sure you take enough time off."

"Easier said than done," she said lightly. "I was thinking I'd have another week off. It took me a long time to relax and I feel as though I'm only just appreciating the time off now."

"That's a good idea. No point rushing to open up again." He glanced at her empty glass. "Do you want more wine?"

She chewed the last piece of her pizza, contemplating the question. If she was intending on driving home she shouldn't be drinking. But she had no idea if Rory expected her to stay. "I better not," she said in between licking tomato sauce from her fingers. "I need to drive home later."

He nodded and didn't comment as he picked up the empty pizza box and took it to the kitchen.

"You could always stay over if you wanted," he said when he returned. "Who's looking after Arran?"

"He's staying with Isla and Logan."

"So you could definitely stay. If you want to?"

"I'd like to." She shuffled along the couch and kissed him, then pulled away again quickly. "What did you mean the other day when you said we should take things slow?"

Sighing, he sank back into the couch. "I'm not actually sure. I was thinking we should do things differently this time. There's no point in jumping back to how we were before, since that clearly didn't work."

"I don't want you to move back in." The words came in a rush and Elspeth barely knew she was going to say them until they were out. "I'm sorry. I feel awful saying that and I know it would be good for Arran, but I think it would be too much too soon."

Rory smiled gently. "I think our entire relationship has operated under the principle of too much too soon."

"Aren't you offended?" she asked. "I was worried you'd be upset."

"No. I think you're right. Everything has always been a rush with us. It had already crossed my mind that moving back in together straight away probably wouldn't be a good move."

"Will you keep living here?"

"No. I thought about asking Angus and Mary if I could move into the bunkhouse. It's been sitting empty since Lexie moved out, and I know Angus was intending to rent it."

"That would be perfect." Elspeth was certain Angus and Mary would agree to it. "It's weird, though, isn't it? What are people going to think if we're in a relationship, and have a child together, but don't live together?"

He pulled her close to him, circling his arms around her. "I don't care what anyone thinks. All I care about is that we're happy. We need to do what's right for us."

"How will it work?" Elspeth tried to imagine it. "Will you still have Arran to stay with you at the weekends?"

"I don't know. Maybe you can both come and stay with me at the weekends! I imagine I might stay at your place sometimes too. But I think it's important that we have our own space and time for ourselves." He pushed her hair from her face and kissed her forehead. "We'll figure it out."

CHAPTER FORTY-THREE

On Saturday, Rory took Arran to his place as usual, leaving Elspeth in peace for the weekend. They'd talked about the three of them spending the weekend together but had decided against it, not wanting to rush things. Instead, Rory would bring Arran home earlier than usual on Sunday and they'd have dinner together.

For once, Elspeth wasn't daunted by the prospect of having time to herself. Saturday afternoon was spent pampering herself with a bath and a face mask and a good book. Reading was something she wanted to make more time for. When she was younger she'd loved to read but didn't often find the time any more.

On Sunday, she woke to a beautiful bright day and ate her breakfast out on the patio. She remained there with her book for the rest of the morning. Occasionally she looked up to watch the sunlight sparkling on the gentle waves of the loch. In the silence, birds of prey circled near the trees at the far side of the loch, and a couple of otters played on the rocky shore nearby, completely oblivious to Elspeth watching them.

A message from her mum came through in the middle of the morning inviting her to have lunch with them. It seemed to be more of a summons than a question and Elspeth didn't dare decline. Not that she wanted to. Having lunch with her parents would be nice, and it would give her time to chat to them about her plan for going back to work.

Except when she set off over there, she registered Alasdair's car and realised it probably wasn't going to be only her and her parents. At the sound of an engine she lingered on the drive, surprised to see Rory's car. She hadn't been expecting him for hours yet.

"You're early," she said, when they got out of the car.

"We missed you," Rory said, slipping his arms around her waist and giving her a brief kiss. "And your mum sent me a slightly aggressive message telling me to make sure we were here for lunch."

They were interrupted by Isla and Logan. "You're coming for lunch too?" Isla asked.

"It seems as though Mum wanted everyone here." Elspeth took Rory's hand as they followed Arran to the kitchen.

"It smells amazing in here," Rory said, before greeting Alasdair and Leana with hugs.

Christine was pulling a tray of chicken legs from the oven and the table was laden with various salads.

"What's the occasion?" Logan asked amid a bustle of greetings.

"We haven't all been together for ages." Christine wiped the back of her hand across her forehead. "I thought it was about time. It's nice to take advantage of the quiet weekends with the cafe closed too."

Logan put an arm around Elspeth's shoulders. "Is the lady of leisure planning on going back to work any time soon?"

"I am actually!" Elspeth shrugged him off and gave him a gentle jab to the ribs.

"That's good to hear," Isla replied. "It'll be good to sell more paintings again. And I won't have to fear you turning up on my doorstep looking for someone to entertain you." She rolled her eyes and gave Elspeth a playful look. "If you want art therapy, go for art therapy."

Elspeth glared at her before turning to her mum. "Are you going to let them get away with teasing me?"

"I can't hold them off forever," Christine said, nudging Rory out of the way to put the food on the table. "You've had several months of no one teasing you, I'd have thought you'd be well rested by now."

There were amused smiles all around as they took their places at the table. Logan and Alasdair didn't waste any time and immediately started filling their plates.

"I'm going to have another week off." Elspeth looked directly at her dad, who was seated opposite her. "Then I'll open up again."

"Whatever you want," he said. "Don't overdo it."

Elspeth felt a lump in her throat at the look of concern in her dad's features. Filling her plate gave her a moment to compose herself.

"I only want to work five days a week," she finally went on. "I know it makes sense to open for six days in the summer, but I don't want to go back to working so much."

"Opening five days a week is plenty," Christine said kindly.

Elspeth put a forkful of salad into her mouth, chewing slowly. "I emailed Megan to see if she could come and help out again for the summer, but I haven't heard back yet. Otherwise I'll have to find someone else." In the peak season, they really needed three of them working in the cafe. Even then, it could still feel hectic.

"I can help," Leana said, putting a hand in front of her face as she spoke with her mouth full. "I can work at the cafe one day a week. I just wouldn't know which days until I get the rota for the pub."

"Then you'd be working six days a week," Elspeth said.

Isla tapped her fork against the side of her plate as though she'd developed a nervous tick. "You're really annoying," she grumbled in Leana's direction.

"What did I do?"

Isla sighed. "You're always so bloody nice. Now I'll look bad if I don't volunteer to help."

"I don't think anyone's expecting you to volunteer to work at the cafe," Keith said gruffly.

Ignoring him, Isla looked directly at Elspeth. "I'll give you three days."

"What?" Elspeth replied.

"I'll work in the cafe for three days a week over the summer."

"Are you serious?"

"Yes. You can choose the days. Just not Sunday because Logan's off on Sundays."

Elspeth put a hand over her mouth as tears welled in her eyes. If Isla helped out and she hired someone else to help out too, it would mean Elspeth could even take three days off a week. It felt as though a weight had been lifted, and it made her realise just how nervous she'd been about getting sucked back into a hectic work schedule.

"Why are you staring at me like that?" Isla demanded, looking at Alasdair.

"I'm not." Quickly, he shifted his gaze and shuffled in his seat. "That's really nice of you, though."

"I keep telling you she's nice really," Logan said with amusement. "She just likes to keep that side hidden."

"It's only for the summer," Isla told Elspeth.

"Thank you." Elspeth walked around the table and wrapped her arms around her sister.

"Get off me," Isla said, shrugging her away. "And can everyone stop looking at me as though it's completely shocking that I'd offer to help my sister?"

"It's quite shocking," Leana said with a grin.

Isla smiled back at her. "Can we change the subject now?"

As they all fell silent, Elspeth slipped back into her chair and gave Rory's hand a quick squeeze. Arran was at the other side of him, happily chewing on a chicken leg.

It was rare for there to be any silent moments during their family dinners, and Elspeth looked around the table in amusement.

"Alasdair and I got engaged," Leana said in a rush.

The announcement shocked everyone into further silence.

"About bloody time," Keith said after a moment, sending ripples of laughter around the room.

"I didn't know we were telling people about it," Alasdair said.

Leana grimaced. "I hadn't planned on it, but the quiet was freaking me out and it was the first thing that came to mind."

"Why weren't you going to mention it?" Logan asked.

"We're not going to have a big wedding or anything," Leana said.

"Small weddings can be just as special," Christine said. "And it's less stressful to organise if you stick to family and close friends."

"We'll probably elope," Leana told her.

"Who will you invite then?" Keith asked.

Leana shrugged. "No one."

"What about witnesses?" Logan asked. "You at least need witnesses. I volunteer."

"Me too," Isla added.

"We can't just have you two there." Leana chuckled. "That wouldn't be fair on the rest of the family. Maybe we'd ask Lexie and Nick."

"Nick?" Isla screeched. "Are you serious? You're going to invite my ex-boyfriend to your wedding but not me?"

"I think this is why it would have been better not to say anything," Alasdair said to Leana with a hint of a smile.

"You're not seriously going to invite Nick though?" Isla asked.

Leana sighed. "Not if you're going to be weird about it."

"We could ask Justin and Kyle," Alasdair suggested.

Isla curled her lip. "That would be better. Though I still think it's rude of you to tell us you're getting married but not invite us to the ceremony."

"I definitely shouldn't have mentioned it," Leana said to Alasdair.

"Have you got a ring?" Elspeth asked.

Leana held up her hand, but there was no ring to be seen. "It needs to be re-sized because I've got fat fingers."

"You haven't got fat fingers," Alasdair said on a sigh. "I just got the wrong size."

Elspeth smiled. "Congratulations anyway."

"Thank you." Leana rested her head affectionately on Alasdair's shoulder as everyone congratulated them.

"Hey!" Elspeth snapped when Rory stole a chicken leg from her plate and took a bite. "I was about to eat that."

"You snooze you lose," he said, handing her the remainder of it.

She gave him a quick kiss, then gazed around at her family as the usual chatter and banter filled the room. For the first time in a long time she had the feeling that everything was going to be okay.

And that was all she wanted.

DON'T MISS THE NEXT BOOK IN THE LOCH LANNICK SERIES...

New Arrivals at the Loch (Book 9)

Dale didn't intend to stay on the Isle of Skye for long, but when he's offered a job at the Old Inn and made to feel at home by the locals, he starts to wonder what it would be like to stick around.

Meanwhile, **Elspeth** is determined to salvage her relationship with **Rory**. After almost losing him, she'll do whatever it takes to ensure they get things right this time.

Over in Portree, **Jess** is hopeful that her streak of bad luck with relationships is over. At least until **Gary**'s teenage niece causes ripples in their budding romance.

When a spate of crimes brings Dale under scrutiny, the locals speculate over his mysterious past, leaving tensions high in the normally peaceful Lannick...

My Kind of Perfect (Book 3)

A Friend in Need (Book 4)

The Lucy Mitchell Series

Beyond the Lens (Book 1)

Beneath These Stars (Book 2)

Hannah has also written a series of children's books aimed at 5-9 year olds under the pen name, Hannah Sparks.

Books in the Land of Stars series:

Where Dragons Fly (Book 1)

Where Stars Fall (Book 2)

Where Penguins Party (Book 3)

ABOUT THE AUTHOR

When she's not writing, Hannah enjoys spending time with her husband and kids. She loves to read and also enjoys yoga and jogging. And tea … she really loves a good cup of tea!

Hannah can be found online at the following places:

Twitter: @BooksEllis

Facebook: @authorhannahellis

Instagram: @authorhannahellis

Website: www.authorhannahellis.com

Feel free to contact Hannah at any of the above or email her at this address:

authorhannahellis@gmail.com

If you'd like to be kept up to date with news about Hannah's books you can sign up to her mailing list through her website:

www.authorhannahellis.com/newsletter

Made in the USA
Middletown, DE
09 August 2021

45643196R00201